Fame & Fortune

A Victorian Crime Thriller

Carol Hedges

Little G Books

For Avalyn & Edward

About the Author

Carol Hedges is the successful British author of 18 books for teenagers and adults. Her writing has received much critical acclaim, and her novel Jigsaw was shortlisted for the Angus Book Award and longlisted for the Carnegie Medal.

Carol was born in Hertfordshire, and after university, where she gained a BA (Hons.) in English Literature & Archaeology, she trained as a children's librarian. She worked for the London Borough of Camden for many years subsequently re-training as a secondary school teacher when her daughter was born.

The Victorian Detectives series

Diamonds & Dust
Honour & Obey
Death & Dominion
Rack & Ruin
Wonders & Wickedness
Fear & Phantoms
Intrigue & Infamy

Acknowledgments

Many thanks to Gina Dickerson, of RoseWolf Design, for another superb cover, and to my two patient editors.

I also acknowledge my debt to all those amazing Victorian novelists for lighting the path through the fog with their genius. Unworthily, but optimistically, I follow in their footsteps.

Fame & Fortune

A Victorian Crime Thriller

E sempre bene il sospettare un poco, in questo mondo.

(It's always better to be a little suspicious in this world.)

Wolfgang Amadeus Mozart ~ Cosi
fan tutte

London, 1867. It is midnight, and a cold, damp autumn wind is sulking around the brick chimneypots. Above, the star-studded sky is barely visible beyond the yellow flicker of gas lamps. A man stumbles along one of the streets leading down to the river. He is being supported by two other men, who hold him firmly by his arms. To the night-constables, sheltering in a doorway and sharing a smoke, it looks as if he has had too much to drink, and is being escorted home by a couple of companions, or perhaps some drinking associates.

This is not what is happening.

The man experiences a sense of unreality. He cannot feel his feet, nor the pavement beneath them. He doesn't struggle or try to escape. He is a survivor, so he guesses that something has been put in his drink earlier in the evening to render him docile and compliant. Mind, he does not remember much of what happened earlier, but he knows with the part of his brain that is still functioning, that this is going to end very badly. The two men stop. A blindfold is placed around his eyes. They walk on. Then stop once more.

The air feels different now, closer, denser. He has the sensation of standing beneath some sort of big overarching structure. A bridge? He is propelled forward. He hears carriage wheels and the clip-clop of hooves passing overhead. He hears water lapping against wooden stanchions close by.

These will be the last things that he hears.

A few hours later, a group of returning revellers will stagger home along the riverside path. They will pass under the bridge, where they will see what looks like a strange shape swinging from a length of rope. It is only when one of the revellers, egged on by his friends, climbs the wooden scaffolding that has been erected as part of the bridge's renovations, that it becomes suddenly and horrifyingly clear exactly what the swinging shape is.

****

The morning starts off drizzly, but as Detective Inspector Lachlan Greig and the officers carrying a stretcher make their way to the foot of the bridge, it brightens, so that by the time they get there, a pale wash of sunlight lies over the river, turning it into lemon-coloured slices.

The body lies on the path, just below the bridge. A couple of constables are engaged in holding back the gawping spectators. A third stands guard over the body. A line of onlookers leans over the bridge. There is a murmur of anticipation as the tall broad-shouldered detective and his men arrive on the scene. The body guard hurries towards them, a self-important expression on his face.

"We took the liberty of cutting him down," he says, indicating the body, which is covered in a large sack. "Don't want to alarm the ladies."

Judging by the faces of the crowd, alarm is the last thing they are worried about. Greig stares down at the sack. He reads the words *Art. Dollimore, Coal Merchant Suppliers, London City Wharf. Business & Domestic.* The sack appears to be brand new. The top of a man's head can just be seen protruding. He finds himself mesmerised by the words. Where on earth did they find a brand new coal sack at short notice?

"What can you tell me?" he asks, getting out his notebook.

"Suicide," the constable says with a knowing air. "I warned them at the time: unattended scaffolding like this is an open invitation, I said. Should have put a guard on it, I said. Or some lights. And now look what's happened," he gestures towards the sack. "A man in the prime of life climbs up the scaffolding and throws himself off. Somebody's going to have to answer for it, you mark my words, sir."

Detective Inspector Greig motions to his men to transfer the body to the stretcher. The crowd on the bridge leans over to better see what is happening. Their expressions are eagerly hopeful. It reminds Greig of a picture he once saw of the crowd at a Roman gladiatorial contest. He hears the usual shouts of *'Was it the Fenians?'* He ignores them.

"Can you show me exactly where the body was found?" he requests.

The constable leads him to the mouth of the archway and points upwards. "Just there. A-hanging from the top scaffolding pole. Group of men coming back from the King's Head spotted him," he says, folding his arms. "Soon as we were alerted, we rushed straight here. I made an assessment of the situation and had the body cut down. I checked his pockets, but there was nothing there ~ see, that's a sure sign he wasn't intending to go home. Suicide, like I said."

His air of self-importance is grating. Greig tries to focus on the facts rather than the interpretation he is being offered. He is not buying the suicide theory. There are easier and far more effective ways to do away with oneself than climbing up rickety scaffolding on a dark night, attaching the end of a rope to a slippery pole and jumping, he thinks. And as for the lack of personal possessions, that could mean anything. He sometimes left his lodgings with nothing more than the price of a drink in his pocket.

He studies the ground. It is a blur of muddy footprints. Unfortunately, the constable, in making a decision way above his pay grade or intellectual ability, has now effectively eliminated any prints that might have provided a clue as to how this man really met his end.

"You writing all this down?" the self-designated expert inquires. "Will you be wanting me to submit a report to Scotland Yard?"

Greig indicates that this will not be necessary, as he believes he has mastered the salient points of the matter. The constable looks disappointed. Greig nods his unfelt thanks, and prepares to follow his men back to Scotland Yard. The sun has now disappeared behind a cloud, leaving the customary smell of decay and rot. A sailing barge is making its way upriver. In its wake, gulls swoop and cry. Greig recalls that they are supposed to contain the souls of the dead. A melancholy thought. It stays with him on the return journey.

****

The man dreams that he is a pastry. Then he dreams that somebody is trying to eat his face. He wakes to find that his cat has crept onto the coverlet and is licking his chin. He pushes her off the bed, deaf to the indignant miaowed complaints.

The man's name is Gerald Daubney; he is an antiquarian and collector. He sits up and calls for his servant. Nothing happens. He waits for a bit longer. No one comes. Eventually he lifts the coverlet and slides his legs from under the sheets. Where is his shaving water? Where is his valet with his razor?

Still furred with sleep, he peers myopically for the accustomed jug and bowl of hot water, the towel, the clothes laid out on the chair, the deferential manservant, but they are absent. He reaches for his dressing gown and slides his arms into the sleeves. He searches for his slippers. They, too, seem to have disappeared.

Walking to the door, he steps over his discarded clothes from the night before. This, he decides, is not good enough. He opens his bedroom door and shouts "Flashley?" His voice echoes down the stairs. There is no sound of hurrying footsteps in response, no deferential wringing of hands. No apology.

Puzzled now, he descends the staircase and enters the drawing room, still shadowy behind its closed draperies at the windows. It takes him a few minutes to sense that something is amiss; another minute to track it to its source: a broken pane of glass in one of his display cabinets. As he hurries to examine it more closely, he steps on a sharp object. He utters a cry of pain and stares down. There is glass on the floor. He has trodden on a shard. His foot is bleeding.

Seriously alarmed now, his eyes scan the room for clues as to what might have happened. All too soon, he realises. The discovery causes his heart to pound. His mind stammers. He reaches out a hand to clutch the top of a chair. He feels the breath leaving his body. The room spins. No, it cannot be! He must've made a mistake.

Frantic now, he goes from room to room, leaving a trail of bloody footprints. He opens cabinet after cabinet and peers inside; he tips drawers onto the floor. He even bends down to check under sofas and chairs but finds nothing but a lot of unswept dust.

Eventually, he is forced to accept the truth. He has been robbed. Someone came into his house in the middle of the night, entered his drawing room, smashed a window in one of his display cabinets, and then proceeded to empty it of the precious contents. And his manservant? What has happened to him? Has he been taken also?

Shocked to the core of his being, Gerald Daubney goes back to his bedroom, wraps his foot in a handkerchief and scrambles into yesterday's clothes. Then, breathless and breakfast-less, he grabs his hat, coat and stick and hurries out into the street. There is only one thing on his mind: he must seek out those who can advise him in his hour of need.

The Antiquaries and Collectors Club, situated off Pall Mall is not as well-known as the Athenaeum, or the Reform. It does not have the cachet of White's or the louche reputation of the 'Gyll'. It is modestly housed in a three-storied building set back from the main thoroughfare.

The club, as its name suggests, provides a forum and meeting place for gentlemen of independent means and individual passions to talk about, or show off, their collections. Papers are given describing the thrills and perils of voyages to far-off shores. Discoveries are displayed, to the amazement and delight of the membership.

Arguments rage over the authenticity or provenance of items brought in. The members might fall out (they frequently do), but they are united in a shared and irrepressible enthusiasm for beautiful and unusual objects from all over the world.

Daubney, his face still white and stricken with shock, arrives at the club entrance, and is shown inside by Withering, the elderly doorman and caretaker. Withering does not inquire after his health, nor what currently ails him, having long grown used to the obsessive and strange nature of the club membership, for whom the term 'not quite all there up-top' could be applied with impunity.

Instead, he silently takes Daubney's hat and stick, and watches him climb the stairs, which creak in a suitably antique manner. Daubney goes straight into the library, where several members are poring over the daily newspapers and muttering under their breath. Upon his entry, an elderly member glances up, recognises him and beckons him over.

"Now then, Daubney, now then, see here: what d'you make of this? Here's Carew, just back from Egypt, says he's discovered a new pyramid, possibly the tomb of some pharaoh and the British Museum says it's his public duty to donate any treasure his diggers pull out of the ground to them. To them! Have you been to the British Museum lately? It's like some gigantic bazaar ~ stuff all higgledy-piggledy everywhere, no proper labelling, no sense of order. Over my dead body, that would be my response, and I intend to write to Carew and tell him so."

At which point another member notices Daubney's agitated demeanour.

"Hello, old chap, looking a bit seedy? Last night's dinner not agreed with you?"

Daubney clasps his hands, works his mouth into several strange shapes. Finally, he bursts out, "Gentlemen, I have been robbed!"

Newspapers are carefully lowered.

"Robbed? When?"

"Last night," Daubney says, clutching the top of the nearest armchair for support. "I awoke to discover that one of my display cabinets was empty. I have been robbed!"

"What has been taken?" someone asks.

"My collection of netsuke."

There is a collective indrawing of antiquarian breath. Daubney is a collector of Japanese miniature sculptures, and in the years since the Japanese policy of *sakoku* ended, and the ports have finally opened up to British traders, he has built up a private collection of netsuke that is the envy of many in London.

"You are sure?" the member asks.

Daubney treats him to a long, slightly unhinged stare. "The cabinet was empty. The netsuke are no longer there. I have searched my house. They have been taken. Also missing is my manservant."

"Ah. Well. There it is then. Find the one and you find the others. Not the first time someone has been robbed by his servants. Have you been to the police yet?"

Daubney flinches at the suggestion, "I am unwilling to subject my private life to the scrutiny of outsiders. The presence of the police inevitably leads to the presence of journalists and subsequently to articles in the newspapers. I thought in coming here, that you might be able to suggest other possibilities."

There is a silence. On the one hand, Daubney has a reputation amongst the members for being slightly eccentric (actually, they are all eccentric to a greater or lesser degree, although they see themselves as perfectly normal). On the other hand, he has asked for advice. Minds are bent upon the problem.

"Perhaps your man might have surprised the intruder," a member suggests. "He could have chased after him, and now returned, with, one hopes, the netsuke."

Daubney considers this suggestion. "It is possible I suppose. I rushed straight here without waiting for his return," he says slowly.

"I'd cut along home then and see if he's there," the member nods. "If he isn't, you may have to resort to the forces of the law. I recommend the detective division at Scotland Yard. I had to avail myself of their services recently. Very professional. Very discreet. Nothing ever got into the newspapers."

There is another silence while all eyes swivel with interest to the speaker, who clamps his lips together firmly and stares them down.

Daubney rises. "Yes. Thank you, gentlemen. You have set my mind at rest. I shall do as you suggest."

He collects his hat and stick and hurries back to his house, where the continued absence of valet and missing items will finally lead him to decide upon the only other suggestion offered, despite his initial reluctance to do so.

****

The chill in the police mortuary is, if anything, even chillier than usual. The smell of chemicals and mortality are fighting their usual battle as Detective Inspector Stride enters. He lowers his eyes and studies the floor intently. It is either that, or looking at the contents of various enamel dishes.

"Ah, detective inspector, I have been eagerly awaiting your arrival," Robertson, the dour police surgeon greets him. "May I introduce my new assistant Mr. Aaron Baker. Fresh from University College Hospital and keen as mustard to get to grips, as it were, with the finer workings of the human body."

A pale cadaverous young man in a white apron moves the corners of his thin lips upwards in what Stride chooses to interpret as a smile. He has a large dissecting saw in one hand. The other hand is resting on what Stride fears is the leg bone of some poor unfortunate.

"Mr. Baker, as you see, is testing the theory that the former owner of this leg could not have been accidentally run over by a cart as the fractures to the upper tibia are of much older appearance. Come closer, I'm sure Mr. Baker will be delighted to explain his findings."

"I'll stand here, if it's all the same to you. No disrespect, Mr. Baker," Stride says.

"You see, Mr. Baker, it is as I explained it to you earlier," Robertson sighs. "The detective inspector is of what one might call a nervous disposition in relation to the sudden, premature or violent deaths of our customers. *In situ*, fine; *in veritas*, less so."

Robertson favours Stride with a wide disingenuous smile, radiating innocence and bonhomie. Stride knows full well that it is a complete act.

"Now, to the matter in hand," the police surgeon continues, removing the cloth covering a body. "You have come about the man found hanging from some scaffolding? I expect you wish to ascertain whether it was a case of *felo de se*? Preliminary examination leads me to conclude that, despite appearance to the contrary, the man in question did not commit suicide. You may express astonishment at my suggestion," he peers at Stride from under his bushy eyebrows. Stride stares back impervious, refusing to give him the satisfaction.

"The evidence I have observed suggests that he was actually hauled off his feet by the rope *after* it was tied round his neck. The level of tightening of the ligature is always higher and more vertical with a hanging than with a case of self-strangulation. Also, suicides tend to jump, which causes the rope to break the neck. I have examined the body and there is no break.

"Another observation I might make is that the ligature employed by a man committing suicide tends to twist, as it is hard for a man to strangle himself. The rope in this case, was not twisted in the slightest degree. *Ergo*, homicide, not suicide. I also refer you to the deep bruising on both wrists, and the abrasions on the sides of his hands, which would suggest some sort of a defensive struggle."

"Lachlan would agree with your conclusions," Stride says.

"Indeed, why should he not? I have observed he is an individual of some sagacity. I shall now proceed further with my examination, just in case there are mitigating matters that I have not noticed. It could be that the strangulation was accidental after all, as in the infamous 1839 case of Elizabeth Kenchan ~ do I need to remind you? I see I do.

"The female in question went to bed intoxicated, with her bonnet on and was found next morning strangled in its strings. She had fallen out of bed, her bonnet becoming fixed between the bedstead and the wall, and was too drunk to loosen the strings."

Robertson recounts this gruesome incident with his usual cheerful relish.

"So, somebody deliberately strung up this man, while he was still alive," Stride muses thoughtfully, shaking his head. "It hardly bears thinking about."

"Well, detective inspector, *Homo homini lupus* as the saying goes."

"Plautus: Man is a wolf to his fellow man," the assistant says, not even bothering to look up from the leg he is studying.

Robertson claps his hands. "Well done, Mr. Baker! I can see you will be a great asset. For far too long I have been wasting my erudition upon the desert air. Now, if you would kindly pass me the large serrated knife on the bench, I shall commence upon an examination of this man's stomach and its contents. I doubt the detective inspector will wish to observe, so I shall bid him farewell with the promise that I will favour him with my report in due time."

Stride takes the hint.

It was bad enough when it was just Robertson, he thinks ruefully as he heads back to the 'desert air' of the main building. *Now there are two of them, it is going to become even more unbearable.* For a moment he contemplates returning to his cramped office and the piles of unread files. Then he dismisses the idea. It is never too early for an early luncheon. Especially after a visit to the police mortuary. He heads for the street.

****

Detective Sergeant Jack Cully regards the individual sitting on the other side of the desk with polite curiosity. The man has the air of an aesthete: pale, thin, with an unhealthy indoor complexion. He wears a black frock coat and crumpled white linen shirt. He is carelessly shaven, with a top hat and lank dark hair, worn slightly too long at the sides. His white hands with long delicate fingers have clearly never done any clerkish or other kind of work. He wears a couple of gold rings with big stones that Cully guesses are probably priceless.

Behind the owlish spectacles, the visitor also has the shiny, staring eyes of a fanatic, and there is something fussily over-refined about the way he produced a handkerchief and carefully dusted the chair before seating himself on it, although as this is Detective Inspector Stride's room, borrowed for the occasion, Cully has some sympathy.

"Will the senior detective be much longer?" the man asks, biting his underlip. He had arrived in the outer office some time earlier, demanding to see 'the senior detective' about a matter of great urgency, and had been asked to wait on the Anxious Bench, where he had been left to his own devices while the desk constable dealt with a brawling fracas on the front step.

"My colleague is engaged on official business, so it is impossible to say for certain when he might return," Cully replies. Privately he is pretty sure that Stride, having braved the police mortuary, has gone to Sally's Chop House for an early lunch.

Sally's Chop House is not a place he feels he could recommend to the visitor, who is currently glancing

12

about the cramped paper-strewn office with an expression of fastidious alarm. He does not look as if he dines on the sort of fare offered at Sally's ('meat from known animal species'). Mind you, Cully thinks, given the visitor's rake thin body and pallid features, he doesn't look as if he dines on anything nourishing at all.

"However, I am quite capable of dealing with whatever has brought you to Scotland Yard," he continues, drawing a piece of paper towards him and selecting a pen. Cully dips the pen into the inkwell and regards the visitor expectantly.

"It is private matter of some delicacy," the man begins hesitantly. "I was recommended to apply to Scotland Yard, as your known discretion will be imperative."

He's being blackmailed by some woman, is Cully's immediate thought. Then he dismisses it. There is something about the man that precludes any suggestion of an emotional entanglement. Any emotional entanglement.

"My name is Gerald Daubney, detective," the man informs him stiffly, "I am a collector of small Japanese carvings, china and such, and the matter upon which I wish to consult Scotland Yard concerns certain valuable items that have gone missing from my private collection ~ items that I now fear may have been stolen by my manservant. I discovered the theft yesterday morning."

Cully proceeds to head up the piece of paper with the man's name, nature of crime, time of discovery, and information about the suspect.

"What items were taken?" he asks.

Daubney stares off. Frowns. Swallows. Takes a deep breath. Falters. His reaction is as if a member of his family has disappeared.

"My entire collection of Japanese netsuke," he says, staring down at his hands.

Cully hesitates, pen poised over his notebook. He hasn't a clue what a netsuke is, let alone how to spell it. Daubney sighs gently, then patiently spells out the word.

"Netsuke are small ornaments of animals, fruit or people. They are carved out of wood or ivory and are small enough to hold in your hand."

"They are toys?"

Daubney frowns. "Not toys, no. Ornaments. In Japan, men carry them tied into their sashes. There are certain craftsmen who specialise in specific forms ~ for instance, I have ... I had," he corrects himself, "several rats, that were made by an artist in the north of the country. They are just beautiful. And very rare."

His face suddenly twists, as if somebody has stabbed him with a knife. Cully tries to feel sympathy for his plight, but truthfully, there are enough real rats running around the streets and back-alleys biting children and spreading disease. The idea that anybody in their right mind would want to make little wooden models of them, let alone collect little wooden models of them, is beyond his comprehension.

"Has anybody other than yourself visited the room where the robbery took place?"

"Certainly not."

"Then I will arrange for myself and another officer to visit you later today so that we can make an assessment of the situation."

Once again, the same wrenched expression crosses the man's face.

"Is that completely necessary, detective?"

"It is certainly usual."

Daubney seems to be engaged in an inner struggle that goes on for some time. Cully sits back and waits for him to reconnect. Eventually, the man nods, albeit reluctantly.

"So be it. I agree to your request. I can offer you and your colleague a brief visit shortly after 4 o'clock. You must understand, I am somewhat of a solitary disposition and I maintain a strict regimen. The loss of my collection has affected me extremely badly. I will show you the broken glass and the display case, and I can also give you a list of the netsuke, if you really believe it will help you find the thief."

Cully is strongly tempted to tell him that if this is how he feels, then he and his colleagues in the detective division have plenty of other work they could be getting on with, including a brutal murder, but something in the man's air of nervous wretchedness halts him in his tracks.

"I assure you, we will disturb you as little as possible," he says. "It is always necessary to see the actual place where a crime was committed. We are trained to pick up clues that a lay person might miss, which can lead us to uncover the perpetrator. We will be with you shortly after four, as you request. Please do not enter the room, nor touch anything in the immediate area."

Cully stands, to indicate that the interview is over. Daubney immediately gets to his feet with a sigh, offers a limp hand, and is accompanied to the main entrance, where he is shown out to the street. Thoughtfully, Cully watches him depart. He decides to see if Detective Inspector Lachlan Greig can accompany him. Detective Inspector Stride might be a little too abrasive for Mr. Daubney's delicate nerves.

A short while later, Gerald Daubney lets himself back into the house. It is as silent as when he quitted it a few hours earlier. Eschewing the drawing room, as requested by the detective, he enters the front parlour. The blinds are down, as they are in the rest of the house, producing the soft restful light that is conducive to the profound seclusion that he enjoys.

He sits down in one of the two highbacked crimson chairs. There is a chirrup, and Zanthe, his small white cat, named after a particular style of Japanese chrysanthemum pottery, appears from under the table. She twines her lithe body around his legs. He bends down and picks her up. The cat gently butts his chin with the top of her head.

Suddenly, Daubney finds himself in a clean space where there is nothing but pain: the Edo cat has gone. He may never again hold its ivory body in the palm of his hand, run his fingers over its smooth creamy back, marvel at the little miracle of its perfection, the alert ears, the tiny pink tongue licking its flank, the intense preoccupied expression in its green eyes.

He remembers building his collection. Each netsuke arrived in a wooden box, wrapped in a silk square, having been packed and crated and sent from Japan by the dealer he met once on his only visit to the strange exotic country. Thirty-eight of them; the tiger, the monkey, the elephant, the rats, the fruits and nuts, the two toads, the tiny squatting beggar, the Edo cat, and all the erotic ones that he did not remember ordering. Each was unwrapped, held in his hand and considered from all angles, then placed carefully on one of the velvet-lined shelves in the bow-fronted cabinet.

He cannot pinpoint the moment when collecting the little carvings went from being an interest to an obsession. He only knows that his collection of netsuke, and this silent, curtained, unvisited house are the only things he loves in the world. Exhausted and heartbroken, he sits on, feeling his body tremble. He wonders whether this is what death from shock feels like, until it occurs to him that he has taken neither bite nor sup since he awoke.

Having correctly diagnosed the symptoms of his distress, he decides to go in search of sustenance. Such matters were always the concern of his man, who, in some mysterious way, produced meals at regular intervals. Without his presence Daubney is as helpless as a shelled crab. He rises, scattering the cat who miaows plaintively. He guesses that she is hungry too. But what to give her? This too, was the province of his servant. Now it is his problem.

Daubney makes his way to the kitchen, *terra incognita* as far as he is concerned. There he finds a stout woman in a cap, print gown and apron. She is setting tea things on a tray. A black kettle is coming to the boil. This is Cook, a formidable female who has been with the family ever since he was a boy, although he does not remember her name.

He pauses on the threshold, uncertain whether to enter, what to say. He has never been down to the kitchen since the day his mother passed away. The woman lifts her head from the tray, regards him thoughtfully, then makes a slight bobbing motion that might be a curtsey.

"Tea won't be long, Master Gerald," she says. "Will you be wanting anything to eat?"

Daubney frowns. "Have you seen Flashley, Cook?"

The cook shakes her head. "Not seen hide nor hair of him. Perhaps he is ill? He hasn't been looking too well of late. I wondered whether it was the influenza. There's a lot of it about. Had you noticed, Master Gerald?"

Daubney tries to recall whether he has observed anything different about the manservant. It is a question he finds almost impossible to answer. Flashley is just somebody who is there on the margins of his life. He makes things easier. And now he is making things difficult by not being there.

"I was thinking of bringing up your tray myself, if that'd be alright," the cook says.

He waves a languid hand.

"Yes, yes, of course Mrs Err …. Cook. And if there is any of the … the seed cake, that would also be quite acceptable, thank you."

Daubney returns to the higher regions of the house to await his refreshments. Their arrival will coincide with that of the two detectives from Scotland Yard, thus requiring an additional two plates, cups and saucers, and adding to his already elevated level of unease.

****

Eventually, having finished their initial investigatory visit, Greig and Cully find a quiet spot to consider what they have learned. Jack Cully's thought processes are interrupted at intervals by a sneeze. He is allergic to cats, and had managed to sit close to what he'd thought at first was an example of rather good taxidermy, until it got up, stretched, yawned, and tried to sit on his lap.

Cats always made a beeline for him. They knew a victim when they discovered one. He was lucky that his small daughter Violet's rescued kitten had decided early on in its arrival to go and be rescued elsewhere.

"A strange gentleman, our Mr. Gerald Daubney," Greig remarks, "though that might be excused given recent events. It is clear he has been very vexed by the theft of his little wooden ornaments."

"It is also clear that whoever entered Mr. Daubney's house was in possession of a key," Cully says thoughtfully. "The front door showed no evidence of force being employed, nor were any ground floor windows broken. Either that, or the thief was a consummate picker of locks. But the absence of Mr. Flashley, the living-out manservant points strongly towards the former thesis. It looks like a simple case of 'rob and run' to me."

"And yet Mr. Daubney swore to the honesty of the man," Greig murmurs. "It is a mystery why a loyal servant, with such an upright character, who has worked in the house for so many years, would suddenly turn around and steal from his master."

"We have his address," Cully says. "I suggest we go there now. There's always an advantage to arriving unannounced and unexpected. If he is lying low, we may catch him out."

Cully knew that the advantage of surprise had little to do with the innocence or guilt of the individual sought, but the *element* of surprise often spurred people towards the truth. They finish their discussion and pick up a cab at the corner. Some time later, they are dropped outside a row of lodging houses.

They rap at the door of one, and wait patiently on the grubby step, until the door is opened a crack. A large-eyed sickly face peers up at them. It takes a second or so for both men to register that it belongs to a child, not a frail old woman.

"Ma says not to open the door," the child declares firmly. Cully squats down until his face is on the same level as the child's. "She is quite right to say that," he says. "Where is your mother?"

The child runs claw-like fingers through its thin wispy hair. "D'liverin' washing."

"And what is your name?" Cully asks.

"Anna Pritchard, 3 Benson Street, London, England," comes the prompt reply.

"That's a pretty name. My little girl is called Violet. Do you know, Anna, whether Mr. Flashley is at home?"

The child frowns. "First floor back? No, he ain't."

"Thank you, Anna. Would your mother mind if we came in and waited for him? We need to speak to him about something. It is very important. Can you help us?"

The child opens the door slightly. Now they see that she has a twisted back. One shoulder is markedly higher than the other. She is clad in an old-fashioned red dress that has been pinned to fit her awkward body. On her feet are a pair of men's carpet slippers.

"I promise you, we won't be any trouble," Cully smiles. "Indeed, we shall be as quiet as little mice." He digs in his pocket and produces a small screw of paper. "Here, would you like a peppermint sweet? My Violet loves them."

The child's face is suddenly alight with interest. She takes a sweet, studies it, licks it a few times, before putting it in her mouth. Cully and Greig seize the moment and enter the house. Cully puts his index finger to his lips. "Quiet as mice," he whispers, as they mount the uncarpeted stairs to the first floor.

"That was a good trick with the sweeties," Greig says, as the two men stand on the landing outside the door to Flashley's room.

"Poor child," Cully says, as they turn the handle of the door, and find it is unlocked. "I pity any little one who has to endure what she has. Life is hard enough without being a cripple."

They go into the room and glance around, seeking clues. They are immediately struck by the sense of order. Clothes hang on a rail. Shoes and a pair of overshoes are lined up underneath. Shaving tackle and hair oil are on the washstand, along with a cake of yellow soap and a neatly folded striped flannel. Everything is neat and tidy.

"The curtains are drawn," Greig observes. "And the bed hasn't been slept in, which suggests to me he left here, but didn't return. He was planning to return, that is quite clear."

Cully crosses the room and opens a drawer in the bedside table. He sees a notebook, a pencil. The notebook lists the man's daily expenditure ~ food, coals, candles and rent, all neatly entered in weekly columns and balanced against his salary. Had he not been a valet, Mr. Flashley would have made an excellent accountant.

"I do not think we are looking for a man on the run," Cully says. "Nor even someone who has gone to ground. He has left too many personal possessions. Unless he has sold the little carvings, and has absconded with the profits."

Greig takes the notebook and turns to the back. "Now, this is most interesting," he says thoughtfully. "Our man seems to have liked a flutter. Here is a long list of bets. Small amounts but noted quite regularly. If this last entry is anything to go by, our man owed a considerable amount of money to somebody."

"I wonder whether it is related to his absence?" Cully muses. "Perhaps here is the motive for his theft?"

Greig's face indicates that he has something else he wishes to communicate, but before he can divulge what is on his mind, they hear the sound of heavy footsteps coming up the stairs to the accompaniment of wheezing. They turn round. A wide, squat woman in a print dress and a large cap stands in the doorway, her meaty arms folded. The small hunchback child peers anxiously round her ample aproned form.

"Ho yus?" the woman says. "Breaking and entering ~ caught red-handed too. Before I calls the police, who the devil are you?"

****

Robertson, the police surgeon, is just putting away his various surgical implements when Detective Inspector Lachlan Greig enters the cold white-washed mortuary.

21

Robertson favours him with his usual quizzical one-raised-eyebrow look. The look he reserves for members of the detective division, and any other officers of the Metropolitan Police who did not have specific medical training.

"Detective Inspector Greig?" he says, snapping shut the velvet-lined case that contained his surgical saw. "I confess I was not anticipating a visit from any of you at this juncture."

Greig agrees that this may well be so, but that he has a member of the public in the main building, to whom he would like to show the clothes of the man found hanging from a bridge.

"The person in question has a lodger of a similar age and description, who has not been seen for two nights in a row," Greig tells him. "It is just a hunch, but worth pursuing."

Robertson gives him a narrow-eyed look, then hands over a bundle of clothing.

"These are what the gentleman was wearing when he was brought in. Please return them after your so-called 'hunch' has been proven, or not."

Greig carries the bundle back to the main building, where the redoubtable landlady, who has been pacified and quite won over by the tall Scottish detective's charm, identifies them as belonging to her former lodger Mr. James Flashley, after which Cully escorts the landlady back home, saying he will call in on Mr. Daubney and inform him of the fate of his manservant. Meanwhile, Greig takes the clothes back to the police surgeon, along with the name of the dead man.

"Ah, I see," Robertson says. "A successful hunch, then. Thank you, Detective Inspector Greig. It is always good to have a name for the unfortunate individuals who end up on the police mortuary slab. I will now complete my report, which I shall submit to Detective Inspector Stride tomorrow without fail. I bid you good evening."

Detective Inspector Greig is in a suitably pensive frame of mind as he makes his way back to his lodgings. The connection that he suspected between the absent manservant and the all-too present body in the police morgue has now been proven correct. It is the same individual. But for the rest?

He remembers his old boss in Leith telling him about the five W's: who, what, where, when, why. Once you can answer each of them, he'd said, you have the case solved. Greig thinks he can probably answer three. The identity of who was in charge of the rope, and why it ended up round the neck of the murdered manservant, however, still remains to be discovered.

****

The district of Bloomsbury has a reputation as the intellectual and cultural centre of the city. The British Museum, that treasure-store of the world's antiquities and curiosities, lies at its heart. Writers, architects, poets, lawyers and educational reformers make their homes in the great tranquil squares, set about with umbrageous plane trees. It is said that Bloomsbury is like the quiet quarter of a country town, set in the midst of the roaring sounds and smells of the greatest city on earth.

Situated between Bernard Street and Guildford Street is one of the odder nooks in its desired WC postal district code. It is known as the Colonnade, and consists of a cobbled passageway, stables, and rather down-at-heel terraced houses, fronted by the structure that gives it its name.

This is where many small tradesmen live and work, some in shops on site, others leaving each day to work in larger factories and stores. Here are tailors, mantua-makers, shabby beer-shops, shoe-makers, dressmakers, the elderly woman who sews pleated fronts for pianofortes and at the far end, over a confectioner's, the dolls' house furniture workshop that employs ten-year old Izzy Harding.

The room where Izzy works is full of long tables at which the workers, mostly small girls, sit all day. Some paint tiny Louis XVI chairs and tables in gold paint. Others assemble and glue small wardrobes, dressing tables, dining sets, and kitchen dressers. None of the children have ever played with a dolls' house, let alone a doll. For most of them, play is an alien concept. As is furniture.

Having little hands is an advantage in this profession, likewise an ability to work accurately and at speed. The orders come streaming in from the big department stores. The overseer, herself not more than fourteen years old, but already a hardened entrepreneur, patrols the room constantly, checking the quality of workmanship, chastising those who slack off.

At noon, when the bells of the city chime the hour, the youthful overseer (her name is Kate) claps her hands and shouts "dinnertime", the signal for a general shuffling of feet, a scraping of boots on the wooden floor, and the noise of benches being pushed back.

Those lucky enough to have something to eat produce heels of hard cheese, pieces of bread and scraps of meat from various pockets and proceed to munch hungrily. For the rest, it is a chance to get their heads down and snatch a few minutes' welcome respite.

Izzy Harding swings her legs over her bench and goes towards the attic window, picking up a stool on her way. She is undersized for her age, with a face that might blossom into prettiness at a later stage. Now, her eyes are too big and hungry, her cheekbones too near the surface for beauty.

She climbs onto the stool and lifts her face to peer out. Birds swoop to and fro in the leaden-coloured sky. Smoke rises from chimneys, forming strange ghostly shapes in the air. A shaft of dust-laden sunshine lights up the planes of her small cat-like face with its pale hair and sea-green eyes that catch and hold the light.

If she stands on tiptoe and looks down, Izzy can see the top of a straggly tree, just beginning to shed its leaves. If she looks further afield, she sees the roof and top floor windows of a house in one of the grand gated squares, where poor people like her are forbidden to go. She can hear carriages, horses, the sounds of construction.

Izzy sucks the end of her ragged sleeve. It is not exactly nutritious, but better than nothing. She has brought no food to eat and supper is a long way into the future ~ if her vagabonding mother has remembered to buy anything. She doesn't hold out much hope.

The church bells ring the half-hour. The end of dinner-break. Heads are raised wearily from folded arms. The last morsels of food are stuffed into mouths. The workers return to their places. Izzy picks up her paintbrush, dips it into her pot of lacquer, and embarks on the line of miniscule cabinets that arrive in a steady stream from the assemblers and gluers at the other end of the table.

All afternoon she toils, the smell of the lacquer making her feel sick. It is the colour of treacle. But it isn't treacle. If it was, she'd probably have eaten the pot, even though she has no bread to go with it. Every now and then a man arrives and delivers more boxes of furniture to be assembled and painted. It is autumn, and the miniature housing market is buoyant.

Eventually, as the light begins to fade, the overseer rises. She goes to the top table and stands with her arms folded. The sign that work is finished for the day. Izzy screws the top back onto the varnish bottle and wipes her hands on her pinafore.

All around her, children are packing tiny furniture into boxes. Two older boys get brooms and begin sweeping the floorboards. Once everything has been tidied to the standard required, the overseer digs out a key from her pocket. The attic door is unlocked, and a steady stream of small pattering footsteps descend the stairs to street level.

Izzy Harding waves farewell to her co-workers. Then she ducks round the side of the building, scurries down a back alleyway, crosses several filth-ridden courts, finally entering a passageway so narrow that an adult has to turn sideways. At the end of the passageway is a small door. She pushes it open and enters a large, hot kitchen full of steam, pans frying, pots bubbling and people in filthy cooks' aprons shouting at each other over the noise.

This is the kitchen of Mrs Sarah McAdam's Select City Dining Room, which caters for the needs of the thousands of clerks who spend all day seated on high stools in dimly lit rooms, entering columns of figures into ledgers. At the end of the day, all they require are big plates of hot dinners served speedily and cheaply. Two nights a week, in the Victorian equivalent of the gig economy, Izzy Harding washes the plates.

As Izzy slides into the room, one of the cooks looks up from the huge pot of potatoes boiling away on the range, shouts, "Oi, you're late!" and throws a ladle at her head. Izzy ducks. She pulls out a box from under the butler sink, steps onto it, picks up the first greasy plate from the pile on the draining board, and sluices it under the cold tap.

This is her second job. For the next few hours she will wash dirty plates and cutlery and keep her head down. It is as boring and repetitive as painting dolls' house furniture. But it has one overwhelming advantage to the day job: it comes with food.

The meat bones, with their tassels of fat and gristle, are put straight into a large simmering stock pot on the side of the stove. But every now and then, when nobody is watching, Izzy will creep over with her box, and surreptitiously siphon off some of the liquid using the cracked cup she hides underneath it. At the end of her shift, Izzy gets paid in leftover bread, which she will cram as soon as she leaves the premises.

It will be dark by the time she finishes. She will make her way back through unlit alleys and foot-streets, occasionally almost tripping over a rat. The rats don't bother her though. In London, a person is never far from a rat. In one form or another.

Tonight, when Izzy gets in, she is going to be informed by Mrs Bridget O'Shaughnessy (widow, washerwoman and mother of five), who rents the first floor back of a dismal tenement and then sublets portions of the floor to make ends meet, that the rent is owing and her 'Ma' hasn't paid it.

Izzy keeps a small secret stash of coins hidden in her mattress, along with her other treasures: a shiny brass button, a length of bright scarlet ribbon she found in the street, a sheet of gold leaf, six farthings and a miniature dolls' tea-set, streaky-painted and deemed therefore to be too inferior to be sold. These are the only things she truly owns in the world.

Reluctantly, she'll dig out the rent money and pay her landlady, who mutters, as she always does on occasions like this something about *'shurely that craiture like yer Ma doesn't deserve a good childer like you'* as she drops the coins into her apron pocket. Too exhausted to worry about her absent parent, Izzy will lie down on the thin mattress on the floor, with her boots still on, and fall instantly asleep.

****

Maria Barklem does not like to describe what she does as charity. Charity, in her experience, comes in the form of stern-faced Christian ladies with condemnatory expressions. Charity sits in cold committee rooms and hides itself under worthy names, while doling out its meagre largesse with reluctant parsimony.

Maria Barklem has experienced enough charity throughout her life to recognise it for what it is, and to have nothing to do with it. She remembers, oh so vividly, the hand-me-down clothes that her mother would be given by the 'Society of Charitable Providers of Clothes for the Children of the Indigenous Poor & Worthy Clergy'. Dresses that were faded from too many washes, and discoloured under the armpits, coats with unmatching buttons, boots that were scuffed and thin-soled, but suitable for the child of a poor vicar.

Then there were the 'Coals and Batter Puddings' women, who used to turn up periodically with covered basins and bags. They always wanted to check that the family were actually deserving of their gifts, poking around the tiny grace and favour cottage on the edge of the graveyard, checking the pantry for any suspicious evidence of food that would mean the gifts would be summarily withdrawn.

Thus, Maria has grown into a slender, dark-haired young woman with a pointed chin and a habit of staring at the world as if daring it to take her on. Her bonnet might be last year's model, her dress unfashionable in cut and colour, but she is determined to do something important with her life. The decision has been forged upon the rocks of much childhood humiliation.

Part of this determination has resulted in Maria enrolling herself at the Working Women's College in

Queen Square, where she attends evening lectures, along with 200 other women. They are an eclectic mix of working women: dressmakers, barmaids, milliners, servants, and shop-workers like herself. Some of the students come from as far afield as Pimlico! Maria is currently learning Latin and mathematics and thinking about becoming a qualified teacher.

The bells of the local churches are in some disagreement about the exact moment when six o'clock arrives as Maria lets herself out of a small local baker and confectioner shop. She takes a key from her pocket and locks the door. She leaves behind an empty shop, still smelling enticingly of baking, though all the shelves are empty save for an elaborate plaster wedding cake in the front window.

Maria makes her way back home. Arriving on the doorstep, she is greeted by a collection of dishevelled children, who eye the cloth bag she is carrying with bright hopeful eyes. Maria smiles at them, makes a rapid head count, purses her lips for a second, then leads them to the back of the cottage, where she unlocks the kitchen door.

"Just teaching my class, Mother," she calls up the stairs. A faint reply comes floating back. Maria ushers the motley crowd into the kitchen, where they distribute themselves round the scrubbed deal table, emitting a variety of smells and odours as they make themselves comfortable.

She takes some battered slates and a packet of chalk from the kitchen drawer and distributes them amongst the scholars. Then she opens the cloth bag and removes a half-loaf of coarse bread. The scholars fix their eyes upon it. Maria fetches a plate and breaks the loaf into pieces.

"Now then," she says, "who can tell me what letter of the alphabet begins the word *bread*?"

A forest of hands.

"Alfie?"

"B! Innit, miss?"

"Quite correct," Maria says, passing him a piece. The child stuffs it into his mouth and chews ravenously.

By the time the word BREAD has been spelled, the actual item has been shared out and devoured. The words PIECE and GONE follow in quick succession. When nothing remains, not even a CRUMB, Maria passes on to elementary maths, using buttons from an old tin box that belonged to her mother. The scholars scratch their heads as they deduct or add buttons and work out the answers on their slates.

Time passes. The class is on their final exercise of the evening ~ sharing stories of their day, when a timid knock is heard on the kitchen door. Maria hurries to open it, her face lighting up when she sees the diminutive figure of Izzy Harding standing on the step.

"Oh Izzy, there you are!" she exclaims. "I wondered where you'd got to this evening. It isn't like you to miss your lessons."

Muttering an apology, Izzy Harding sidles into the room, shucking off her battered hat and coat. She slides onto the end of a bench, picks up a stick of chalk and a slate, and laboriously writes her name at the top. The others watch her curiously and in silence.

After a few minutes of scratching, Izzy looks up. She sets down the chalk and hands the slate to Maria, who reads:

Sory I was lat. Ma had a hedake.

Resisting the urge to apply corrections, Maria hands back the slate without comment. She can read between the lines and behind the spelling. Izzy wipes off the words with her sleeve. The lesson stutters to a halt. The scholars pile up their slates, hand over their chalk (with the exception of a lumpen-faced boy called Jonny

Farringer, who has eaten his) and file out of the kitchen door.

Maria watches their ragged shuffle back towards the street. It saddens her that Izzy Harding, the brightest and best of the class, has not been able to share in the food, but she knows better than to keep her back. Any sign of favouritism will be noted and begrudged. Her mission is to teach the rudiments of reading and writing, not to dispense charity to a select few.

She sets the kettle onto the stove, and prepares the simple supper that will sustain her invalid mother and herself. Maria wonders whether her best and most able pupil will eat tonight. She suspects not. One day, she promises herself, when she has her own school, things will be different for children like Izzy Harding. In the meantime, she will continue to do what she can to help them get along.

****

Bright and early next morning, Detective Inspector Stride arrives at Scotland Yard, refreshed by a mug of morning coffee purchased from his usual stallholders, who have reappeared on the corner of the piazza after a mysterious absence.

He enters the outer office, where a small group of last night's drunks are being processed by the desk constable before being released into society to become tonight's drunks. He progresses through to his office, noting that a selection of the morning papers has been placed upon his desk. Atop of them sits the autopsy report on James Flashley, late valet to Gerald Daubney, collector of small wooden Japanese carvings.

Stride opens the autopsy report, skimming over the medical terminology and Latin phrases with which Robertson likes to pepper his writing. Then he pauses, reaches for a pencil and makes a mark in the margin. Some time and several cups of coffee later, Stride catches up with Greig and Cully.

"Robertson's report on Mr. Flashley is done," he tells them. "He writes that the deceased's stomach contents were mainly liquid. Beer, he says. I think we should take a likeness of Mr. Flashley round some of the public houses near to where he was discovered. Somebody might remember him, and the company he was keeping. Worth a try. We can't sit around all day hoping something will turn up."

Greig exchanges a wry look with his colleague. Stride's assumption that they have been idly passing the time is, as usual, somewhat misplaced. A small team of police constables has already been scouring the neighbourhood, making door to door inquiries on the lines of: Had anybody seen anything unusual on the night in question? Had anybody seen a group of men in the vicinity of the bridge? Had anybody seen activity around the actual bridge itself? Had anybody seen anything at all? A negative response on all counts. To be expected. No one wanted to get drawn into something that might set them at odds with the community.

"We'll get on to it straight away," Cully says reassuringly.

Some time later, the two detectives arrive at their first port of call. The Ship Inn is a low public house. If it got any lower, it would be resting on the actual mud of the river itself. There is an ooziness about its aspect, a drippy quality to the green door, as if it needed to be wrung out. The bricks look as if they would feel clammy to touch. The small ground-floor windows are water-stained and cloudy. Even the painted sign over the door, chafing on its rusty hooks, exudes dampness, as if the billowing main in the picture was leaking over the edges.

Greig and Cully enter. The Ship Inn is ill-lit, cavernous and almost totally empty. It smells of musty disuse. As they cross the floor, two matted dogs get up from their place in front of the smoky fire and start barking at them. A thrawn-faced barmaid, who could have breakfasted on lemons, screams incomprehensible abuse at the dogs, who look as if they might burst into tears as they slink off to a far corner. She leans on the bar, smiling with radiant falseness.

"'Morning gents. What's it to be?"

"Some information, if you please," Greig says, showing her his card. Stepping forward, he places a photograph onto the bar. The woman studies it for a second, then shakes her head.

"No. Never seen 'im before."

"He could have been in the company of a couple of other men. They are the ones we're seeking."

The barmaid pretends to consider the suggestion.

"Sorry, gents, wasn't working that night."

"I don't think I said what time of day I was interested in, did I?" Greig says, turning to Jack Cully.

"No, I don't think you did," Cully rejoins.

The barmaid closes her mouth firmly. The silence extends, settling round them. Greig and Cully wait. They have outwaited masters of suddenly-developed-muteness many times before, and they can outwait her if they have to.

"Look, you really don't want to know about them," she says finally.

"We do, that's why we're asking you," Cully says.

The barmaid purses her lips and goes silent again.

"Withholding information from the police is a crime," Cully says sternly. "Refusing to answer our questions is a crime. Lying to the police is a crime …"

A customer emerges from the far end of the room.

"Watering the beer is also a crime," he says, placing his empty pint pot on the counter.

The barmaid rounds on him in fury.

"Oi, you ~ this is a respectable house. We do not water the beer!"

The man shrugs. The barmaid glowers. The man catches Greig's eye, holds his gaze for a full second before slightly inclining his head towards the door. The two detectives watch him leave, then, ignoring the still spluttering barmaid, they silently follow him out.

The man is leaning on a wall, waiting for them to emerge. He touches his cap in greeting.

"Jonas Mellows, midshipman on The Golightly," he says. "My ship's due out of the Port of London this afternoon. I overheard what you were talking about."

He holds out his hand and Cully gives him the photograph. Mellows studies it for a few seconds, then nods.

"Aye, I recognise him. Comes in occasionally with Herbert Black and his brother Munro Black ~ black by name and black by nature. I guessed when Emma said you didn't want to know in *that* tone of voice, that it'd be something to do with them."

Greig names the specific evening they are interested in. The man scratches his head, frowns, then agrees that as far as he remembers, Munro Black was drinking in the Ship Inn in the early part of the evening, possibly in the company of another man, not his brother this time. He did not recall them leaving at any point.

"If you're going after the Black brothers, you'll need to keep your wits about you, gents. There's evil, and there's pure evil, and there's Herbert and Munro Black. As I know to my cost."

He rolls up his left sleeve and shows the two detectives a long scar, running from wrist to elbow.

"Knife fight with Herbert. He's the younger brother. Charmer on the surface. Nasty piece of work underneath. I grew up with them. They run things around here, if you get my drift," he nods at the police photograph, "Your man in the picture ~ dead? Thought so."

"If everyone is so afeard of them, why are you helping us?" Greig asks.

The midshipman smiles thinly. "As I said, my ship's due out of the Port of London on the afternoon tide. By the time the Black brothers realise who's shopped them, I'll be halfway to Lisbon. By the time I return, you'll have them both behind bars, if there's any justice in this world. Besides, Herbert Black and I have history, as you might say. And if you want to know what it is, go ask Amy Feacham ~ you'll find her behind the bar at the Mermaid's Arms in Earl Street. They don't water the beer there."

He touches his cap in farewell, then turns and heads off down one of the numerous small side streets. Greig and Cully watch him go. Cully checks his notebook. "The Mermaid's Arms ~ I don't think we've visited that one yet."

"Then I suggest we go there forthwith," Greig says. "Let us see what this Miss Feacham has to say."

The two detectives make their way through foot-streets that lead them in the direction of the wharfs and docks that line the river, until eventually they smell the raw stink of river mud, hear the slap of water against wooden stanchions, and see, in the distance, a forest of masts above the rooftops and tall chimneys belching clouds of black smoke.

Greig and Cully lose themselves, ask directions, lose themselves again, finally finding themselves on a swing-bridge overlooking a busy wharf, where lighters, schooners carrying coal from the north-east coast, sailing barges and watermen's skiffs are berthed or unloading cargoes.

Beer barrels are being rolled off a barge and up a narrow plank to the jetty. There is a row of dilapidated houses, some with their windows hanging over the water, their white-painted house-boards stained and peeling.

A small child leans out of a first-floor window, watching a stray dog searching for scraps on the runway down to the river. The air is full of hammering and sawing and the smell of wood, for there are a couple of ships tied up being refitted, their foretop masts and yards unshipped, their rigging and stays slackened.

At last, exasperated by their inability to locate it, Greig hails a man piloting a hay barge stacked high with bales and heading upstream, and is given directions to the Mermaid's Arms. The detectives cross the bridge, walk down the rather precarious plank and handrail structure that leads to the wharf and head up a small alleyway between two rows of houses, thus entering that part of the city known as Down by the Docks.

Down by the Docks is home to a great number of people, many of whom are out and about. The street is littered with oyster shells, fish heads, vegetable peelings, stray cats, small children, crawling babies, fighting dogs, women with unbonneted heads and bandanna kerchiefs floating from their shoulders, and seamen with bare tattooed arms and hands in pockets.

Every building in every court and every alley is a low boarding house, with posters in the front windows advertising 'Lodgings for Travellers' or 'Clean beds'. These places are rented by dock-labourers, sailors, sack workers or people who make their living by the waterside.

There are slop shops galore, run by swarthy bearded Jewish merchants, who have managed to suspend vast curtains of red and blue flannel shirts, nor'-wester hats and waterproof overalls outside their shops. There are sail-maker shops, shops supplying gear for ships or gear for sailors, provision-agents and customs offices all crammed together.

They pass a ship lying broadside-on to the wharf. Two stout gangplanks connect her with the wharf, and a row of carts and vans are transferring their cabbages, cheeses, tubs of butter, barrels of beer, milk, loaves of bread, sacks of flour, potatoes and boxes of biscuits from wharf to deck.

Greig and Cully side-step the various goods lying on the wharf, and continue their journey until they finally reach a public house. The sign over the door depicts a golden-haired young woman rising out of an azure-blue sea. She wears a welcoming smile at one end, a bright green fishtail at the other, and very little in between.

They push open the door. In contrast to the Ship Inn, this public house is brightly lit and welcoming, not least due to the attractive young women in spotless white aprons standing behind the gleaming bar.

The only customers at this time of day are three elderly men, with 'sea-dogs' written all over them. They have cloth caps and hunched shoulders and sit playing cards, their drinks at their right hands. One tosses a card, face-up, on the table, followed by his companion. The third gathers up the cards and re-shuffles them. His fingers are bent and gnarled, the tips stained brown with tobacco.

The old men glance up quickly as the detectives pass by their table, approach the bar and order their drinks. Then, as Greig and Cully pass their table once more on the way to a vacant corner booth, they deliberately glance down at the cards in their hands. Greig and Cully sit down. In a couple of minutes, the younger and prettier of the barmaids arrives, carrying two tankards.

"Your drinks, gents," she says, placing the tankards down on the scrubbed oak table. She stands back, arms folded. "I'm Amy Feacham. I know who you both are, and I know what you've come about."

They are not surprised. The speed with which a rumour can run round the city is a well-known phenomenon. Sometimes, the rumour is even up and running before the starting pistol has been fired.

Greig produces the photograph of James Flashley and lays it on the table. "Have you ever seen this man before, Miss Feacham?"

The barmaid raises her eyebrows at the polite appellation. She looks down. "Might have. He don't look too happy, does he?"

"On the evening we're interested in, we think he was in the company of a Mr. Munro Black. Mr. Black was possibly drinking in the Ship Inn."

"Ah. That'd explain the look on his face. They water the beer at the Ship. Everybody knows it."

Cully attempts to pull the conversation out of the quagmire before it settles in.

"Mr. Munro Black. You know where we might find him?"

Amy Feacham's face takes on a set expression. Her lips tighten.

"Maybe. You won't find him round here, I can tell you that for nothing."

Greig gives her his most winning smile.

"What can you tell us then? It would be very helpful if you could point us in the right direction."

"I'm sure it would. But how would it help me, is what I'm thinking."

Cully leans in. "We are talking murder here, Miss Feacham," he says quietly. "A brutal murder. Robbery too. It is your duty to help the police with their enquiries.

Any information you give us will be treated with the utmost confidence, I assure you on my word."

Amy Feacham laughs harshly. "You think I trust your word, Mr. P'liceman? Or the word of any man in this city?" She stares into the distance, her dark eyes solemn, her face remote and thoughtful.

The two detectives await her decision. Finally, she sighs.

"Right. This is what I'll say. If you want to find Herbert and Munro Black, don't go looking around here. They left this place behind them a long while ago. Too low for the likes of them now, we are. Ask in Russell Square, where the nobs of the West End live. I'm sure somebody will direct you to their door. And if you do find it and knock, you might care to ask about Rosa ~ say we haven't heard from her in a long while, eh."

Ah. Greig remembers the sailor's words. So this is the 'history' he spoke about. A row over a girl. He had thought the remark referred to something less prosaic, more swashbuckling.

"Who is Rosa?" Cully queries.

"My sister," comes the surprising reply. "She's only sixteen. Got lured away by Herbert Black. We warned her against him. Said he was no good for her. But she wouldn't listen, coz he bought her clothes and jewels and such. Made her all sorts of promises about being a fine lady.

"Next thing, she went off in a carriage, and we ain't seen nor heard from her since. Ma hasn't had a night's sleep for worrying, and my little sister cries her eyes out every time she sees Rosa's empty chair by the fire."

She stares fiercely at the detectives. "You say you want the Black brothers for murder? Well, I want them for taking away my sister. So, if you find them, you come straight back and let me know, eh? Let's call it my reward for 'helping the police with their enquiries', shall we?"

Having imparted her conditions, Amy Feacham picks up the drinks tray and goes back to the bar, leaving Greig and Cully staring thoughtfully into their pint pots. They had come looking for answers, but now, had discovered more questions. The investigation into the death of James Flashley, which seemed a fairly simple one, has just developed mission creep.

"Murder, robbery, and the abduction of a young woman," Cully murmurs. "I predict Detective Inspector Stride isn't going to like this at all. Not one little bit."

****

Gerald Daubney, antiquarian and collector, finds himself suddenly a ghost in his own life. His fortress walls have been breached. The empire is crumbling, the barbarians are at the gates. In the past week, he has been robbed by persons unknown in conjunction with a known person, whom he trusted, and who has been brutally murdered. His privacy has been invaded by policemen, who have asked him all sorts of questions while walking round his domain, one of them *picking things up and handling them.*

The horror! The horror!

Nobody has ever visited his shuttered and heavily curtained abode since the day his beloved mother passed away in the front bedroom. Not many people visited it before this event took place, truth to tell. And now, there appears to be a constant stream of people knocking at his door, sitting on his furniture and offering sympathy while eyeing his precious objects with greedy accumulative eyes. He feels violated by visitors.

Here are two more of them: fellow antiquarians, shown in by a maid who is some relative of the cook, and has been appointed on a temporary basis. By whom? He did not appoint her. He does not know her name, but her shoes squeak in an alarming fashion. The visitors seat themselves on two of the small, antique, velvet upholstered occasional chairs, relics from his childhood, and not meant to take the weight of their ample bulky bodies.

The maid inquires, in a deferential voice, whether it is his wish that refreshments should be served. His wish is that he'd be left alone with his cat, and his sorrows, but proprieties must be adhered to, so he inclines his head in agreement.

"Now then, Daubney, now then, how are you doing, old man?" asks Charles Warren, collector of the sort of paintings generally hung in a locked study away from innocent female eyes.

Daubney winces. He would hardly describe himself as an 'old man' and the interlocuter's tone of voice suggests he is suffering from some chronic and painful condition.

"We were passing your door, so we thought we'd look in," says his companion, antiquarian Augustus Roach-Smith, acquirer of British urns and Roman vessels.

Nobody 'just passes his door', Daubney thinks. There is a high wall and an equally high iron gate, leading to the tall flat-faced white house which is itself situated at the end of an unpaved road, in an unfashionable part of the city. Its charm lies in its obscurity. Before the robbery, he could go for weeks without seeing another human being, save for servants or tradesmen, who didn't count. It was a state of affairs that suited him admirably.

Now, seemingly, it is open house. The world and its friends beat a path to his door, all eager to give their opinion on what happened and how it might have happened and why it happened. Everybody is an expert.

Everybody has a theory. Everybody wants to tramp round the rooms, view the empty cabinet, shake their heads, and ask him the exact value of what he has lost. They are like the crowd at a public hanging. He should sell tickets, he thinks bitterly, as the unnamed small female servant enters with a tea tray.

The two collectors spoon sugar into their cups, fill their plates with tiny sandwiches and shortbread biscuits. Daubney takes a cup and plate but eats and drinks nothing. His appetite, like his precious collection of netsuke, has left him.

"We gather that the police have identified the body they found swinging from the bridge as that of your manservant," says the acquirer of urns, his mouth full of sandwich.

Daubney stares at him. "What is this? How have you 'gathered' it?"

"Oh, it was in one of the morning papers. They quoted you: apparently you said what a terrible business it was and how you'd never suspected your own manservant of being capable of such a heinous crime as robbing his own master."

Daubney blinks. He spoke to the newspapers? He does not recall saying anything to the newspapers. He would never say anything to the newspapers. And he had impressed upon the two detectives that they must not speak to the newspapers and his name must be kept out of the public arena at all costs. So how has this happened?

All at once, a fleeting memory crosses his mind, hovers, and settles. Oh … wait … yesterday morning, when he was leaving the house to take a short walk, there was a man standing on the pavement outside. A vulgar man in a loud waistcoat who had hailed him by name and called him 'squire' and said he'd come to offer his condolences on the death of his manservant.

Daubney had assumed, from his low demeanour and unwelcome air of familiarity that he was some acquaintance of James Flashley, possibly even a family member. Thus, he had attempted some platitudinous remark, uttered in a low monosyllabic voice, purely for civility's sake. Then he had hurried away. When he returned, the man had gone, and he had thought no more of the encounter.

Now he discovers that from one brief insignificant meeting, this duplicitous individual has confected a story, throwing him into the lurid limelight of unwelcome publicity. His hand, holding the fine porcelain teacup, trembles so much that liquid slops into the saucer. He places it down on the rosewood table and clasps his hands between his legs, fixing his gaze upon the floor. The two collectors exchange glances over his bowed head.

"Do buck up, old man," Charles Warren says.

A tremor runs through Daubney's etiolated frame. He has heard the same words shouted by various brutes of games masters as he lay winded, wounded, bruised or bleeding on some muddy playing field. Though 'old man' was usually replaced by 'stupid boy'.

Silence falls, deep and profound.

All three men know that in the minds of their contemporaries ~ the ones that inhabit the world outside that of the avid collector, they are regarded as life's losers. Weak, obsessive, and in some eyes, comical figures. They also know that their devotion to 'things' is caricatured in the popular journals.

Daubney recalls that only last week, Punch referred to it as *Chronic Chinamania*, accompanying the article with a cartoon portraying a group of shabbily clad collectors weeping uncontrollably over a dropped plate (a couple of whom were instantly recognisable as members of the Club).

It is at such a time as this that public opinion may have a point. The antiquarians and collectors are, so to speak, the limpets of the human race, clinging onto their small rocks for survival as the tide of indifferent humanity washes past them.

Augustus Roach-Smith eventually breaks the silence that has fallen, like the dust of ages, upon the conversation. "So, what's the plan, old man?"

Plan, the limpet thinks? What plan? Why does he need a plan? He has no plan. Just an empty cabinet and a feeling of deep, dark despair. He bites the inside of his mouth, tasting his own blood, hot and ferric. He shakes his head.

The two antiquarians exchange a glance. The glance says: *we have fulfilled our obligations. We cannot do more with such uncompromising material.* They rise, as one, mutter a few farewell platitudes and make their way out to the badly lit hallway, where they help themselves to their own hats and coats and see themselves out.

"Well," Warren says when they are far enough away from the house. "What do you think?"

"Always was a rum chap, Daubney," Roach-Smith replies. "Remember a lecture he gave last year on those little Japanese wooden things ~ couldn't understand a word."

"Do you think he'll ever get them back?"

The other shakes his head. "Not a hope. Miles away by now. Probably sold to some other collector for a tidy sum. Might even have been exported. Sad, really."

"Yerss ... sad," Warren sighs. Then brightens. "Spot of dinner?"

"Why not. Gives you an appetite, all this sympathy lark."

The two hail a cab and are shortly dropped off at their club, where a plate of beefsteak pie and potato soon dispels the last vestiges of sympathy that was threatening to linger around, like a bad smell.

Gerald Daubney waits until he is sure they won't return. Then he rises, fetches a chair and sits down in front of the empty cabinet, his gaze fixed upon the shelves, his mind still seeing them filled with his treasures: the tiger, the monkey, the elephant, the rats, the fruits and nuts, the two toads, the tiny squatting beggar, the erotic ones he always placed at the back of the cabinet, and his beloved Edo cat.

Time passes. He is not aware of it. He feels as if he is retreating into an immense empty space. A desolate state of being. There are a lot of ways of being lost, not all of them involve being missing. Sometimes you could get lost right there in plain sight, stepping out of your life or disappearing into it.

Meanwhile the white cat, who has been sleeping under the drawing-room settee, emerges, leaps onto the side table and starts to investigate the sandwiches. Discovering a bloater paste one, she picks it up in her soft mouth and carries it back to her hiding-place to eat.

****

Let us move to another part of the city, where we discover Mrs Riva Hemmyng-Stratton, novelist, sitting at a writing desk, and glancing, in a meditative way, at the damp trees in the garden. She is the author of many books depicting the fashionable life of the English aristocracy, popularly known as 'silver fork novels'.

Her works include such titles as: *Astley Tremaine or The Man of Refinement*, *If Only She had Known*, *The Recipe for Diamonds*, *The Adventures of a High-born Lady*, and *Cecil Danvers*, her most recently published and by far her most popular book to date, a thrilling tale of secret liaisons, scandal and divorce in the higher echelons of society.

The writer is engaged in a tricky segment of her current manuscript, which features gallant Edgar Blakelock (*fine black moustache and glittering eyes*) and her heroine, Clarissa Ferrers (*golden curls, retroussé nose, and slender rose-tipped fingers*).

The plot revolves around a French snuff-box, something the novelist is not familiar with, but is now introduced as an *objet* of great interest (the insertion of French or Italian words elevates the prose and lifts the reader out of their mundane parlours and straight into the exotic *milieu* of the affluent upper-classes).

Mrs Riva Hemmyng-Stratton mentally identifies as 'the Author', as in: *'the Author knows that it is nearly time to bid farewell to the characters and go about the business of the day.'* Indeed, the small ormolu clock on the mantelpiece has just struck three, a reminder that the world outside the window awaits her attention.

The pen is laid down. The fates of Clarissa Ferrers and Edgar Blakelock are put aside, albeit temporarily. The Author has an appointment at one of the discreet little tearooms off the main thoroughfare, where a well-born gentleman could entertain a wife or a lady friend without causing eyebrows to be raised, and a middle-aged woman of outwardly impeccable rectitude might spy on them from a discreet corner, purely for the purposes of literary research, of course.

Mrs Hemmyng-Stratton dons an inconspicuous mantle and a harmless bonnet with a veil, tucks her bag (containing her notebook and trusty pencil) under her arm and sallies forth to catch the omnibus. A few stops later, she arrives at her destination, and settles herself at a corner table, where, having ordered a pot of China tea and a small slice of sponge cake, she removes her gloves, lifts her veil and peers hopefully round the room.

Ah. She spies some likely prey. An elegantly dressed man with dark hair and neatly-trimmed beard is entertaining a young Beauty. The Author mentally notes the bloom on the Beauty's cheeks, the chestnut curls peeping out of a fashionable straw bonnet, trimmed with blue ribbons and prettily dyed feathers, the well-fitting gloves.

Her companion is wearing the sort of suit that bespeaks access to a personal tailor. His linen is impeccable. (In her books, the Author sets great store by the cut of a coat, the tying of a cravat, the crispness of a linen shirt. It depicts manliness as well as class. As for shoes and boots ~ there is so much that can be deduced from footwear).

A notebook is extracted from the bag and opened. Feigning indifference to her surroundings and those who occupy it, the Author begins to write, pausing every now and then to sip tea and crumble cake. She sees the man lean forward and say something *sotto voce*, to his fair companion; the words bring a blush to the Beauty's cheek.

(*'Why, my beloved girl, how fast the hours speed. 'Tis almost time for us to part, I to the gilded saloon of Clubland, and you, my cherished blossom, to the bosom of your aristocratic family.' A sigh convulses his manly frame. 'Ah, Clarissa, you know that I desire your happiness above all things. How to procure it ~ therein lies the chief interest of my life.'*)

Before she has time to turn the page, the man rises, offers his arm to the Beauty and together they make their way out of the tea-room. Mrs Hemmyng-Stratton presumes that his carriage is waiting in a side street. Liveried footman in attendance. A fine pair of matching bays awaiting the instruction to 'trot on'. She cannot imagine that they would be conveyed by anything as mundane as an Atlas omnibus.

On the return journey, the highborn gentleman will hold Beauty's pretty soft fingers and she will shed a tear, upon which her escort will tenderly offer her his handkerchief, which will smell of Bond Street musk and millefleur. Ah, she can almost picture the scene, such is the benefit of a vivid imagination and several very successful novels.

Meanwhile, she must make her own way home. She pays for her tea, her head full of ideas for the next scene of her novel as she walks to the stop. The omnibus arrives. She hails it and climbs aboard. The only vacant seat is next to a mother with a loud, sticky child. The Author does not like children, loud, sticky or otherwise. Children, in her opinion, should neither be seen nor heard. There are no children in any of her novels, and her personal experience of the state is so far in the past as to have been obliterated by the mists of time.

She is relieved when the omnibus eventually reaches her stop and she can pay, alight and wend her way to the peace of her fireside, where it is her intention to enjoy a further cup of tea, the drink that *'cheers but does not inebriate'*, as William Cowper (a poet of whose work she is a great admirer), so aptly put it.

But Mrs Hemmyng-Stratton is not going to enjoy her peace and simple fare for long. A letter awaits her, propped up on the mantelpiece by Dulcie, the maidservant. It is from Charles Colbourne, her book publisher, and its unexpected contents are going to cause her a great deal of perturbation and sleepless nights.

****

There are many things that Detective Inspector Stride does not like. New boots, paperwork, cold foggy mornings, his wife's scrag end of mutton stew, and having to run the gauntlet of Robertson's acerbic personality, feature high on his list of pet hates.

He is also extremely lairy of members of the press (mentally filed under 'scum of the earth') door-stepping him on his way to work. Thus, when a familiar figure in a loud check coat, soft cap and waistcoat steps from an alcove and hails him jovially, Stride's first instinct is to ignore. Then to quicken his pace.

"Oi Stride, got a bit of news for you," Mr. Richard Dandy, aka Dandy Dick, calls out. He is chief reporter on *The Inquirer* ('One of Fleet Street's Finest Papers') and Stride's nemesis.

"That's Detective Inspector Stride to you, *Mr.* Dandy," he replies with barely concealed venom.

"Whatever you say, squire, whatever you say." Dandy shrugs. He folds his arms and smiles in an irritating manner.

"What I *say* is, you are blocking my path. Kindly step aside and allow me to get to my place of work."

Dandy Dick doesn't move. "So you're not interested in what I've discovered about your Mr. Flashley, then? Shame. Never mind, I'll have to inform the Man in the Street first. See what he makes of it. Sheds a whole new light on why he ended up swinging on the end of a rope."

Stride bites down on his anger.

"Aha ~ you are interested?"

"Go ahead," Stride says between gritted teeth.

"Well then, since you asked so nicely, hur hur: a little bird ~ and it's a reliable little bird, told me that your man liked a flutter ~ gee-gees, cards, boxing, and the like. Keen as mustard. Only he wasn't as keen on paying up when he lost. There were quite a few debt-collectors with his name at the top of their lists. I'm talking about the kind of coves who'd be happy to be paid in 'kind', if you take my meaning. Bag left under the public house table. No questions asked."

"Go on," Stride says.

"That's it," Dandy Dick says. "I'm naming no names. Over to you detective inspector. Can't expect me to do all your work for you. Oh, and while I'm here, how's the Scottish one getting on with his new lady-love? They were spotted holding hands in the park the other Sunday. Very cosy. *Tray romanteek,* as the French say. Has he named the day yet? Tell him to invite *The Inquirer* to the nuptials. We'll give him a good write-up. Page five, with a nice picture of the happy pair. Always willing to support the forces of law and order, as you know."

Stride shudders. "Yes, thank you. I think I can confidently speak for my colleague when I say he will be delighted to decline your offer. On your way, Mr. Dandy. On your way."

Dandy Dick throws him another maddening grin. Then he saunters off in the direction of the Strand, his hands in his coat pockets, leaving a thoughtful Stride to make his way to Scotland Yard, where the report from Greig and Cully's earlier investigation awaits his attention. And indeed, as Jack Cully predicted, he isn't going to like it. One little bit.

****

Rays of golden autumn sun light up the hedges, as Mrs Hemmyng-Stratton makes her way towards Salisbury Square. Idly, she wonders whether this is what Moses saw ~ a bright patch of sunshine on a hedge, and thought it was holy fire. She reaches the dingy building that houses Charles Colbourne & Co., publishers of popular and classic fiction (there is no '& Co.' but it makes the business sound grander than it is).

She enters the outer office. The office clerk is in the middle of writing something down in a large black ledger. He holds up a finger, indicating he will be with her in a minute. The finger then points to a seat in the far corner. A man who can communicate so much in so few words, she thinks. Or no words at all. Just a single digit.

Mrs Hemmyng-Stratton sits and waits. She tries to conjure up a plausible reason why, out of the blue, Mr. Colbourne would write her a letter like that. '*Certain matters of import have been brought to my notice*' was what he wrote. '*It is imperative that we meet to discuss them at your earliest convenience*'.

Somehow, even with the most vivid imagination (and the Author's imagination has no limits to its vividness) this does not sound like good news. Time passes. Eventually, the inner door opens and her publisher appears. He is a thickset man in his early forties, his dark hair shiny with boar's grease. He has small pale blue eyes and a thin nose that angles slightly to the left-hand side.

"Ah," he says, upon spotting the Author.

An unpropitious opening. Given her sales and popularity, she expected more than this greeting. She follows him into his inner sanctum and places herself on what she privately refers to as The Writers' Chair. Mrs Hemmyng-Stratton likes to imagine that the spirits of many great authors from the past, who have sat where she is sitting now, have imbued the faded, burgundy damask upholstery with their inspired thoughts.

Colbourne retreats to the far side of the desk, where he picks up a cream manila envelope, upends it, and extracts a letter. "This communication was received yesterday. It comes from Strutt & Preening, lawyers who represent Lord Edwin Lackington ~ does the name ring any bells with you?"

She frowns, shakes her head.

"Well, it should. According to this letter, it has been drawn to his attention that you have taken certain events surrounding his divorce case, in particular, events involving his wife and another person, and written them into your novel. Now then, what do you say?"

Her jaw drops open.

"But … but … I do not know the Lord, nor his situation, so how is this possible?" she stutters, clasping her hands.

"The lawyers write that the circumstances leading up to the divorce case, which was based upon the separation of Lord and Lady Lackington on the grounds of her scandalous behaviour with a member of the London artistic community, and the placing of the unfortunate lady into a lunatic asylum for her own protection, are minutely depicted in your novel *Cecil Danvers.*

"I quote from the letter: *The book incorporates details of the affair, the device of the umbrella, the railway carriage and the small discreet apartment behind Oxford Street. It is an exact replication of the events that caused such distress to the Lackington family, and friends of the family. My client, Lord Edwin Lackington awaits your response to this letter, and may seek damages and compensation in the High Court to restore his reputation in the public eye.*"

The Author feels cold. Sick. Dizzy. Bewildered. She racks her brains to see if she can find any remembrance at all of the events she is supposed to have replicated.

"I do not know how to answer this charge," she says finally. "My books are works of fiction. They come from my own head. I have never taken events or individuals from real life and placed them in any novel. Never. Nor would I."

Colbourne treats her to a long, level stare.

"You'd be prepared to stand up in a court of law and swear to this?"

The Author swallows. "If I have to, yes."

He nods. "Then I shall reply to the lawyers and tell them what you have said. As far as you are concerned, this is an unfortunate coincidence and cannot be seen as a deliberate attempt to make fiction from unfortunate events that you never read about, nor heard of, nor knew had taken place, am I correct?"

"Yes, yes. That is how it was. Pure coincidence. Please make that quite clear. I am happy to rewrite the book if the lawyers demand it. Anything to show Lord Lackington I never meant any hurt to him or his family."

Colbourne nods and stands, indicating that the meeting is at an end. The Author reties her bonnet strings, then gets shakily to her feet and totters out of the office, still rigid with shock. Colbourne waits until he is sure she has left the building. Then he summons his clerk and orders him to take down a letter at his dictation.

Privately, he knows that writers like Hemmyng-Stratton are two-a-penny. He has a pile of unsolicited manuscripts stuffed in his cupboard, most of which are pretty well the same quality and content. But publicity such as this cannot be bought or manufactured. It only comes a small publisher's way once in a lifetime, and he intends to make the most of it.

As soon as news of what has happened comes out, and it will come out, even if he has to go to every newspaper in the city, copies of *Cecil Danvers* are going to fly off W. H. Smith's station bookstalls and out of Mudie's lending library like hot cakes. There will be second and third impressions. Orders galore from small booksellers. He is going to make money. More money than he could ever dream of.

Colbourne dictates. The clerk writes. Then Colbourne signs the letter with a flourish and instructs the clerk to deliver it by hand to Strutt & Preening at their Gray's Inn Chambers, but not to bother waiting for an answer.

As soon as the clerk has gone, Colbourne reaches down his hat and coat, and sets out to speak to his printer. There is much to organise. He swaggers along the pavement, swinging his walking stick in a debonair fashion. Publish and be damned, be damned! Publish and be damned rich, that's more like it!

****

While Charles Colbourne is counting his prospective wealth and gloating over his good fortune, in another part of the greatest city on earth, three detectives are pooling information and trying to come up with a way of taking their investigation forward.

"Is this not what our Mr. Robertson would call devising a *modus operandi?*" Greig remarks cheerfully, stretching his legs to the almost non-existent fire spluttering in the grate.

Stride shoots him a glance. *Don't you start*, it says. "As I see it," he remarks, drumming a pencil against the side of a coffee cup, "We have several lines of inquiry: There is the local one ~ not that anybody is speaking to us, of course, good law-abiding lot that they are: saw nothing, heard nothing, saying nothing. Then there are the Black brothers ~ who sound like criminals who've moved up-market. The third line of inquiry is asking round our sources if they know who owned James Flashley's debt and how much it was."

"If he was gambling and losing money, that would certainly explain the theft," Cully says. "But I don't understand why he was murdered. It doesn't make sense. You don't hang a man because he owes you money. You certainly don't hang a man if he's just paid up."

"I think the answers to all these questions are to be found in Russell Square," Stride says. "Yes, that is where they lie. With the blackguard Black brothers ~ a good description, I think. We must go at once and make inquiries, but we will need to tread warily ~ this is where the so-called 'better class' of people live and they won't take kindly to being treated like the sort of people we usually deal with. I shall accompany you, just to make sure you don't make any missteps."

Stride's confidence in his own investigative abilities is not shared by the rest of the detective division, but luckily for him he is too busy rearranging his desk prior to leaving to notice Greig & Cully exchanging a quick rueful glance.

****

The large townhouses of Russell Square are inhabited by merchants, bankers, the Sirs and my Noble Lords. Not as upper-class as Hanover Square, whose inhabitants look down upon it as a poor neighbour, but still possessing a private garden, surrounded by green-painted railings and planted with great plane trees.

There is a statue of Francis Russell, Duke of Bedford at the centre of the garden, a reminder that the privileged inhabitants owe their circumstances to someone even more privileged. Detective Inspector Stride enters the square, accompanied by Detective Sergeant Jack Cully. Lachlan Greig has remained at Scotland Yard to instruct a couple of new recruits who are not convinced about the concept of joined-up writing.

The two men pause at the north end, contemplating their next move. After a few silent minutes have elapsed, Cully says, "We have been here before, haven't we?"

Stride turns to face him. "Exactly what I was thinking. It was 1860. Seven years ago. Almost the same time of year when we found the body of that Romanian Countess. Impaled on the railings."

"If she was a Countess," Cully murmurs, and Stride nods, pulling a wry face.

What they had discovered on that terrible night has haunted both men for many years afterwards. Indeed, Stride still has the occasional nightmare, from which he emerges cold and shaken in the small hours. Always the same thing: Something with black fur and glaring yellow eyes is stalking him through the empty streets of the city.

"Number 55, if I'm not mistaken," he says. "South end of the square. Might just as well start there with our inquiries as anywhere else. Come on."

The two detectives cross the square. They arrive outside Number 55, which has undergone a makeover since their last visit. A glazed cast-iron porch now extends from the gate to the front door. There are fresh blinds at the windows and the chipped black and white chessboard tiles on the front path have been replaced by newer versions.

And yet.

Something about the house still exudes unease. It is as if the ghosts of the past linger on, albeit tamed and modernised. Cully is reminded of a previous case: the brutal murder by a man of his wife and two children. Questioning the neighbours, he was told over and over again that the house in which they'd lived had a 'reputation' ~ misfortune of some kind had always affected everybody who'd inhabited it.

At the time, he'd dismissed it as local folklore. Then the house got blown up in a gas-leak. Now, as the detectives open the wrought-iron gate and walk up to the black-painted front-door with its elaborate new brass furnishings, he is prepared to give folklore the benefit of the doubt.

Stride's brisk knock brings a small housemaid to the door. Her eyes widen at the sight of the two detectives and her mouth falls ajar. Stride fixes her with an official stare. As a young police officer, he quickly realised that the emotion he most often inspired in people was alarm followed by pre-emptive guilt. It had its uses.

"Is your master within?" he inquires loftily, proffering his card. The girl gapes at him, wipes her hands on her apron and eyes the small cardboard rectangle suspiciously. She does not take it.

"Is he wivvin what?" she asks.

Cully smiles inwardly. Just because the 'better class' of people inhabit these luxurious houses, it doesn't follow that they employ the 'better sort' of servants. This servant-girl, little more than a child, has a scared, half-witted look about her.

"We are looking for two gentlemen who we believe live in the Square. Their names are Mr. Munro and Mr. Herbert Black," he says in a slightly softer tone than his colleague. "Do they live here, in this house? Or if not, do you know where we might find them?"

The girl frowns. Her eyes dart from side to side as if seeking an answer in the ether that surrounds them. Stride and Cully stand and wait.

"Is it about business?" she asks, at length.

Stride nods. "It is indeed."

"Umm. I'll have to ask," she says, and before they can stop her, she closes the door in their faces.

They wait a little longer. Then Stride knocks loudly on the door again. This time, nobody comes to open it.

"Aha. Well, well, it looks as if we may have found them," he says, rubbing his hands together. "That was a piece of unexpected luck!"

Cully considers the possibility that Stride is right. Or that he has just terrified a young servant half out of her wits and sent her scurrying back to her basement scullery without passing on the message.

They walk back down the path.

"We will call again soon," Stride says. "Meanwhile, these Watch Boxes need to be manned. I'll go and round up some of the local beat constables."

As they turn to cross the square, Cully glances back at the house. His eyes stray upwards to the third floor. At one of the windows, he suddenly spies the pale triangle of a woman's face, framed in dark curls. Their eyes meet. Her mouth opens, but she is too far away for him to work out what she is saying. Then she disappears, and the blind is pulled down.

"I'll keep watch until the constables arrive," he says. "I can use one of the boxes."

Stride nods, "If you're quite sure."

He hurries away. Cully stations himself inside an empty Watch Box. Its narrow aperture gives him a clear view of the house. He has a sudden sense of déjà-vu, remembering how, as a very young constable, still wet behind the ears, he took his turn at being on duty in just such a Watch Box on the edge of one of the exclusive London squares.

He recalls the cold, the sense of isolation, with just a rattle and a candle for company. The rich inhabitants of the square barely acknowledged his presence as they came and went in their private carriages or on horseback. He, like the box, was just part of the outdoor furnishings. A way of preserving their privacy and keeping themselves and other poorer neighbours apart.

But that was long ago, he reminds himself. And now, here he is, a member of the detective division, with a wife and two beautiful daughters. He hears the clatter of hooves as a carriage drives past the box. Cully applies his gaze to the small wooden aperture. The carriage sweeps round the side of the square and comes to a halt outside Number 55.

****

Mrs Riva Hemmyng-Stratton, novelist, sits at her small walnut writing desk. It is furnished with all her writing accoutrements: the bottle of black ink, an assortment of pens and pencils, a blotter and a stack of white paper. Beyond the window, leaves are dancing madly in the wind. Little puffed clouds are scudding across the grey sky and smoke rises upwards from numberless chimneys.

She does not notice. With hot glowing cheek and palpitating bosom (as befits a true tragic heroine), she is thinking about the awful predicament that has suddenly befallen her. She is quite sure that the events described in her book were not copied. She cannot recall ever hearing of the affair that she is supposed to have fictionalised. But how, oh how, can she prove it?

The Author rests her elbows on the desk, her chin propped up by her cupped hands. There is a small teapot, a cup and saucer, and a plate of macaroons next to her elbow, but neither bite nor sup has passed her lips since she got in.

What to do ~ oh what to do? Will she have to change her name? To retire from the literary scene, wherein she has enjoyed modest success? Must she go back to once again writing worthy Sunday school stories for small children?

Perish the thought! A shudder of horror runs through her artistic frame. She cannot go back there. Not now she has entered, (albeit fictionally) the glittering world of the aristocracy. The bible is all very well and good in its way, but it cannot compare to silk dresses, frogged coats or the chandelier-lit ballrooms and intrigues of the fashionable elite.

Listlessly, she picks up the top page of her new *oeuvre*. Her beautiful heroine (possessor of a refined *cinquecento* profile) is dressed in a delicately folded and draped ivory silk gown adorned simply by a long and slender chain set with uncut jewels. She is waiting for the arrival of her dashing suitor.

The heroine waits. The Author sighs. Her Muse has quite forsaken her. She has nothing to add. Her heroine will have to wait a little longer. Her creator has more important problems. Mrs Hemmyng-Stratton breaks a piece off one of the macaroons and pops it absentmindedly into her mouth. Her fate, unlike that of her heroine, lies in the unsteady hands of an unknown woman incarcerated in a lunatic asylum.

It is exactly like the plot of a novel. A wronged Lord, a beautiful Lady (she assumes she is beautiful) shut away from the world behind stout walls. And she, the innocent party, dragged unwittingly into the story.

All at once, she sees herself in a new light. Her predicament resembles the plot of a book written by Mr. Wilkie Collins, a writer she very much admires. The Author cogitates, then rises, goes to her little walnut bookcase and withdraws a copy of *The Woman in White*. Abandoning her heroine entirely, she takes the book and the plate of macaroons to an easy chair and starts turning the pages.

Fiction has brought about her awkward predicament. Therefore, let fiction extract her from it. The resolution to her current dilemma lies within these covers. It must do. She has only to peruse the plot, and then use her imagination.

****

Meanwhile, peering through the aperture of the police Watch Box, Jack Cully sees the carriage door open. A stout matronly woman, dressed in respectable black, alights. There is a pause. Then, one after another, two young girls descend. Slowly.

From his unseen vantage point, Cully can tell there is something not right about them. Their movements are slow and languorous, as if they were swimming through treacle. Their eyes stare straight ahead and their faces show no emotion at all, as they are pushed and pulled through the gate, then dragged up the path to the front door of Number 55.

There is a brief pause, after which the woman returns with the two girls, now accompanied by a third. Cully focuses upon the little group. He is sure she is the girl whose face he saw at an upper window. The woman hustles them all into the carriage, then gets in herself, tucking some notes into her bag.

She slams the door, and they are driven away, leaving Cully to ponder upon what he has just witnessed. If this is what he thinks it is, and he is pretty sure it *is* what he thinks it is, then they have uncovered something far darker than the theft of some miniature Japanese wooden carvings. Darker even, than the taking of a man's life.

A short while later, two constables from C Division enter the square. Cully extracts himself from his vantage point and invites them to accompany him. Positioning them at a discreet distance, he knocks on the door of Number 55.

This time, the door is opened by a different parlour maid wearing a black dress, an afternoon apron and smart cap. Cully inquires as to the occupants' whereabouts, and is informed tartly that '*Mr. Black is occupied with business at the moment and is not receiving visitors.*'

Cully states his wish to wait. Smiling affably, he steps over the threshold. He has acquired, over the years, the knack of endearing himself to house servants, unlike Stride, who has a tendency to speak hectoringly, and make demands which put their backs up.

His affability pays off. The maid disappears, leaving him to his own devises. Cully sits on one of the two gold-painted hall chairs placed on either side of a small table. He has retained his coat and hat in case a speedy getaway is on the cards.

A grandfather clock ticks mechanically. Apart from that, the house is absolutely silent. Cully strains his ears trying to make out any voices, possibly in distress, but the thick carpets and closed doors mask off any sounds.

Ten minutes pass by. Slowly. Cully sighs. For all he knows, he could be here for hours. There is a fireplace with a mirrored over-mantel close by the staircase. He gets up and goes to check his appearance. The Watch Box had not been dusted for a long time.

The over-mantel contains a brass dish on a stand for visiting cards, a china shepherdess, and a little cat, carved in ivory. The cat has green eyes; its head is turned to one side as it washes its flank with a small pink tongue. It has 'clue' written all over it. Cully picks it up. Could this possibly be what Mr. Daubney calls a netsuke?

He turns it over. There are some black painted marks on the underside. They might be Japanese writing ~ Cully has never seen Japanese writing before so he can't be sure. He puts the little cat carving down and makes a quick memorandum and a sketch in his notebook. He checks the time and decides not to wait any longer.

After instructing the two constables to maintain a close watch on the house and alert him or Detective Inspector Stride to anything unusual, Cully sets off at a brisk pace towards Scotland Yard. He intends to consult the list of missing netsuke when he gets back, just in case it contains a small ivory cat. If it does, then this might be the breakthrough they have all been waiting for.

****

Maria Barklem is also counting on something. In her case though, it is not breakthroughs but buns. Stale buns. Buns that have sat on a shelf in the shop window all day. Buns that are about to be reduced in price so that the Scottish baker for whom she works can eke out his slender profit margin, and nothing goes to waste.

Since first light, Maria has toiled behind the bakery counter, serving breakfast rolls and loaves to the servants and children sent out to fetch them. After that, there were the passing lines of workers, stepping inside to purchase a penny loaf or a bun. Later, housewives dropped by to fill their shopping baskets with the family's daily bread (and the odd cake as a treat).

Now it is late afternoon, and the rush has turned into a trickle. A few individuals, the sort that turn up regularly for the remaindering of produce, are waiting by the door for the signal that bread prices have dropped. Unlike earlier customers, these have poor quality clothing and faces pinched with want.

And there are so many of them, Maria muses, as she cuts bread into quarters, slipping a couple of buns into a bag under the counter, where the loaf of bread that burned in the oven, also awaits the end of her shift.

It does not escape her that a few yards away, in the majestic townhouses with black and white tiled steps leading up to the big front doors, people will be preparing to dine in warm comfort on turtle soup and roast pheasant, served by an army of cooks, maids and butlers.

Here, the poor and desperately needy jostle and push for quarter loaves of bread, stale cake and rock-hard buns, grateful for anything to stave off the pangs of hunger. They will hunker down in some cold damp room or doorway to eat, the children trying not to cry over the state of their cold, blue, shoeless feet.

Once she has dealt with the poverty rush, Maria Barklem is free to leave. The premises will be taken over by the baker himself and his assistants, who will work through the night in the back shed, mixing and kneading and feeding the hot ovens, so that the next batch of loaves is piping hot and ready for the morning.

Eventually, the local church bells strike the half hour and Maria takes off her pinafore and hangs it on a hook. She slides the bolt on the shop door, then picks up her basket (carefully covered with a cloth) and makes her way out of the back, murmuring a greeting to the young boy who has arrived to weigh out flour, get the fires going and grease the tins.

As she walks home, the first fallen leaves blowing around her feet, she reminds herself that what she has in her basket is not stealing. Jesus commanded his followers to feed His lambs, did he not? Her mind throws up the picture on the cover of the Sunday School prize book she won, age six, for reciting, by heart, five whole psalms.

The picture was of a kindly man in a flowing white robe. He had long fair hair, blue eyes and a beard. In the picture, he was carrying a small sheep under his arm, while at his feet clustered numerous children in very clean pinafores and tuckers. The message couldn't have been plainer.

Besides, who knows which of her small class might be the 'angel unawares' that she is commanded, in scripture to entertain? Maria no longer believes in God, but He occasionally comes in useful to support her minor larcenies.

Reaching home, she lets herself in quietly. For a moment, she stands in the small kitchen, relishing the peace. Then she fills the kettle, sets it on the hob, and cuts some bread and butter. Her mother will be wanting her afternoon tea. She sets the invalid's tray with an embroidered cloth, and the pretty pink china. Anything to tempt her to eat.

Having delivered the meal and spent some time plumping pillows and talking about her day, she goes back to the kitchen to prepare. This evening, Maria is holding a special class for her most promising student, who has missed the past two weeks' lessons for reasons she suspects, but is far too discreet to ask about.

****

Meanwhile, over at Scotland Yard, Detective Sergeant Jack Cully is presenting his theories, based on observations made during the recent visit to Number 55, Russell Square. His two colleagues hear him out in silence. Then Detective Inspector Stride thumps the desk with his closed fist.

"Blackguards!" he exclaims. "How right I was to call them so! Is there any crime they are not guilty of committing? Theft, murder, luring an innocent girl away from her family, and now, seemingly, selling young women into prostitution?"

"I fear the last two are connected," Cully says, pulling a face. "The maid told us Herbert Black was abroad. I am guessing he has gone to arrange the sale and delivery of these girls to some brothel on the continent. It may be that Rosa Feacham is one of them. I saw a young woman looking out of the first-floor window. She then left the house with the other two girls."

Greig shakes his head. "How many times have we come across this sad story, gentlemen?"

"Too many times," Cully says grimly. "But it never ceases to shock. Of course, we have no proof, but the young women I saw being delivered looked as if they had been given drugs, and the woman who brought them was clearly placing money into a bag as she left the house."

"Can we track her down?" Stride asks.

"I gather many of these vile individuals hang about the big railway stations, hoping to get into conversation with some youngster fresh from the countryside. They pretend they have a room to rent or know of some domestic employment."

Stride frowns. "Sadly, we don't have the manpower to watch every station in the city. So we may have to pass this on to another force. Besides, our real investigation is theft and the murder of Mr James Flashley, not the trade in young women. And returning to Mr. Flashley ~ have you checked the list we got from that collector?"

Cully nods. "There is an ivory cat on the list. I am not sure if it is the one I saw in the actual house. I shall write to Mr. Daubney and ask him to come down to Scotland Yard, where I can question him more closely. If the cat is indeed one of the items stolen from his collection, then we have reason to return to Number 55 and insist on being seen by the occupants."

"Meanwhile I will call in at the Mermaid's Arms tonight and tell Miss Feacham, the barmaid, that we have discovered the address of the Black brothers. I shall also mention we saw the face of a young woman at an upstairs window and give her a description." Greig says. "*Carpe diem*, as our surgeon Mr. Robertson always says."

Stride gives him a hard stare. *He may well say it*, the stare says, *but that does not mean you have to*.

****

By the time that Izzy Harding's boots are heard on the path, Maria has sorted the lesson, made some more tea, and placed a small fruit cake, purchased from a rival establishment, on a serving plate upon the Welsh dresser.

Izzy enters the warm homely kitchen, shaking the rain from her battered hat.

"We had to finish an order for one of the big shops," she says, shucking off her thin coat and taking her usual seat.

Maria wrinkles her nose at the pungent aroma of varnish. "Never mind, you're here now," she says, placing a bun by Izzy's slate.

Once the bun has been consumed, along with a mug of hot milk, the pair get down to the mysteries of nouns and adjectives, followed by a brisk foray into the bewildering world of the apostrophe. Izzy is a quick study, asking for clear explanations when she doesn't understand. Maria is delighted with her progress, and the time passes all too quickly.

Eventually, glancing at the kitchen clock, she informs her young pupil that the lesson is ending, as she herself has to go out to attend a class, much to Izzy's surprise.

"I fort you didn't need to learn anything, Miss," she says.

Maria tells her that a life spent not learning something is a life wasted and Izzy nods in agreement, though inwardly, she guesses that her own life-lessons are probably not what her teacher has in mind. She pushes her slate away and reaches for her coat.

Such a thin coat to be wearing on a chill Autumnal evening, Maria thinks sadly. She notices that one of the pockets has come adrift and is flapping uselessly.

"Here, Izzy ~ let me sew up that pocket for you before you go," she says.

Maria fetches her workbasket, taking out her green velvet pincushion, some black thread and a pair of gold sewing scissors in the shape of a crane. Izzy is fascinated by the spiky pincushion. She picks it up and stares at it intently.

"So pretty," she breathes.

Maria ladder-stitches the pocket, biting off the thread when she is done. Meanwhile, Izzy continues to marvel at the pincushion, turning it over and over, studying it from every angle, as if it were priceless treasure. Maria is amused. She holds out her hand, and after the little girl has returned the pincushion, she takes out the glass-headed pins and fine needles, then gives it back to her.

"Here, take it. A reward for a hard-working pupil."

Izzy's eyes light up with joy. She smiles. Maria catches her breath. The girl's face is so pale and thin, the cheekbones even more prominent. On impulse, she rises, goes to the dresser and cuts a large slice of fruit cake. She holds it out, expecting Izzy to grab it and cram it into her mouth. But she does not. Instead, she takes it very slowly, and looks at it intently for some time. Surprised, Maria asks why she isn't eating it.

"Coz I want to remember what it looks like when it's gone," Izzy replies simply.

She carries the cake to the kitchen door, where she eats it in very small bites. When she has finished, she picks up a few fallen currents from the floor and eats them one by one, before pulling her coat tighter around her thin body. Then without saying another word, she slips out of the door and disappears into the darkness.

Later, when she returns to the overcrowded lodging house, where she and her mother share a room with two other families, Izzy will secretly add the pincushion to her other treasures: the shiny brass button, the length of bright scarlet ribbon, the sheet of gold leaf, the six farthings and the miniature dolls' tea set.

****

An Autumn evening in Babylondon. Music blares out of various venues and halls. At almost every corner of the West End you may come across a magnificent public house, all shiny brass fittings, gilt and mirrors. Streets are lit by whispering gaslight. Pavements throng with every kind and class of person.

Stop awhile and watch.

Here are glistening expensive clothes brushing shoulders with semi-rags. Here are the young, the old, the fair, the wrinkled, the be-jewelled and the paint-begrimed. Here are modest young girls with sweet keepsake faces returning home after their labours, being jostled by street beggars and ruffians.

See a drunken tramp, shuffling along until he is almost pitched into the path of an oncoming cab by a gang of rich and titled youths, who are in turn overset by crowds of jovial clerks and spruce law students pouring out of the Haymarket Theatre in search of supper.

In Babylondon, if you are very rich, you may dine on pheasant and partridge stuffed with truffles at the Café de l'Europe, all washed down with fine wines. If not, enter one of the many taverns or supper rooms, where chops, pork pies, sausage rolls and a glass of pale ale await your consumption.

Meanwhile, out in the noisome streets, the poor frequent the still-open chandler's shops looking for dubious mutton pies, ounces of ham, heels of Dutch cheese, or bargain for bits of plaice or flounder at the fried-fish shops while their children fetch beer from a public house for 'father's supper'.

By two o'clock, the shops will long be shuttered, the halls darkened and the public houses unlit and unwelcome. The Strand is so silent that you may count the footsteps as they sound. The city now occupies that interval between the death of the day and the birth of the coming day. It is in an undead state.

Look more closely.

A man approaches. One of the night-walkers, inhabiting the city at night-time as they feel exiled from it during the day, though this individual is a recent convert. Since the robbery, Gerald Daubney has come to prefer the nights. Nights are when things seem clearer, cleaner. Nights are when he does not have to contemplate the shattered ruin of his life. Darkness and solitude are his friend, for since his great loss, he feels homeless at home.

And so here he is, walking the nocturnal streets. These are the witching hours, when he can chase the moon across the city's skyline, spying it around chimneys or through the gaps between houses. Sometimes he passes building-sites shrouded in hoardings, where the old has been torn down to make way for some new city, rising like a Leviathan from its ancient ruins.

His night-time peregrinations take him past great churches, where he averts his face from the stone-eyed gaze of other people's saints. Hidden in the shadows, packs of children watch him with glittering eyes, vanishing from view whenever he turns to look at them.

At night, there is almost no light between the flickering gas-lamps. Just enough from the moon to pull the street's cobbles from the ink-dark. His footsteps seem to fall away. *'Hell is a city much like London, populous and smoky'* ~ he learned these lines at school.

Recently, he has also learned that Hell lurks in the shadows at the edge of his mind. In blank walls and labyrinthine, claustrophobic streets. In hidden secrets. And in the sure and certain knowledge that there is no escape. No way back. Just a slow progression into more and deeper darkness.

****

It is a damp, windswept morning, and outside Number 55, Russell Square, the same servant-girl who shut the door upon the two Scotland Yard detectives is down on her hands and knees scrubbing the front step.

So preoccupied is she in her thankless task that she fails to hear the front gate open, and the sound of boots marching up the tiled path. The boots stop just short of her bucket of scummy water.

The girl looks at the boots, then lifts her eyes slowly to the wearer. A young woman with dark corkscrew curls and snappy black eyes is staring down at her. Her cheeks are red from the whippy wind and her mouth is set in a firm line of disapproval.

The girl sits back on her lean haunches and puts down the scrubbing brush. Her face assumes a mulish expression. "What you want?" she says sullenly.

Amy Feacham bends down and hauls the girl to her feet by the simple device of grasping the shoulder straps of her apron in one strong, pint-pulling, awkward-customer-ejecting movement.

"Well, well, and who do we have here? I heard you was trying to 'better' yerself, Ida-May. I heard what you'd gone Up West. Still ended up on yer hands and knees, though. Now then, before I allows you to get on, you can let me into the house, coz I got a bit of business I need to see to in there."

The unfortunate Ida-May struggles to free herself, but Amy's grip is like iron.

"They ain't in," she says sullenly.

"You never was a good liar, were you?" Amy says scornfully. She extends a leg and kicks over the bucket.

"Oh my! What a clumsy person I am, eh? Now you'll have to go get some more water. Off you toddle, Ida-May; I'll be right behind you."

Muttering darkly, the maidservant picks up the empty bucket and carries it down the area steps, closely followed by the barmaid. Once inside the kitchen, Amy checks for the presence of any servants but finding the place deserted, she darts across the kitchen floor, heading for the baize-covered door on the far side that will take her up to the ground floor of the house. She wrenches open the door, then spins round to face Ida-May.

"Not a word. You get me: Not. A. Word. You ain't seen me, you ain't heard me and if you try any of your old tricks, Ida-May, you'll be picking your teeth up from the floor."

With this parting threat, Amy Feacham closes the kitchen door behind her, and mounts the unswept and uncarpeted steps that will take her into the hallway of Number 55. Once she has gained the hallway, Amy begins her search. She opens doors, goes into rooms richly furnished with antiques and paintings in gold frames, searching everywhere and calling Rosa's name.

On the first floor, she opens wardrobe doors, because as children, they'd play hide and seek in the tiny rented terrace and it was always surprising where her sister could hide. But if she is hiding in this empty house full of strange ghosts, Amy cannot find her this time.

Slowly it dawns on her that there is actually no evidence of Rosa's presence anywhere in the place. No clothes in wardrobes, no familiar bits and bobs on any dressing table, no indication whatsoever that her sister has ever lived here or is living here now.

Puzzled, Amy goes out to the first-floor landing, where she stands still, listening to what is not there. "Rosa," she whispers, "it's me, Amy. Come out."

But there is no reply. No laughing sister emerges from her hiding place with the accusation that she was there all the time but Amy didn't look hard enough. And then, just to complicate matters further, she hears footsteps coming up the path, a key turning in the lock. She looks through the bannister rails and sees the front door open. A man enters. From her vantage point Amy observes the top of his expensive beaver hat, the set of his powerful shoulders, and she recognises Munro Black.

"Amy Feacham ~ I know you are somewhere in the house. Come out, come out wherever you are," he calls in a sneering singsong voice.

Ida-May must've told him, she thinks. *Little traitorous snitch that she is.* Amy descends the stairs, her hands automatically bunching into fists, as they always used to do whenever in the presence of this man or his brother.

Black watches her in silence. He is a handsome man, his stocky brutal body resembling that of a fairground strongman (which was his former career). He wears an expensive handmade suit and very shiny leather boots. His whole demeanour bespeaks a man always used to getting his own way, violently if necessary.

"Where's Rosa? I know she was here," Amy inquires, reaching the bottom step and deciding to stay there.

Black cocks his head on one side and pretends to think.

"Rosa? Rosa? Do I know a Rosa? More to the point, did I invite you into my home? Because if I did not – and I think I did not, I might have to call the police and have you arrested for breaking in."

Amy ignores the threat. "Where's your brother Herbert then? Coz he's the one who lured my innocent little sister away from her home and her family. What's he done with her?"

Black folds his arms. "My brother isn't here. And where he is, is none of your business, Amy Feacham. And as for your sister, she knew quite well what she was signing up for. Not quite the innocent little lamb you think she was. She isn't here either and I can tell you for sure she isn't ever coming back. Now, as we have nothing further to say to each other, I'd like you to leave my house. Or I shall have to throw you out into the street, where sluts like you and her belong."

Amy feels a hot molten lava of anger rise up. Something seems to snap inside her. Without even thinking of the consequences, she marches directly to the mantelpiece, picks up the china shepherdess and hurls it at him. It falls to the ground and shatters into pieces. Instantly, Black's face turns from sneering contempt to a mask of fury.

"What the hell, Amy! That was a Meissen! Worth a fortune!"

"And now it ain't."

He comes towards her. Something in his expression tells her she has only two options: fight or flight. Her hand reaches out and comes to rest on the ivory cat. She picks it up. It sits snugly in her palm, its back seeming to mould itself to the shape of her skin, as if it had always been there.

Black grabs her left arm. Amy raises her right hand and smashes the cat straight into his face with the full force of her barmaid's strength. He screams, staggers back, blood pouring from his nose and mouth as he spits out a tooth. Amy seizes her chance. She races to the front door, wrenches it open and escapes out into the street.

On and on she runs, weaving in and out of the crowd, never slackening her pace until she reaches one of the river bridges, where she stops and bends double, gasping for breath. The adrenaline that gave wings to her feet has vanished. And with it, her former bravado.

The reality of her position begins to dawn on her. What has she done? She can hardly believe it. She certainly does not think she will get away with it for a second. He knows her name; he knows where she works. He has powerful friends in the underworld. He has only to say the word and her life will be snuffed out like a candle-flame in the wind.

The little cat still sits in her hand. Its green eyes stare up at her accusingly. *I saw what you did back there*, it seems to say. As a swift comet's tail of fear runs down her spine, Amy leans over the parapet and hurls the ivory cat into the swirling lead-coloured water below.

****

It is not just in fiction that unlikely events happen. Sometimes real life tosses a fortuitous scenario into somebody's unsuspecting path. The eighteenth-century writer Horace Walpole coined the word 'serendipitous' to describe such a happening.

Mrs Riva Hemmyng-Stratton has possibly never heard the word, and probably could not even hazard a guess at its meaning. And yet, arriving at the offices of *The Gentlewoman's Home Journal and Fireside Companion* with an article in her hand, she is about to experience a serendipitous event herself.

Standing outside the building is a young woman carrying a manuscript tied up in green ribbon. She has very bright blue eyes, hair the colour of toffee and the air of somebody who is remarkably pleased with herself.

As Mrs Hemmyng-Stratton prepares to enter the outer office to hand over her article (a paltry thing, but the fee will pay this month's rent), the young woman impulsively reaches out a hand and touches her arm.

"Excuse me," she says, "We have not met, but I feel I must share my good fortune with somebody, or I will absolutely burst!"

The Author regards the young woman with some surprise. "Indeed, we have not met," she says a trifle stiffly.

"Then let me introduce myself at once. My name is Miss Lucy Landseer and this" ~ here she waves the manuscript she is clutching ~ "is my debut novel! It really is! And it has just been read by the publisher, who likes it and might want to publish it, and I am so excited!"

Mrs Hemmyng-Stratton has a sudden moment of déjà-vu: she recalls that heart-stopping moment, so long ago now, when her own first tentative foray into the world of fiction was met with approval. She unbends and bestows a smile upon the young woman.

"I am so pleased for you, Miss Landseer," she says warmly.

"I see you are a fellow writer," the young woman continues. "Would you consider it *very* presumptuous of me to invite you to celebrate my success in a cup of tea and a piece of cake?"

Mrs Hemmyng-Stratton considers the offer. Her plan for the day was to hand in the article, pocket the fee, and then walk to her own publisher to reassure herself that the matter of the Lackington divorce accusation was being taken care of satisfactorily. But the young woman's face glows with such a rapturous delight that she cannot refuse her request. It would be like kicking a friendly puppy.

"I shall be delighted to accompany you," she says. "Let me hand in my own little piece first and then I will be at your disposal."

Thus, a short while later, the Author finds herself sitting at a small table in one of the newly-opened little tea-rooms that are springing up all over the West End to cater for the needs of ladies who shop.

Then, even more surprisingly, after two cups of tea and a buttered scone, she is unburdening herself to this total stranger, who listens intently, her pretty head on one side, and a half-eaten scone in her hand.

When Mrs Hemmyng-Stratton has talked herself to a standstill, there is a pause, while the rest of the scone is conveyed to Lucy's mouth. After which, having dabbed off any crumbs onto the linen napkin provided, she leans forward in her chair, her blue eyes alight with interest.

"I am so glad we met, Mrs Hemmyng-Stratton, for I believe I may be able to help you in your predicament. Let me explain: a while ago, I found myself in a situation where my powers of observation were useful to the detectives at Scotland Yard. Indeed, the information I provided led to the apprehension and incarceration of a serious criminal!

"I have always been interested in solving things ~ I am seriously considering the possibility of setting up as a female detective ~ yes, I see the smile on your face, but think about it: so many crimes take place as a result of affairs of the heart, in which women detectives would make far better investigators than men, for they are considerably more sympathetic, and less likely to attract attention.

"But to revert to your own matter: if one could prove that this Lady Lackington had read, and was influenced by your book, it would stop her husband pursuing you, would it not? He wouldn't have a case against you. And you wouldn't have to pay him a penny in compensation. So, we must devise a plot whereby we can meet with the unfortunate lady and find out whether she took events from the book to help her arrange her extra-marital affair."

"We?" Mrs Hemmyng-Stratton queries.

"I assume you wish for my help?" the astonishing young woman says, flashing the Author a winning smile.

"After all, you can hardly turn up at the Asylum yourself ~ that would be rather too obvious and might be seen as coercion of a witness."

"Turn up at the Asylum?"

"Is that not the most obvious plan?"

"But I do not know into what Asylum she has been placed. Nor where it is."

Lucy Landseer waves a dismissive hand. "Not a problem. That is easy to find out. I shall consult the archives at one of the newspaper offices. I have contacts. We are dealing with aristocrats here, so there are bound to be articles 'in the public interest'. The press loves this kind of scandal: a betrayed husband, a lover and a guilty wife etc. It is meat and drink to them. Once I have traced the information, we will meet and plan our next move. Oh, this is wonderful! My first novel and maybe my first case! What a perfect day."

Mrs Hemmyng-Stratton demurs. "It is very kind of you to offer your assistance, but I am sure it will not come to this, Miss Landseer. My publisher has written to the lawyers affirming my complete ignorance of the affair. That will be enough to end the matter."

The fledgling detective butters another scone, pours some more tea and begins scribbling away in a notebook very similar to the one currently residing in Mrs Hemmyng-Stratton's own capacious bag. She tears out the page and places it on the table.

"Very well. But here is my address. Believe me, if you do require my help, I shall not fail you."

She flashes the bemused writer a beaming smile, finishes her scone, then places some coins upon the table. "I await your summons, fellow scribe," she says, and sticking a vicious-looking hatpin determinedly into the side of her hat, she shrugs on her coat and departs, leaving Mrs Hemmyng-Stratton to wonder whether she has just dreamed up the past hour.

But if it was a dream, her subsequent visit to her publisher soon dispels the supposition, for there she discovers that the solicitors of Lord Lackington are not to be put off by the assertion of her innocence and intend, unless ample compensation is offered, to take the matter further, and instigate legal proceedings against her for producing a work that brings his noble name into disrepute.

After restating her position yet again, Mrs Hemmyng-Stratton is left to creep home, feeling sheer dread dog her every footstep. Once back in her little sanctuary, she throws herself into a chair and contemplates her current position, and the choices open to her. That she has the funds to pay the vast amount of money that she suspects will be demanded, is out of the question.

She cannot afford to leave the country and make a new life for herself abroad under an assumed *nom de plume*, even if she wanted to, which she does not. Nor is she willing to take that dark and lonely road that leads to a silent grave in a lonely churchyard (she *is* a novelist, so she does tend to think in rather dramatic and clichéd terms).

Eventually, having exhausted all her options, she picks up her pen and writes a letter to the impulsive young woman she encountered a few hours earlier, who, despite being almost an unknown quantity and of dubious provenance, now appears to be the only person left who might possibly be able to salvage her reputation and save her from public humiliation and utter financial ruin.

****

Meanwhile, Stride and Cully are attempting to breach the outer ramparts of Number 55, Russell Square once again. This time, their efforts are rewarded. A maid servant answers their knock, and shows them straight into a sitting room, where a big brutish man with a waxed moustache is relaxing over coffee and a cigar.

The room's furnishings are lavish: thick Turkey rugs cover the floor and there are numerous small occasional rosewood tables full of ornaments and small china figurines. The fireplace is black marble, with a pair of unusual Oriental gold-handled daggers mounted in a crossover pattern above. It is clear that no expense has been spared in the fixtures and fittings.

The man rises at their entrance. Extends a hand. Introduces himself as Munro Black. Apologises for his absence on a previous occasion. Indicates that they might like to sit. Orders coffee for them from the servant. Asks how he might assist them, in an unctuous manner that suggests that he is pretty sure he can't. Or probably won't.

Throughout these procedures, Stride and Cully observe their host closely. They note his hulking body under the well-tailored suit, the starched cravat, the gold rings and watch-chain. They also observe the broken nose and grossly swollen mouth.

"Oh dear, you seem to have been in the wars, sir, if I may say so," Cully remarks.

Black laughs thickly through his bruised lips. "You should see the other bloke."

His voice has an incongruous lisp resulting from a missing front tooth.

They sit. Stride produces his notebook. He flicks through the pages, taking his time. Through many such interrogations, he has learned the power of building suspense, especially when he suspects he is about to be manipulated by a skilled operator, such as the one facing him now.

"We are sorry to disturb you, Mr. Black, but we are investigating a murder."

"Oh yeah?" Black observes.

"A manservant called Mr. James Flashley ~ and, as we are reliably informed, Mr. Flashley was an acquaintance of you and your brother, we decided to pay you a call. Am I correct in this assumption? Do you know the gentleman?"

Black raises his hands, his eyebrows and the level of his voice.

"Jem Flashley? Murdered? No – I can't believe it! Not Jem. Why, I'm sure only the other day we were sharing a yarn about the good old days over a pot of ale."

He regards them wide-eyed with horror. He is either genuinely upset, or the theatrical profession has lost a valuable asset. Both detectives assume the second option.

"Indeed. And that is the reason we are here," Stride says. "We have been told that you were spotted drinking with a friend on the exact night and close to the exact place where the murder happened. Can you confirm this?"

Black looks towards the heavily curtained window. He shrugs. "I go out for a lot of drinks. Business, pleasure, sometimes somewhere between the two. I don't keep a note of them all. Can you be a bit more specific. What night? What pub?"

Stride consults his notes. Tells him the date. "You were seen that evening in the Ship Inn, near St Catherine's Dock."

There is a pause. Black seems to be paging through some mental directory.

"Can't say I remember the place. Who said they saw me there? Was it the barmaid said so?"

"The point is, you were seen there," Cully cuts in. "And a short while later, Mr. James Flashley, a man you were once sharing a yarn with about the good old days, was found dead."

"Well, when I was talking with him, he clearly wasn't dead, was he?" Black snaps, the colour rising to his bruised cheek.

"Perhaps your drinking companion might vouchsafe for your movements?" Stride says.

"Like I already told you, officer, I meet a lot of people in my line of work. I don't remember who I was drinking with that night."

"Maybe you could try to remember?"

Munro Black makes a big performance of scratching his head and screwing up his face in concentration. Then shakes his head. "Nope. No idea, sorry."

"What a pity," Stride says evenly. "He could have given you an alibi."

"For what?" Black replies. "Did this barmaid see me doing any harm? Did anybody else?"

He stares at them. The silence thickens.

"Thought not. So, gents, you are clearly wasting your time."

"What was your relationship with Mr. Flashley?" Stride asks.

Black shrugs his massive shoulders. "We go back. Born in the same street. Played in the same gutter. Only one of us managed to climb out of it and make something of themselves. Guess which one? I run several clubs. Successful ones, naturally. Gambling, cards, for those who like that sort of thing. Drinks and entertainments for those who don't. People work for me, not the other way round. Jem wanted my kind of lifestyle and thought he could get it by gambling."

"Did he owe you money?"

Black considers this carefully. "Most people do."

"We have reason to believe debt might have contributed to Mr. Flashley's demise," Stride says, studying Black thoughtfully.

Black shrugs in a nonchalant 'nothing to do with me' manner.

"What is your brother's business?" Cully asks. "And can we speak to him?"

"He does a bit of this, bit of that. He buys and sells stuff. Paintings, furniture, that sort of thing. And he isn't here, so you can't speak to him."

"What does he buy and sell specifically? Collectables? Valuable items from overseas? Maybe from the Far East?" Stride asks.

Black's face is wiped of everything except the bruising.

"I couldn't say. He does what he does, I do what I do. Mostly, he lives abroad, which is where he is at the moment."

"You see, we have reason to believe that Mr. Flashley's employer was robbed of a collection of priceless Japanese netsuke on the night that his manservant was murdered. The night when you and an unremembered companion were seen in the same vicinity as the victim, who owed you money. Perhaps you could shed some light on that?"

Black looks puzzled. "Sorry gents, you got me there. Don't understand. Nets of what?"

"Netsuke," Cully repeats. "They are small Japanese carved ornaments."

"Never heard of them, sorry."

"Oh, I think you have," Cully says. "In fact, I am sure you know exactly what I am talking about, because I have recently seen a netsuke in your house. And it matches one on the list of stolen articles supplied to Scotland Yard by Mr. Flashley's employer."

He rises, walks to the door, opens it and goes into the hallway. The other two follow him. But there is no little ivory cat on the mantelpiece. Jack Cully blinks, checks again. He turns, meets Stride's eye and shrugs sheepishly.

"Right then," Black says briskly. "Like I said, I don't know what you are talking about and it is nothing to do with me. Jem's death is nothing to do with me either. Or Herbert. Now, I have an important business meeting, so if you have no more questions, I'll bid you both good-day. Sorry I couldn't be more help. Any time you're passing the house, please feel free to pass, eh."

He throws a fake smile at them, then snaps his fingers to summon the servant, who opens the door. They are shown out into the street. The door slams behind them. They walk away in silence. Halfway across the square, Cully glances back at the house. The blinds are pulled down at every window. The house seems to exude a hostile, even malicious air.

"There was a small ivory cat on that mantelpiece. I saw it with my own eyes," Cully murmurs.

"I'm sure you did," Stride says. "Mr. Black is clearly a smooth-tongued operator. As is his always-absent brother who 'buys and sells stuff' ~ and some of that stuff is clearly human. Come Jack, we will park Mr. Black here for the time being and try to work out another route to reach him. Perhaps Mr. Daubney might be able to tell us a little more about his stolen cat."

Upon their return to Scotland Yard, Jack Cully writes a letter to Gerald Daubney asking whether he might call round, at his earliest convenience, as he wishes to consult him upon some matters pertaining to the recent robbery.

He tries to keep it as vague as he can, given that the evidence is no longer available, and he does not want to hold out false hopes. He has a feeling that Mr. Daubney isn't the sort of individual to whom the term 'stoic' might apply.

$$****$$

Letters, and their possible outcomes are currently the focus of Detective Inspector Lachlan Greig's attention. Here he is at his desk in his small rented room, chewing the end of a pen as he stares at one of the most frightening sights in the world: a blank piece of paper.

Greig has always served in the police force, first in Leith, now in London. He has seen many developments in policing, some good, some less helpful. He has never really stopped and thought about the trajectory of his life. Events happened, he dealt with them, and then more events arrived to take their place.

And now?

Greig thinks about his colleagues. He wonders how they will react to his decision. He writes a couple of words, crosses them out and screws up the paper. This might be the most important letter he has ever had to pen. He must get it right. He has only one shot at it and the consequences of making a mistake are too great to contemplate.

He stares out of the small window into the back yard. The apple tree still bears some late fruit. A blackbird perches on one of the branches and as Greig watches, it suddenly opens its beak and lets forth a trill of careless notes.

Heartened by the bright song, Greig takes up his pen and begins to write. Twenty minutes later, the page is covered. The pen is set down. He reads through what he has written and is satisfied with it. He blots the letter, folds the paper and inserts it into an envelope. The die is cast.

Next morning Greig is walking to work, the important letter in his pocket. He is adopting the *head-down-no-I-am-not-a-member-of-the-police-force-so-do-not-approach-me* stance. It has always astonished him how members of the general public, so quick to avoid him if he wants to question them, are so keen to address him if they have the slightest trivial problem.

Greig has given up musing upon how they know he is a member of the Metropolitan Police, given that he does not wear a police uniform. They just do, though. His fellow detectives have also remarked upon the same phenomenon. Despite seeing no difference between his own work attire and that of any other city employee, some invisible aura surrounds him, and it draws individuals to his side like a magnet draws iron filings.

He crosses Covent Garden piazza, stepping over and around various bits of detritus, vegetable, animal and human, and is about to make his way to one of the coffee stalls, when he is suddenly hailed. Greig looks around.

"Down here, mister."

Greig looks down. An overlarge cap is sitting on the head of a small boy, who is in turn sitting in the gutter, hands clasped around his knees. His eyes are red-rimmed, and his clothes smell of neglect, tobacco and woodsmoke. Greig has a soft spot for small waifs and strays, having been abandoned as a baby, and something about the utterly miserable expression on the boy's face touches his heart.

He squats down. "Hello, laddie. What's your name?"

"I'm Brixston. Dunno yore name, but I recognises yer," the boy says. "You came into the Ship, didn'tcha? While back, it was. With anovver man. Asking questions."

Greig nods and makes a 'go-on' motion with one hand.

"I heard yer talking to Janet what works behind the bar. I used to work there, see. Pot boy. An' I stayed there at night too. Wasn't meant to, but they never bovvered to turf me out. I slept with Fang and Biter. All curled up together by the fire. Them doggies was my pals."

Greig remembers the two vicious dogs. He also notes the use of the past tense. A tear trickles down the boy's face, making a clear white path through the grime.

"But you don't work there anymore?"

The boy wipes his eyes on the back of his sleeve. "Place has burned down. I was lucky to get out alive. Had to climb on a chair and break a winder. But the doggies didn't get out. Burned to death. Heard them barking, but I couldn't get back to save them. My pals, gone. My home, gone."

He buries his face in his hands and sobs piteously. Greig waits for calm to be restored. Then he asks, "How did the fire start?"

The boy shrugs. "Just did. I woke up and the bar was full of smoke."

So, a couple of days after his colleagues were questioning Mr. Munro Black about his whereabouts on the night of a murder, the public house that he was drinking in was burned down. Some might call it an unfortunate accident. Some might call it a deliberate attempt at intimidation of any possible witnesses. Greig belongs to the latter camp.

"Where do you live now, lad?" he asks.

The boy shrugs once more. "Doorway up west one night, tarpaulin back o' Spitalfields Market last night. There's five of us sharing it now, so I ain't sure where I'll kip tonight."

"I see. And how would coffee and a slice or two of bread go down?"

The boy's face brightens. "It'd go down a treat, mister."

He scrambles to his feet, brushing filth off his worn trousers.

"Mebbe you could answer some of those questions you heard me ask?" Greig suggests, as he leads the way across the Piazza.

The boy nods. "Maybe I could an' all. Coz I was there on that night, working in the bar. I know all the regulars wot come in. And them what isn't regular, too. And I know what they talk about. Nobody ever sees me, though."

"Let's get some food and a hot drink into you first, eh?" Greig says, putting a kindly hand on the boy's shoulder. "Then we'll talk."

A short while later, the tall figure of Inspector Lachlan Greig and the very much shorter figure of Brixston enter the portals of Scotland Yard. The boy looks decidedly more cheerful and is wearing Greig's striped muffler round his neck.

Greig directs him to the Anxious Bench, where citizens come to wait for news of their nearest and dearest who might have been taken up for various crimes and misdemeanours of which, naturally, they are totally innocent. Brixston stares around him, bright-eyed with wonder, while Greig goes to locate Jack Cully.

When the two detectives return, the boy is leaning against the front desk, working his way through a bag of toffees supplied by the duty constable.

"He was telling me all about his dogs," he says apologetically in response to Greig's raised eyebrow. "I used to have a dog when I was his age. Poor little tyke."

Greig and Cully steer the poor little tyke to a vacant interview room and sit him down.

"Is this where the wrong'uns come?" the boy asks, staring at the plain whitewashed walls and small high window.

"It is," Cully says. "But you are not one of them. You are helping us to catch some."

"Now, Brixston, can you tell the detective exactly what you told me," Greig says. "And while you tell him, I shall write it down so that we have a record of what you saw on that night."

The boy glances from the bag of toffees to the two detectives and back again. Then, with a sigh, he shoves the bag into his coat pocket, folds his arms, and begins his tale. It does not take long in the telling, and once it is told, Cully and Greig leave the room for a quick discussion in the corridor. After which Greig returns, telling Brixston to sit tight and not to leave the building under any circumstances.

The two detectives then head for Detective Inspector Stride's office, where they find the incumbent shifting folders around his desk with the air of a man in desperate need of a filing system. His face expresses relief when they knock and enter.

"Paperwork, gentlemen! Damn paperwork! The curse of the modern-day detective. I would rather hunt down the vilest criminal through the city streets than deal with endless memoranda from Home Office wallahs who wouldn't recognise a crime if it was being committed in front of their eyes in their own drawing-room!"

Greig and Cully, who have heard this rant, in various forms, many times over, make placatory noises and seat themselves in front of the desk.

Stride hunts around for his mug of coffee, fails to locate it, utters a few more expletives, then fixes them with a baleful stare. "Yes?"

Greig gets out his notebook. "We have just come from interviewing a young lad who worked at the Ship Inn ~ I don't know whether you've heard, but the pub has been burned to the ground in what we think was a deliberate arson attack."

"We believe it was carried out at the bidding of Mr Munro Black," Cully says. "Either to intimidate anybody who was drinking there on that night, or to serve as a warning to the local community not to engage with us. It is too much of a coincidence."

"The lad survived the fire ~ he was lucky," Greig continues. "We have him in an interview room for his own safety. We described Mr Black to him, and this is what he told us: on the night in question, he saw Black drinking in the bar together with another man. He heard Black saying that he was going to collect on a debt later that night and the man in question had better pay up this time or it would be the worse for him. The two men stayed in the pub drinking for several hours, then they got up and left. Black told the barmaid that they would return to settle up later. They never came back."

Stride abruptly shunts a pile of folders onto the floor, the better to rest his elbows on the desk.

"The picture is emerging, gentlemen. Black the elder refreshes himself at the Ship Inn with another man, name currently unknown. They then meet up with Flashley, who either had the collection of Japanese carvings ready to hand over or was going to break into his master's house and remove them."

"I have spoken to some of my contacts," Greig says, "Black was in the habit of buying up various debts and then using his power to extract money or favours from the debtors. We know James Flashley liked to gamble, and I saw lists of sums he owed at the back of a notebook in his room. When added up, and if unpaid, they amounted to a tidy sum. So you are right, Flashley has to be the man they were going to meet."

"And he decides to pay off his gambling debts by stealing from his master. That is either a lot of debt or a lot of fear," Stride says.

The three detectives sit in meditative silence.

"The trouble is, it's all hearsay at the end of the day; we can't *prove* any of it," Greig says. "The boy is nine years old, so his evidence, such as it is, would never stand up in court. A good defence lawyer would hang him out to dry in ten minutes. The brothers can and will deny everything. The younger one seems to have disappeared altogether. We do not know anything about this third man, and the only other party to the whole business is dead. Where, gentlemen, do we go from here?"

"I am awaiting a response from Mr. Daubney to my letter," Cully says. "I have asked when it might be convenient to call upon him. I'd like him to tell me some more about the Japanese cat he listed as stolen. Obviously, I shall tread cautiously: we don't want to build up false hopes."

Faces brighten. Then unbrighten, as Stride observes that whatever the strange collector of antiques and Japanese ornaments might say, the small ivory cat is no longer on Black's mantelpiece, and he has only to deny its existence in court to further distance himself from the theft.

"We will just have to sit tight," he says. "It is the hardest part of any investigation, but it must be done. We have shaken the tree, and now we must wait and see what falls out of it. And let us pray that it is something that will put both these brothers behind bars for a very long time."

"Let us hope so," Cully says. "In the meantime, I shall get the boy to sit down with our police artist and see if he can produce a likeness of the man who was drinking with Black on that night. It might just be worth our while circulating it amongst the riverside taverns. I'll get copies sent to the local police stations too."

"And I will find somewhere safe for the lad to stay until we close the case," Greig says. "He is not safe to roam the streets, not with a ruthless operator like Mr Munro Black on the prowl."

****

It takes a lot of horsepower to keep the population of London moving. 40,000 horses are needed just to pull the omnibuses that daily transport the clerks and office workers from the newly built suburbs to their jobs. Add to this, dray horses, carriage horses, cart horses, pet ponies, costermonger horses, and riding horses, and the importance of the horse, in all its various manifestations, alive or dead, cannot be overestimated, and can be judged by the number of London public houses bearing their name. There are 25 Black Horses, 54 White Horses, 27 Horse and Grooms and sundry other equinely named watering holes. In contrast, Queen Victoria has a mere 21 pubs named after her.

Leaving aside the question of the various by-products, though many of the ambulant inhabitants of the city wish they wouldn't be, there are horses in mews, horses in sheds, in stables, in back yards and tethered on common land. And right at the top of the tree, leading the most privileged lives, are the fine carriage horses and riding ponies of the rich.

Here, at Bob Miller's Livery Stables in St John's Wood, head groom, William Smith is supervising the re-shoeing of a fine dapple-grey mare, property of Lady Fanny Windermere. The mare is a thoroughly pedigree animal. She has a skittish temperament. A bit like her owner.

William holds the bridle and croons soothing words as the blacksmith cradles Araminta's hindleg on his lap and begins removing nails from the first worn shoe with a pair of pincers. A brazier burns brightly nearby, and there is a bucket of cold water on the ground. The smith's tools, and the new shoes are awaiting the fixing.

It is a picture that could be placed at almost any period of history, thinks Lachlan Greig as he steps into the yard. Behind him, the boy Brixston hangs back, staring round-eyed at the busy scene.

The mare shakes her head impatiently and blows out a whickering neigh of indignation. William leans his face along her smooth neck and makes small clicking noises. Greig motions the boy to stand still.

A black and white sheepdog suddenly emerges from one of the stables, shakes itself, yawns, and pads across the yard towards the visitors, its tail wagging. The boy lowers himself to the ground and stretches out a hand. The dog, sensing a friend, comes to investigate.

By the time the mare has been shod, and William is free to shake Greig by the hand, Brixston and the dog have disappeared, which conveniently allows Greig to outline the boy's story, and the urgent need to hide him from possible recriminations by the dangerous villain currently the focus of Scotland Yard's attention.

"If they are prepared to burn down a public house to send a warning to the community not to talk to us, killing an innocent boy would be like squashing an inconvenient insect," Greig says.

William Smith, hands in trouser pockets, listens intently, occasionally nodding. He too, began his life in the gutter as a lowly crossing sweeper. He was rescued from this life of grime by Josephine King, owner of the flourishing business King & Co., who took him in and cared for him.

Now, Greig suggests, it is time to repay some of his good fortune by helping the boy Brixston, another waif and stray in a desperate situation. "There must be some jobs he can do around the place," he suggests. "Sweeping up or mucking out the stables."

William considers the offer. "We are a stable lad short at the moment," he admits. "It would only be temp'rary though, until he returns."

"Temporary is fine," Greig says, adding, "And it would be better if he stayed on the premises and didn't stray too far."

"Fair enough," William agrees. "Let's go and see if it suits him."

The men look around, searching for the boy. One of the grooms comes out of a stable, leading two fine matching carriage horses on halter reins.

"If you're looking for that lad, he's in the far box with Molly and her pups," he says.

They find Brixston lying in the straw, curled around the sheepdog, who is suckling six tiny puppies. It is a scene of utter contentment, boy and dog in perfect accord. The boy glances up as the two men step into the box.

"Look at them fine pups," he says, stroking Molly gently on her soft head. The dog moves her head sideways and licks his hand.

"Brixston, how would you like to stay here for a while?" Greig asks. "We need to keep you out of harm's way until we have arrested Mr Black."

The boy's face lights up. "Could I? Really? Oh my ~ that'd be prime, that would. Can I sleep here, with the dog too? Only I'm used to sleeping with dogs, you see, and I'd have the pups for comp'ny as well."

Greig turns to William, who is regarding the boy with an amused expression.

"I reckon that'd be alright," William says. "You can help out in the yard during the day, to earn your keep as it were. I began as a stable lad, and so can you. We'll see if you have a knack with horses like you have with dogs. Moll hasn't let any of us near her pups since they were born."

Brixston utters a great sigh, then buries his face in the dog's warm fur. They leave him there and return to the yard, where Greig gives William some money 'to pay for the training'. Then the two shake hands once more, and he departs.

On the way back, Greig buys a copy of the *Police Gazette*. The burning of the Ship Inn is on the inside page. According to the journalist, the fire was started by a candle carelessly left alight, that fell onto the bar where it set light to some spilled alcohol. The fate of the two dogs is described in graphic detail. The article ends by saying that the animals were the only casualties, apart from the building itself.

Greig, who knows from Brixston, that there were no candles that night, wonders whether Black and his accomplice have read the piece. And whether they've realised that there is a lone survivor of the tragedy. And who he is. Because if they have, judging upon what the boy has told them, the brothers will move heaven and earth to find him, and shut him up. Permanently.

****

Mrs Riva Hemmyng-Stratton has not yet received any reply to her letter to Lucy Landseer. She has, however, received a letter from her publisher, Charles Colbourne & Co. enclosing the copy of a communication from Strutt & Preening, the lawyers representing Lord Edwin Lackington, declaring that as they have had no offer to meet their client's demand for monetary compensation for his suffering and humiliation at the hands of the writer, they are instructed by their client to take the matter further and prepare court papers. They await a response etc. etc.

The Author does not understand. She was assured by her editor, in whom she has placed her absolute trust, that the matter would proceed no further. But it is proceeding, and apparently at an alarming pace. Too upset to break her fast, she dons her bonnet and outdoor mantle and sets off in the murky grey light of the morning to discover what has gone wrong.

Reaching the publishing house, she is even more alarmed to see Charles Colbourne himself standing on the step with a copy of *Cecil Danvers* in his hand, and a group of scribbling reporters gathered in a semi-circle around him. She secretes herself in a convenient doorway, the better to observe without being spotted.

"This book," Colbourne declares, holding the copy above his head, "is one of the publishing sensations of the age. Look long and hard at it, gentlemen of the press. My author, the popular and talented fiction writer, Mrs Hemmyng-Stratton has written a book ~ and what a book, gentlemen, a book that has sold many copies; that has been loved and devoured by young ladies throughout the land, but which now, by some peculiar twist of literary Fate, has been seized upon by a certain noble Lord who believes it is the true story of his wife's scandalous love affair.

"I will not name the noble Lord, but I assure you, gentlemen of the press, there is not a shred of truth in his allegation. Not. A. Shred. And we will fight him in every court in the land to prove it."

The Author clutches a convenient pillar, her eyes almost starting out of her head with shock and surprise. Colbourne, still not perceiving her presence, continues.

"I intend to republish this wonderful book, and send copies of it to every station bookstall, every library and every bookshop in the kingdom. Let it be read far and wide. Because this is censorship, gentlemen, an attempt to silence a woman novelist, just as they were silenced in the past, or forced to write under an assumed name. We live in more enlightened times, my friends. Just as you are free to publish your articles, so must any writer be free to publish his or her work. Male or female. Am I right?"

The reporters cheer. Colbourne waves the book above his head.

"The lawyers representing the noble Lord hope, by taking this author to court, to set a precedent that will frighten off other writers. If they are allowed to win, how long before the vultures of the legal profession descend upon you? Eh? We are dealing with the freedom of the press, friends. The. Freedom. Of. The. Press. How long before your attempts to set some matter of great import before the general reading public has to pass across the desk of an aristocratic censor?"

"Never!" comes a voice from the crowd.

"How long before you are told that you cannot write about some crime or misdemeanour because it concerns an aristocrat or member of the rich elite?"

"We will always write what the Man in the Street deserves to know!"

"You speak the truth, my friend," Colbourne agrees. "And now, gentlemen, I must return to work. There is much to do. Write your pieces. Tell the Great British Public how a rich aristocrat is trying to sue a poor impecunious woman writer and let the verdict of the Great British Public upon his deeds and actions ring out across the land. I thank you."

He bows. The clique of penny-a-liners cheer. Colbourne goes into the building. The reporters go into a huddle. They swap notes, light up cigarettes, then saunter off in the various directions of their newspaper offices to write up the story.

As soon as the street has emptied, Mrs Hemmyng-Stratton advances upon the publishing house. She feels as if she has been subject to some medical procedure that has taken place without either her consent nor any anaesthetic. She barrels into the office, barges past the secretary's desk and bursts into Colbourne's inner sanctum, where he is seated behind his desk, feet upon it, and a big cigar in his mouth.

"I have just been standing outside your office, where I have witnessed the most disgraceful display of flagrant audacity," she exclaims. "You ~ the man I trusted with the precious output of my literary endeavours ~ are intent upon turning my work into some grubby sensationalist story for the newspapers? How dare you!"

Colbourne's smile is that of a crocodile waiting on a riverbank for an unwary swimmer, who has just stepped into the water.

"No such thing as bad publicity, Mrs S."

"But I TOLD you I had not based the story on any real events and you SAID you believed me and that once you had written to the lawyers, there would be no further trouble."

"Ah well, second thoughts on all that, you see, Mrs S. I took on your book in all innocence," Colbourne says, craftily. "I paid you in good faith. I published it in good faith. How was I to know that you had ~ or had not ~ copied the story from true life? It is up to the author to prove their integrity, not the poor hapless publisher. Now, my business could possibly go under, if my name becomes associated with you. So, at the end of the day, I have to do what I have to do to save it. If you are innocent, Colbourne & Co. makes money. If you are guilty, I will have to pull the book. No more money."

She stares at him, thunderstruck.

"So, what you are saying is that you intend to profit, one way or another, at the expense of my literary career and reputation? That you are using me for your own sordid pecuniary purposes?"

Colbourne picks up an editing pencil and twirls it. "Something like that."

"You would throw me to the wolves of public opinion?"

"Got it in one."

"But what am I supposed to do?" the hapless Author cries, wringing her hands.

"You'd better hope Lord Edwin Lackington changes his mind. Or if he don't, you'd better come up with some money. Or a good lawyer."

She rises, stands tall, wrapping the tattered cloak of her broken world around her with as much dignity as she can muster.

"Be assured, whatever the outcome of this disgraceful business, I will never offer Charles Colbourne & Co. another of my precious novels. Ever. You, sir, are no gentleman!"

"Fair enough."

"I bid you good day, Mr. Colbourne."

He waves a careless hand, not even bothering to rise from his seat.

Mrs Hemmyng-Stratton totters back out into the bleak uncaring street. She is utterly alone in the world. She has no friend, no helpmeet, neither chick nor child who will come to her aid. And the sharks, oh the sharks are circling!

****

Midday in London marks the traditional dinner hour, and for millions of workers it is a chance to escape from their daily drudgery and snatch a bite to eat. For some, a mug of milk and water and a bun has to suffice ~ Maria Barklem belongs to this group and consumes her meagre meal while standing behind the counter.

She has temporarily turned the shop sign to closed so that she can eat, but the enjoyment of her brief period of rest is offset by the number of small grubby faces pressed to the window, and the poor pinched women with their half-empty baskets who hurry by, hungrily eyeing the delicacies on offer.

Elsewhere, stoop-shouldered City clerks slide inkily from behind their desks and betake themselves to various local eating houses to enjoy a cheap meal, washed down by something inexpensive and barely alcoholic that will not impede them from performing their post prandial task, for to be discovered drunk in charge of a ledger is a sackable offence.

Factory girls, sharp-set and ill-clad, swarm out of their Stratford manufactories at the sound of the dinner bells, heading for the fried fish shops, where their penny buys them a piece of fried fish the size of their palm, and a slice of bread. Some go to the hot soup establishments, to buy a halfpenny basin of thick pea soup, to be eaten standing in the street.

After a hard morning avoiding paperwork, Detective Inspector Stride also heeds the call of the noontide bell and heads for his favourite watering hole: Sally's Chop House, a dark low-ceilinged place off Fleet Street, presided over by the eponymous Sally, who used to be a prize-fighter with failed criminal inclinations, and has a broken nose and an air of assumed innocence to prove it.

Sally's customers sit at long wooden tables or inside small wooden booths. There is sawdust on the floor and chips in the chinaware. But Sally's customers are the sort of people who do not care about such matters, being focused more upon price and portion size.

Stride sits alone in a back booth. He has been coming to Sally's for so long that the booth he occupies is always free around lunchtime, because the usual crowd of diners recognise an officer of the law when they see one, and do not wish to get too close. Just in case.

He places his order. Then sits staring at nothing in particular, until Sally arrives at the back booth, carrying a plate of steaming beef stew and potato, and a drink. At which point, Stride glances up at him thoughtfully.

"Netsuke," he says.

"Bless you, Mr. Stride, sir," Sally says, setting the chipped plate in front of him. "That's a nasty cold you've got there."

"Have you ever heard of netsuke, Sally?"

Sally frowns and looks off. "No, can't say I have, Mr. Stride," he answers, because it is better to deny everything upon principle, in case you end up one day having to deny it upon oath.

Stride conveys food from the plate to his mouth. "Small Japanese carvings of animals, Sally."

The only animal carvings Sally knows are those that arrive at the back door under cover of darkness. They are generally carried by men in flat-caps and handed over with the assurance that they are not of equine origin.

He nods. Stride eats. Sally hovers deferentially by the booth watching him consume his meal, on the basis that the sooner Stride finishes eating, the sooner he can remove his plate and send him on his way.

"And yet it appears that there are people in England who are willing to pay a small fortune for them," Stride continues after a pause. "I do not understand why, do you?"

As a provider of dinners, the stupidity of the general public (especially their inability to read a menu board clearly) is a topic Sally could hold forth upon for hours. Ditto their tendency to steal cutlery.

"No idea, Mr. Stride, sir," he says, shaking his head. "None whatsoever. Bit more potato?"

"No, thank you, Sally. Excellent lunch, as always. I must now return to Scotland Yard. Crime waits for no man, eh?"

Sally pushes the corners of his mouth into a broad, fake grin.

"As you say, Mr. Stride sir. As you say."

Stride hands over payment for his lunch. Sally thrusts it into a grubby apron pocket. He can almost see the other diners bending sideways to avoid coming into contact with Stride's aura of law enforcement as he threads his way between the tables.

As Detective Inspector Stride enters the busy thoroughfare, the clanging bells of the city proclaim the hour of one, and all the shopworkers, labourers, navvies, and clerks are summoned back to their toil.

Meanwhile, another individual is also making his way towards Scotland Yard. In response to Jack Cully's letter, Gerald Daubney, collector of Japanese artefacts, has emerged from his reclusive isolation. He does not wish for his sanctuary to be invaded once more by clumsy members of the Metropolitan Police, so he has chosen to take himself to Scotland Yard instead.

Daubney has not experienced the delights of the city by day for some time. In his heightened state of emotion, the shock of it is almost unbearable. The noise of traffic rumbling through the insufficiently wide streets falls upon his ear like thunder. Coaches, drays, and carts jostle for street-space and lock wheels.

A hundred voices are raised in dispute. Whips are brandished, insults exchanged. Daubney treads cautiously, hugging the inside of the pavement, continually starting back in trepidation as some completely innocent member of the public passes too close to him for his comfort, for who knows what rogues, what villains, pickpockets, thieves and murderers he might be rubbing shoulders with unknowingly?

The usual quotient of street beggars is regarded with horror as they perform their various money-inducing tricks. In Daubney's over-heated imagination, each one seems to be sizing him up, working out whether his pockets contain anything valuable, or whether he looks the kind of individual whose home might be worth breaking into.

By the time he reaches Scotland Yard, and is directed to wait on the Anxious Bench, he is a quivering mass of nervous energy, the last person to be the first person Stride encounters as he returns from luncheon. Daubney struggles to his feet as Stride enters. The collector's cheek is hectic. His eyes dart from side to side. His hands shake. He is a human bundle of sensitivity and apprehension.

"Good day, detective," he says, panting slightly from the effort of rising from the bench. "I have received a communication from one of your colleagues, Detective Sergeant Cully. He has discovered something, I believe, about the theft of my precious netsuke. I have come to find out what it is. Please inform him I am here."

Stride issues a curt command to the desk-constable to seek out Detective Sergeant Cully at once. He then smiles in what he hopes is a professional manner at the agitated visitor, before heading for the sanctuary of his own office, where he intends to have a brief post-prandial doze on a pile of folders.

But the meeting is not going to take place, for unbeknown to both men, Jack Cully left the building a short while ago on a personal quest. It is his daughter Violet's birthday, and he has decided to surprise her with a present. It will also be a surprise to Emily his wife, who firmly believes that men cannot possibly be trusted to buy gifts for small girls.

Cully has gone in search of a pink ribbon for Violet's pretty curls. Luckily, one of the haberdashery shops at the lower end of Regent Street has a good supply. The trouble is that the supply is far too good. Cully finds himself faced with a positive rainbow of ribbons. A superfluity of choice, from which he has to pick just one ribbon.

Deep pink, pale pink, shell pink, apple-blossom pink. Who knew there were so many shades of pink in the world? And so many types of ribbon: silk ribbons, satin ribbons, velvet ribbons. Cully set out a man with a mission, now he is a man with a problem.

Finally, after the saleswoman has pitched him various scenarios, and unrolled numerous ribbons, laying and overlaying them upon the glass counter, he makes his choice. The pink ribbon is rolled and placed in a small box, and Jack Cully emerges from the shop with a new appreciation of the problems facing fashionable female members of society.

Upon his return, he is informed by the desk constable that a certain Mr. Gerald Daubney came inquiring for him, was seen instead by Detective Inspector Stride, and emerged from the meeting a short while after, tight-lipped and unhappy.

Cully does a mental eye-roll. He can imagine the encounter between the two men, one upper-class and a bit odd, the other running on strong black coffee and prejudice. He goes to track Stride down.

"Ah, Jack, there you are," Stride greets him. "You just missed Mr. Daubney."

"So I gather."

Stride shakes his head bemusedly. "Strange man. Very strange. Accusing Scotland Yard of all sorts.

Anybody'd think we were the ones who stole his precious little toys."

Cully pulls a face. "I hope you didn't refer to them as toys."

Stride's expression tells him all he needs to know.

"His manservant is brutally murdered, and the only thing preoccupying Mr. Daubney is where his blessed collection might have gone to. I may not be a 'collector of Japanese artefacts', but at least I care about tracking down and arresting the blackguards who killed a man in cold blood," Stride says, slightly defensively.

"What did you tell him?"

"I said you would write and arrange a further meeting at a mutually convenient time."

Cully is pretty sure this can be interpreted as sending Daubney off with a flea in his ear. He rises with a sigh.

"I will write to him straight away."

Stride grunts, then mutters something about the upper classes, snapping fingers, and beck and call. Cully pretends he hasn't heard. He returns to his own office ~ a crowded room he shares with several other detectives, and dashes off an apology for his absence coupled with a request to visit tomorrow.

He could call round on his way back, but he is not going to. Tomorrow will do. Mr. Daubney and the ivory cat netsuke can wait. Cully knows his priorities. He has a small daughter with a birthday, and the length of pink ribbon that is burning a hole in his coat pocket.

****

Halfway up Ludgate Hill, where the shops are largest and their silk and Indian shawls most precious and tempting to the female eye, is a small gateway. It leads to a labyrinth of streets, courts and small lanes, unpaved and strewn with litter, orange peel and noisy children.

Ludgate Hill turns eventually into Fleet Street, 'the street of ink'.

Here are the printing shops, newspapers, publishers and wholesale booksellers. Here are the all-purpose newspaper offices, and here, wearing her best hat and coat, and carrying a satchel, is Lucy Landseer.

She turns left into a narrow street, skirts round two little girls with hoops, and finally reaches her destination: a small square containing two trees behind an iron railing, some sparrows, and a black painted door with the words *'Illustrated London Express'* in bright copper lettering.

This edifying newspaper, published fortnightly, advertises itself as the 'social conscience' of the Londoner, claiming to tap into the tone of advanced public opinion. It is known for its illustrations, sometimes erring on the lurid side, as the editor knows that 'the more blood, the more copies sold'. Lucy has supplied the paper with occasional articles, and on the strength of this, has made an appeal to the editor for help.

It is ten minutes past ten o'clock as Lucy knocks firmly on the door, which is opened by an elderly porter. Lucy states her mission in a firm voice, (she has discovered that firmness is the trick in getting her own way with members of the male sex) and is handed over to a messenger, who leads the way into the interior of the building, along an empty corridor, and down a flight of stairs to the unwindowed basement room containing the shelves of leather-bound back copies of the newspaper.

This is the domain of Armand Malpractis, indexer, archivist, producer, and Keeper of The Catalogue ~ always referred to in hushed tones and capitals. It is widely speculated amongst the journalists, who regard him with bemused perplexity, that when he was child, he probably kept a record of all his toys. In a black ruled notebook. And arranged them in a specific order only known to himself.

If he had a wife (unlikely), she would be labelled *Wife: duties domestic*. It is also speculated in the newsroom that when he finally departs from this world (*Mortal coil: shuffle off*), the word Catalogue will be found engraved upon his heart.

Knowing nothing of this, however, and intent only upon her quest to help her new writer friend, Lucy Landseer knocks at the door. Then, head held high, she enters the room and marches (firmly) across to the desk.

She positions herself directly in front of it and waits. Malpractis continues writing something in neat copperplate on an oblong card. He seems totally absorbed in his work. There is a pile of similarly written cards to one side of him. An unwritten pile on the other side.

After a few minutes' silence, Lucy coughs in an introductory sort of way. Malpractis drops his pen, starts, utters an exclamation of surprise and glances up. His glasses slide down his long nose and hang precariously off the end, fighting for precedence with a small drop of moisture.

"Oh. Ah. I see. No. Well. Yes. There you are. Aren't you?"

Lucy stifles a smile and agrees. Armand Malpractis rises. He is a tall, spare man, with a lean face, fringed by wispy locks of greying hair, a grey beard, and the sallow complexion of one for whom fresh air and brisk exercise are unknown phenomena. His shirt and black suit are crumpled and there are numerous pencils sticking out of the top pocket of his jacket.

Malpractis regards her with a puzzled frown, as if he is inwardly searching for a category under which to file her: *Young woman: provenance unknown*? He pushes his glasses back up his nose and waits for enlightenment.

"My name is Miss Lucy Landseer. I am a writer. I applied to your editor asking if I might search the newspaper for a story that interests me."

Malpractis shuffles through his mental card index: *Editor: request from writer?*

"Yes. Ah. Let me see. A moment, Miss ... Landseer," he says. His voice is thin and reedy. He riffles through a tray labelled: *Queries?* until, with a murmur of satisfaction, he draws out her letter. There is a pause while he reacquaints himself with the contents. Then he nods a few times.

"Yes. I understand. Good. You wish to inquire about a certain Lord Edwin Lackington and his wife. I believe I may be able to help you. Let us now proceed forthwith and without further delay to The Catalogue."

He emerges from behind the desk, and shuffles over to a large cabinet of dark wooden drawers, each with a small brass place holder containing a written alphabetical indication of the contents. Malpractis pauses, stands awhile in silent contemplation of his life's work, as a priest might stand in rapture before the altar of the Lord. Then he pulls out one of the drawers and starts flicking through the cards inside.

"Lackington, Lord Edwin Ripley St. John ... letter to the Times opposing railway expansion ... letter to the Times re: fox hunting ... stag hunting... grouse shooting ... opposition to female education. None of this pertains to your inquiry. Yes. Ah. Here we have it. *Lackington, Lady Georgiana Artemisia: scandalous affair... report of Commissioners in Lunacy ... petition to the magistrate ...* Now we are progressing."

"But this is exactly what I want," Lucy exclaims, clapping her hands delightedly. "Wonderful! Thank you. How do I proceed?"

Malpractis regards her quizzically, as if she were some strange object that needed to be identified and categorised (*Female: excitable nature?*).

"You do not proceed, Miss … Landseer. At least, no further than one of the desks at the far end of the room. I am the one who proceeds upon your behalf. I shall write down the year, month and date of each article, followed by the relevant page. I shall then fetch you the monthly bound copy containing the article, clearly marked, which you may then peruse at your leisure. Notes are permitted to be taken.

"Please also bear in mind that the Archive Room closes for luncheon at midday, reopening at one in the afternoon. It then closes at four-thirty promptly. If you would now take your place, I shall endeavour to supply you with the first volume of the newspaper."

Lucy sits down at one of the two unoccupied desks. She retrieves her notebook and her pens and pencils from her satchel and tries to contain her impatience. Meanwhile, Malpractis begins jotting down references upon slips of paper, which he then takes over to the shelves of brown leather-bound volumes. As he searches, he emits a toneless humming, rather like a preoccupied bee. This is punctuated sporadically by a whispered: "Ah, yes."

Lucy Landseer, writer and imminent detective, turns to a clean page in her notebook and writes: The Case of the Unfortunate Author. She underlines it. Twice. Adds an exclamation mark. Then she sits back to await further developments.

****

Further developments are also about to occur elsewhere in the city. Here is Detective Sergeant Jack Cully knocking at the door of Mr. Gerald Daubney. After a long wait, and just as he has decided to give up and return to Scotland Yard, he hears a heavy tread on the other side of the door, accompanied by huffing and puffing.

The door is unlocked from the inside. A couple of bolts are shot back. A length of chain is unhooked. The door is then slightly opened and a round, red, elderly face in a mob cap peers through the gap.

"D'liveries to the basement," it says, puffing.

Cully introduces himself. The face identifies itself as belonging to the cook. The door is opened and Cully steps into the gloomy hallway.

"I'm sorry sir, them stairs'll be the death of me! Nearly missed you."

Cully makes polite please-do-not-concern yourself noises.

"How does your master find himself today?" he inquires, as the cook divests him of his outdoor coat and hat.

"He mopes, sir. As he did yesterday and the day afore that. I've worked for the family since the master was a lad, sir, and they were all of a moping disposition. His Ma was a great moper, Gawd rest her soul. Mind, she had good reason, what with all them babbies coming and going so fast. Five babbies, sir. Four tiny coffins. Only Master Gerald survived."

The cook heaves a great sigh and shakes her head sadly.

"His Pa was a champion moper too, sir, especially over matters of business, and stocks and shares and the railway, but Master Gerald beats them both for moping. He seems to have inherited a double dose of it. He just sits in that blessed room of his hour after hour, day after day, curtains drawn, moping. Just him and that white cat. It's not normal, is it?"

"I am sorry to hear that."

"No sorrier than I am," the cook grumbles. "I have got a girl in to sweep and dust ~ so long as he don't notice and isn't pertickler, and I can send out the laundry, but as for the shaving of his face, and the brushing of his clothes and his boots and such things what a gentleman requires for his daily wellbeing, it ain't my job. And so I told him straight the other day."

"And what did your master reply?" Cully asks, intrigued by this insight into another person's life. Or half-life.

"He moped," the cook says laconically. "Shall I announce you now, sir?" She knocks at a closed door, half opens it, says, "A p'liceman to see you, Master Gerald."

Cully steps into the room, with its dim light idling through the heavy curtains, throwing everything into shadow, so that it seems more like entering a tomb than a gentleman's drawing room. The air smells stale, as if all the goodness has been breathed out of it.

Gerald Daubney sits in a velvet spoon-backed chair by a miserable fire. He has a catalogue on his lap, and a pencil in one hand and appears to be listlessly ticking items off a list.

The white cat, who has been curled up by the fire, rouses itself, gets up from the hearthrug, and chirrups its way across the room, tail erect in friendly greeting. Once arrived, it begins to wind itself round his ankles, purring enthusiastically. Cully sighs. Cats. Why?

Daubney indicates the seat opposite. Cully sits. The cat launches itself onto his lap, turns around a couple of times, then hoists its back leg and begins to wash enthusiastically. Cully tries not to sneeze.

"Detective Cully? You have some good news for me at last?" Daubney asks.

Cully observes the bright, almost feverish eagerness in the man's expression and voice, and is glad he has had time to think through carefully what he is going to say. He doesn't want to build the eccentric collector's hopes up.

"Not as yet. I have come because I want to find out more about how netsuke, like those in your collection, come into this country," he says.

Daubney's face falls. It is as if a light has been switched off behind his eyes.

"I see. Well, it has only been eight years or so since Japan allowed traders to enter, so it is still, as it were, a specialist area. I pride myself upon having ~" he pauses, a spasm of pain contorting his features, "that is to say *I had* one of the finest collections in London, not to say the whole of the country."

"And from where did you obtain the collection?"

"I bought my first netsuke from a dealer in Japan. Unfortunately, my health then declined so I was never able to make the long and arduous journey again. I now order them from the only reputable business in London that sells authentic netsuke. The shop is called Mortlake & Devine, and is situated in Sloane Street."

"This shop possesses lists and bills of sale to their various clients?"

"I should imagine so. I have a folder of my own orders and payments. Why are you asking me these questions, detective? What is their purpose?"

"I was just wondering how many people might have similar collections, sir. Or might wish to acquire some of your items. For instance, I see from the list you supplied to us that one of the items stolen was an ivory cat," Cully indicates the white cat, who is currently kneading his trousers lovingly with her sharp claws.

Now Daubney's inner light is suddenly switched on again. He leans forward, clasping his hands between his knees and stares unblinkingly at Cully.

"You are referring to my rarest and most beloved netsuke: the Edo cat. It was carved in the seventeenth century by the famous carver Hidari Issan who lived in the Edo region of Japan. I do not know of anybody else who has one similar. I cannot tell you how much its absence pains me."

Cully mentally files this information while trying surreptitiously to persuade the real cat, whose presence is paining him, to relocate.

Daubney rises, goes to a sideboard and opens a drawer. "Here are the bills and receipts for my netsuke," he says, thrusting some paperwork at Cully. "I hope this will speed up your investigation, detective. It seems to be taking an inordinately long time to find and return my precious collection to me."

Cully bites his lip to stop him making some inappropriate comment. He nods his thanks, folds the documents, brushes off the cat (who miaows indignantly), and walks to the door. His departure coincides with the arrival of the cook. She is carrying a tray.

"I brought some coffee and shortbread for your guest, Master Gerald," she says.

"But the guest is just leaving," Daubney tells her sharply. "And I do not require any refreshments at the moment."

He turns his back on them. Cully and the cook exchange raised-eyebrow glances.

"Moping," the cook whispers.

Cully helps himself to a piece of shortbread, then goes to retrieve his hat and coat. Outside, rain has started to fall, grey and relentless. Cully did not bring an umbrella. He tucks the paperwork more carefully into his jacket pocket, puts his head down and starts walking.

****

Izzy Harding has no umbrella either. She hurries along the pavement, trying to avoid other people who have umbrellas but no spatial awareness, so keep knocking into her. Izzy is carrying a cardboard box, which contains two sets of tiny dolls' house drawing room furniture, painted gold, two shiny varnished dining-room tables and chairs, two wardrobes and various minute paintings in gilt frames.

The frames were especially fiddly to paint, and so were given to Izzy, because she has the smallest and most nimble fingers. As a result, her eyes ache and there is a tight band stretched across her forehead. This special hand-delivery is supposed to be a 'reward' for her hard work, though tramping the rain-sodden streets with leaky boots and a bedraggled bonnet hardly constitutes much of a reward, especially as Izzy knows the teenage overseer has only farmed out the job so that she can stay in the warm and dry.

Izzy reaches Oxford Street. Now all she has to do is find the right department store where her box is to be left. It is a rush order ~ the store had a request from a very rich client who has an account there. He wanted two identical dolls' houses for his twin daughters' birthdays. The problem was identified when the department manager instructed his shop assistants to parcel up the houses and was told that the miniature inhabitants were without the basic necessities for a comfortable existence.

Such things happen.

Izzy slows. There are many big department stores lining the street, and her task is to find the correct one. Her instructions are to hand the cardboard box to the man on the door, telling him that 'this is Mr. Pritchard's order. It is expected.' Then she is to return promptly, as there is a new batch of furniture to be varnished.

Izzy has never visited Oxford Street before. It is out of her limited area of expertise. The street takes her breath away. The gold and plate-glass windows of the big shops are crammed with wonderful things. Some have whole rooms with real dining tables covered with cloths and set with silver cutlery and glasses and dinner plates.

Well-dressed ladies are stepping out of carriages and being bowed into the shops by liveried doormen. Other well-dressed ladies are returning to their carriages, carrying parcels. There are glossy horses and shiny carriages parked axle to axle all the way down the street as far as her eye can see.

Izzy glances up, checks the names over the various front entrances, then walks on until she arrives at John Gould & Company. It takes a few minutes to attract the attention of the doorman, who is staring at the rain from the porticoed entrance where he is staying nice and dry, but finally he deigns to look down and notice her.

Izzy hands over her box, repeating the memorised words. The box is taken into his gloved hands, without any thanks, and the instructions to 'cut along sharp.' Izzy cuts along as far as one of the display windows, where she is brought up short. She stands, staring in awed amazement.

The window shows a beautiful nursery, crammed with wonderful toys. Tiny lead soldiers march across an imaginary battlefield. Drums and trumpets play silent music to accompany their advance. There are wooden bricks, rocking horses with dapple-grey sides and red leather bridles, wooden pull-along sheep and dogs, furry cats, teddy bears and stuffed animals galore.

Dolls with rosebud mouths, pink cheeks, frothy dresses and cascading yellow hair sit around a tea-table set with pink cups and saucers and plaster of Paris delicacies. There is even a large wooden dolls' house, its front open to display the contents. Izzy presses her nose to the window trying to see whether any of the furniture came from her attic workshop.

Lost in wonder, she does not notice the small girl with the fur tippet and muff, who has just come out of the store and is walking towards one of the splendid carriages parked in front of the main entrance.

The girl wears shiny buttoned boots, a blue velvet hat, and a warm navy woollen coat. Her ribboned and ringleted hair falls gracefully onto her shoulders. Her pink and white complexion resembles that of the dolls in the window. The girl spies Izzy. She stops. Fumbling in her pocket, she extracts something. She comes over.

"Here, poor little beggar-girl. This sixpence is for you," she says, handing Izzy a small coin.

Izzy Harding is so astonished that she is rendered temporarily speechless. The girl gives her a friendly nod, then skips over to her mother, who is organising a footman laden with parcels. She tugs at her sleeve.

"I just gave the poor beggar-girl over there my silver sixpence, Mama. Was that not extremely kind of me?"

Her Mama smiles indulgently at her. She glances briefly at Izzy, then looks away. The little girl scrambles into the carriage. The parcels are loaded on board. Mama is handed in, and the carriage swings out into the busy street and sets off at a brisk pace towards Hyde Park.

Izzy stares at the silver sixpence in her palm, the words 'poor beggar-girl' ringing in her ears like a slap. Is that what she is? She considers her appearance: the leaky patched boots, the coat, of a cut and colour long out of fashion, several sizes too big and torn at the cuffs, and the hat, which has pancaked and is dripping water down her neck.

For a moment, her heart sinks, as the gap between her world and that of her small benefactress opens up in front of her like a bottomless chasm. To hide the tears springing to her eyes, she turns to the window again. **'Give Them the Gift of Happiness'** says the sign above the rocking horse. She reads it laboriously, spelling out each word through a hot, wet blur.

Izzy takes a deep breath. Swallows. Wipes her eyes on her ragged coat sleeve and reads the sign again. And again. And then it dawns upon her. She managed to find the right store to deliver her box. She has just read a sign in a display window. She. Can. Read!

Suddenly, Izzy Harding feels a great wave of happiness break over her. She is no beggar-girl: she is a reader! She has all the riches of the printed word at her command. A gift more precious than anything else.

Later, after her shift at Mrs Sarah McAdam's Select City Dining Room finishes, Izzy will go home and add the silver sixpence to her other treasures: the shiny brass button, the length of bright scarlet ribbon, the sheet of gold leaf, the six farthings, the miniature dolls' tea-set and the green velvet pincushion.

****

It is three in the morning, and some urge to fear wakes Gerald Daubney, lifting him to his feet beside his bed. Fully awake in an instant, he tries to remember the dream that shocked him, but it has gone. Stranded in the darkness, he drinks a glass of water and racks his brains.

The conversation earlier with the detective from Scotland Yard disturbed him. Yes. The man's questions seemed illogical. He did not understand their purpose. He had been upset by them. He still remains upset by them. It seems that nobody *understands* how he feels.

He goes to the window and draws back the blind. He can hear the rain lashing the building and beating on the cobbles below. He has a sudden vision of what it must be like to live on the streets with nothing to eat save what one can forage, nothing to warm oneself and to be in constant fear of predators lurking in dark alleyways.

Daubney hears a small whimpering sound and is shocked to realise it is coming from his own throat. A shiver runs down his spine. Want of sleep, want of food has led to dark thoughts gathering. He must not give way to them. He must resist them with every ounce of strength in his body, and be robust.

He stretches out his hands, inching his way across the room to the door, where his dressing gown hangs. He will go downstairs and sit in the dark in front of his empty cabinet, and think about days that are over, and dreams that are done. There will be no more sleep tonight.

****

Morning arrives, bringing with it a postman carrying a letter for Mrs Riva Hemmyng-Stratton. She does not recognise the handwriting on the envelope and, fearing that it contains further bad news, leaves it by the side of her plate. Only after consuming the sort of miniscule breakfast that would barely sustain one of her romantic heroines, does she finally slit open the envelope. The contents are as elliptical as they are short.

Dear Fellow Scribe (she reads),

Let us meet outside Verey's in the Strand at 12 o'clock. I have so much to impart!

Yours etc.

L. Landseer

The Author spends some time puzzling over these cryptic lines, her emotions swinging from elation to despair. But in the end, curiosity gets the better of her and so, wearing her best hat, her face shrouded in a heavy veil, she catches a Waterloo omnibus.

By midday, the sun has bullied its way through the clouds that shroud the city. Mrs Hemmyng-Stratton alights, and walks the few yards to the venue, where Miss Landseer awaits her arrival, tapping her foot impatiently. The Author approaches and makes her presence known.

"Ah," Lucy Landseer exclaims, shaking the proffered fingers. "I did not recognise you under the veil."

The Author explains that she is currently being hounded by reporters from various newspapers, all eager to hear 'her side of the story'. They lurk in the bushes outside her house. They creep up on her in the street. They jump out of doorways and accost her. They are everywhere. Achieving fame through her literary output is one thing, having infamy thrust upon her is quite another. She has to be constantly alert and could do with someone to watch her back (because sadly, one cannot have two fronts).

"I do hope you have good news to impart," she murmurs, as Lucy leads the way into the restaurant.

They are soon seated at a nice table, away from the door. Lucy orders a roast chicken, two slices of ham, and potatoes ("It is only a shilling!"). While they wait for their food, Mrs Hemmyng-Stratton lifts her veil and looks cautiously all around. She notes that the clientele consists exclusively of single women, some governess types, and ladies with parcels. Her companion has chosen well.

"Now then," Lucy says, drawing an impressive notebook from her bag. "Here is what I have discovered …"

Later that afternoon, refreshed physically and newly invigorated mentally by Lucy's information, Mrs Hemmyng-Stratton returns to her writing desk and prepares to rescue her heroine from the desperate clutches of writer's block.

Let there be a grand dinner party, she decides, with the tinkle of silver voices and silver cutlery. The conversation will be about horses, hunting, dogs and partridges. The anti-hero, (oh yes, she is going to introduce one, though any resemblance to a certain publisher is purely coincidental) will attend and is going disgrace himself by *eating peas with the assistance of his knife!*

Meanwhile Lucy Landseer betakes herself to the British Museum, where she spends an interesting hour or so amongst the Ancient Egyptians. She has been commissioned to write a series of instructive articles for a ladies' magazine ~ nothing too laborious, one cannot have the female brain over-taxed ~ yes, it is *that* kind of magazine, but it pays the rent.

While she wanders from display case to display case, she thinks about her recent meeting with the author of *Cecil Danvers*. It was almost too easy to prove that the newspaper articles depicting the sad state of the Lackington marriage and the subsequent tragic events that followed, were published *after* the novel appeared in print.

There was no way that Mrs Hemmyng-Stratton, whose connections to the aristocracy were always purely fictional in nature, would have ever been privy to the unfolding drama. Lucy is satisfied that she has supplied the writer with sufficient evidence to present to her publisher and possibly to face down any future accusation of libel.

Sufficient certainly, but not entirely conclusive. For Lucy Landseer still has two unanswered questions. Why has Lord Lackington chosen to attack the innocent author of *Cecil Danvers*, when to do so will only bring the whole scandal back into the public realm? And what of the hapless woman, whose life is even now being passed behind the high walls of an asylum? What can she add to the story?

There is more to this than meets the eye, Lucy thinks to herself. Yes, indeed. And it is her intention to discover what it is. But to do that, she first needs to acquire a small dog. A cocker spaniel, golden in colour, for preference.

****

Detective Sergeant Jack Cully is also the possessor of an inquisitive mind. Right now, he is taking it to certain premises in stylish Sloane Street, listed in the London business directory as 'An Emporium of Antique furniture, Oriental China and Curiosities'.

This is the newly relocated showroom of Mortlake & Devine. It has broad plate-glass windows and a heavy front door painted black and latticed in gold. The window display of blue and white china is artistically arranged to draw the eye of the passing Chelsea and Knightsbridge crowd, several of whom are lounging artistically in front of it.

As he approaches, the showroom door is flung open and a long-haired man in a flowing cloak strides ostentatiously out, to be greeted by the crowd as a returning hero. Throwing his arm theatrically around someone's shoulder, he sets off towards Chelsea, declaring loudly that he is borrowing a large Oriental blue jar from Morty, which will be just right for his next painting of Fanny.

Cully enters the shop and is greeted politely by a tall distinguished man in a dark bespoke suit with a wing collar that looks as if it has been tailored by Pythagoras. His hair and beard are artfully cut. His black shoes are as shiny as the metalwork on the railings outside. This is

Thomas Mortlake, dealer in antiquities and a connoisseur of fine art and collectables.

All around him are the fruits of his expertise and collecting endeavours: display cases filled with blue and white ceramics, teapots with dragons painted on them, tiny enamelled bowls, figurines, vases. The walls are hung with silk paintings, regalia and strange sword-guards. Mortlake & Devine specialise in Chinese paintings, and Japanese artefacts, though given Cully's infinitesimally minute knowledge of Asiatic antiquities, it could just as easily have been the other way around.

Cully shows the man his card.

"The detective police? We have never had a visit from you before. Three shops I've owned and run, and never a brush with the law in all that time. I hope there is nothing amiss?"

Cully explains why he is here.

"Ah. Mr. Daubney. I read about the sad business in the newspapers. What can I tell you, Detective Sergeant Cully? He is one of my customers, yes. Every time we had a delivery from our agent in the Far East, I would alert him, and he would be here within the hour. A good customer, indeed. Over the years, his collections of blue glaze china, and netsuke grew to be the finest in collecting circles. I know he was held in high regard by other *Japonistes,* as some have started calling them. And now, the entire collection of netsuke has been stolen! What a terrible thing. How is the poor gentleman bearing up under the loss?"

Cully shrugs and shakes his head.

"You do not surprise me, detective sergeant. Not at all. For some, just collecting beautiful or rare items is not enough. It becomes an obsession, a life's purpose. The lure is like a drug. The gentleman you inquire about is of that disposition, if I may judge him as such. He must be in extreme mental agony over the loss ~ the more so as it was so unexpected and sudden."

"Did he buy from anybody else?"

"No. I think not. You see, we can always assure our customers that whatever we sell is genuine. That is important. Some shops ~ I name them not, display articles that are fake and pretend that they are genuine, or poor quality, and say they are the finest. Not here. For example, the blue glazed plates over there in the display case, detective sergeant, are genuine Imari ware. The flowered teapot is Katieman. Feel free to take anything you purchase in the shop to the greatest expert in the kingdom, and he will verify that they are the genuine article."

As Cully is never going to purchase anything ~ he has already worked out that the lack of price-tickets probably means everything is way beyond his salary, and the presence of two small and lively girls in a tiny rented terrace house would be deterrent enough to displaying valuable china, he contents himself with a murmured concurrence.

"I am interested in other customers who may have bought netsuke from you," he says, pulling his notebook from his inner pocket. "Especially this gentleman." He shows him the page in his notebook where he has written down the name of Mr. Munro Black, and his address.

The man studies the name, then shakes his head. "I do not recall the gentleman, nor the address," he says. "I will make a note of it though and see whether my partner recollects anything." He gives Cully a sharp look. "Is this in relation to the robbery?"

"Possibly," Cully says, looking off. "I must say that Mr. Daubney seems *most* upset about the theft of a small ivory cat," he adds.

"Ah, I remember that netsuke well. The Edo cat. A beautiful piece. I have been trading in netsuke for many years, but I have never come across one like it before. Or since. It is a one-off. The item is as rare as it is priceless. I can quite understand his grief."

Cully mentally notes this down also. "What do you think has happened to the collection?" he asks.

Mortlake shrugs. "I have not heard of it coming onto the open market, so either it has passed into the hands of another private collector somewhere in the country, or, and I think this scenario the more likely, it has been broken up and taken abroad to sell as individual pieces."

The shop bell rings. A couple of potential customers saunter in. Mortlake's gaze drifts towards them. Cully takes the hint. He pockets his notebook, thanks Mortlake for his time and heads for the door. There is much to think about. And it is midday. He decides to think about it over a ham sandwich and a cup of coffee.

****

The misnamed 'dinner break' is also happening at the dolls' house furniture workshop. Very little dinner is being consumed, though some of the child workers are profiting from the downtime to snatch a quick break under the tables with their eyes closed.

Not Izzy Harding, though. She has nothing to eat, but for once, she does not care, for she has food for the mind. Here she is, sitting apart from her co-workers. In her hand is a small book entitled: A Simple Tale for Christian Children. It has a drawing of a group of flaxen-haired tots sitting at the knee of someone wearing a long robe.

Now that she can make out words, Izzy Harding is on a literary journey. It is amazing how much stuff there is to read, once you master the ability to spot it. Wonderful words are everywhere: on news vendors' boards:

Author Accused in Lord's Adultery Agony! She read that this morning on the way to work.

The sides of omnibuses have directions to exotic places never before encountered ~ Knightsbridge, Lyceum, Victoria. Admittedly, Izzy often hasn't a clue what the words actually mean, but that is not the point: it's her ability to put random letters together and create something new that counts.

Every shop she passes has something to work on: food items, prices, appeals to the prospective customer. Even here, in the dingy half-light of the workroom, she has discovered unexpected reading matter: *Arsenical Green. Gold leaf. Do not ingest contents. Beware fumes*, she'd read, as she sucked the end of her brush and dipped it into the bright green paint. The tiny crib she is working on needs a steady hand and an ability to paint round corners. That is why it has been entrusted to her. Not just a reader, but a reliable worker. Her status is truly advancing in leaps and bounds.

If she closes her eyes tight, Izzy can still see the look of utter delight on her teacher's face when she announced, proudly, that she could read. It was as if the sun had broken through. The other students, still struggling to get to grips with the mysteries of the alphabet, had looked on in wonder as Izzy read some words, then some more, then a whole page of words from a reading primer her teacher had given to her.

At the end of the lesson, replete with stale bun and satisfaction, Izzy had been handed a little book. Her teacher had told her she'd received it as a Sunday School prize when she was younger than Izzy. All the way home, Izzy had hugged the precious book to her thin chest. She'd slept curled around it. She'd awoken to the joy of it.

And now she is about to read it. Her own book. It is a simple tale about a naughty boy who, after some truly dreadful acts of nastiness, is brought face to face with the consequences of his actions and learns to be a good boy thereafter. She turns the pages, enthralled by the unfolding story. She has just reached the bit about the dog, when the book is rudely plucked from her hand.

"What's this then, Izz?"

Izzy glances up into the sharp, streetwise face of Angel, a girl who has spent her whole life defying the name she was given at birth. Angel sits opposite her. Her speciality is varnishing tables and persecuting weaker children. Her current employment gives her ample opportunities to do both.

Izzy gets to her feet, holds out her hand. "Give it back."

Angel's small weasel-coloured eyes dart war-flames. "Make me."

A few children saunter casually over to where some unexpected lunchtime entertainment is about to kick off.

"It's mine," Izzy says, her hand still outstretched.

"Where'd you buy it then?"

"Didn't buy it."

"Stole it then? So you're a thief, Izzy Harding, is that how it is?"

"It's a present," Izzy says, her eyes fixed on the book, the pages of which Angel is now flicking rapidly between her hands in a menacing manner. "Please Angel ~ don't harm it."

Too late. With a dismissive snort, Angel casually rips the book apart. Izzy feels a sob choking her throat. She launches herself at the other girl, screaming abuse, fists flailing. All the child workers gather round, chanting: 'Fight! Fight! Fight!' Despite the difference in their height, Izzy manages to land a few good punches before the teenage supervisor arrives on the scene and pulls them apart.

"Enough. I ain't got time for this. We've got a big order to fill. Angel, go and start work now. Izzy, you can pack the boxes."

Packing boxes is the lowest rung on the ladder, as it involves no skill whatsoever.

"But she started it," Izzy protests.

"And I'm finishing it," the youthful supervisor says. "You want a job here? You do what I say, or it's out on the street for you, quick smart. Understand?"

Izzy glares at Angel, who thumbs her nose in response as she stuffs the broken book down the front of her varnish-spattered overall.

"Thanks for this, Izzy. We could do with some more paper for the privy. Very kind of you," she grins.

Izzy spends a miserable afternoon packing boxes while standing in a draft from the open door. The thought of all those precious pages being used to wipe the backsides of Angel and her rough costermonger family is almost more than her poor heart can bear.

At the end of the day, reluctance dogging her every footstep, she makes her way round to her teacher's house to confess and face whatever rebuke awaits. She hasn't eaten all day, and the lack of food, combined with her feelings of misery and despair, means that when she arrives, and finds no bright welcoming light in the kitchen, it is too much to bear.

Izzy Harding retraces her steps, then sits down on the step, curling her arms around her knees. She leans her back against the front door and allows her head to go heavy. Dark thoughts circle for a bit, like ominous birds of prey, before she feels herself slipping away into another, kinder place.

This is how Maria finds her when she returns from her college lecture, slumped against the door, motionless and still. For a moment, Maria's heart misses a beat. She bends down, shakes Izzy's shoulder gently, calling her name.

Eventually, the girl unlocks her eyelids and raises her head. The light from the street-lamp emphasizes her pinched pallor, the purple rings round her eyes. Maria is shocked by the state of her star pupil. Izzy's hands are black with grime. She has bruising on her left cheek (some of the punches were returned), and a small chunk of her hair is missing.

Maria helps her to her feet, unlocks the front door and steers her through to the kitchen, where she places her on a chair. She sets a bowl and a washcloth on the table. Then she fills the kettle and places it on the hob, before going upstairs to make the invalid comfortable for the night.

On her return, she fills the teapot, and toasts some bread. Izzy wolfs the toast down in record time. Maria says nothing, merely keeping the plate filled until Izzy's colour has returned and she sits back with a sigh.

Tea is poured. Izzy loads spoon after spoon of sugar into her cup and stirs it vigorously. Still Maria says nothing. She watches as Izzy gulps down the hot tea, running her now cleaned index finger around the inside to get the last drops of sweetness. Then she speaks.

"How old are you, Izzy?"

Izzy frowns, does some rapid calculations on her finger. "I think I'm ten, miss."

"And when did you last have a good meal?"

Izzy brightens. "Just now, miss, thank you very much."

Maria rolls her eyes. "Izzy, you have managed to teach yourself to read in a few months. You can do basic mathematics. You have a brain. You're bright and intelligent. You could make a life for yourself. A better life"

Puzzled, Izzy looks at her. "But I have a life."

128

Maria shakes her head. "No, you have an existence, Izzy. And not a very pleasant one, if those bruises are anything to go by. When I first met you, you told me you wanted to better yourself, do you recall? Well, now you have a real chance. Have you started reading the little book I gave you?"

Izzy's face falls as she remembers why she came here in the first place. Sighing, she relates what happened. She has let her teacher down. She has let herself down. Now, instead of buttered toast and sweet tea, she will eat and drink the bread and water of affliction. She waits, head down, hand clasped in her lap, for the scolding.

It does not come. Izzy raises her eyes. To her amazement, her teacher is looking at her with such love and compassion in her eyes. The response is so unexpected that, all at once, Izzy cannot bear it. She covers her face with her hands and sobs as if her heart would break.

Silently, Maria lets her cry, merely passing a clean handkerchief across the table. Unbeknown to Izzy, she is remembering a similar journey: a bright, curious child of whom nothing was expected other than dull obedience and as much absence from the parental sphere as possible. It was hard growing up in the shadow of God Almighty and the church Elders.

Eventually, when Izzy reaches the sniff and gulp stage, Maria leans across the kitchen table, covering the small damp hand with her own. Everything about her young pupil screams neglect and waste. She chooses her words with care.

"Izzy, I know how sorry you are. It doesn't matter about the book. It wasn't your fault and I do not blame you. I have plenty of other books you can borrow. But Izzy, have you ever thought of your future? You could go to school: there is a wonderful school not far from here called Queen's College. They have classes for girls your age. Anybody can attend."

Izzy stares at her. "Don't it cost?"

"There are fees to pay. But I'm sure we could find the money from somewhere. It must be possible. There are charitable institutions galore all over London. Think of it, Izzy: a new world! A better life."

Izzy shakes her head. "I know you mean well, Miss. But places like that ain't for girls like me. I have to work, and besides, there's Ma to consider. If I don't bring home a wage, we'll lose our place and be out on the street." She stands. "Thank you for the tea and such. And for not being cross about the book."

"Would you like another book, Izzy?" Maria suggests.

Izzy shakes her head. "Better not." She wraps her shawl around her shoulders. "I'll be off now, miss. See you next lesson time, perhaps."

Maria accompanies her to the kitchen door. "Izzy, if you ever need a friend, or a place to stay, this door is always open to you. You know that?"

Izzy nods. Then she stuffs Maria's handkerchief up her sleeve and goes out into the gloom of the city.

****

At this time, there are still a few lunatic asylums that live down to the worst the human mind could imagine: long gloomy corridors leading to bare wards or unheated cells, where the air is rent by wild, passionate, despairing cries; where the mad are left to gibber and rave for the amusement of the general public, deprived of liberty, deprived of dignity, locked in after nine at night, and chained and strait-waistcoated during the day.

Such places might have manacles, socklets, and cold baths; they separate the inmates according to class,

130

gender, and keep the 'excitables' well away from the non-violent. In 1867, among a population of approximately 23 million souls, 63,743 individuals were certified as insane, the majority confined to public institutions like county asylums, or to workhouses as pauper lunatics. For them, the only way out was rescue, escape or death. It was like being buried in a living tomb.

But Cedar House Private Asylum is not like that. Set amidst pleasant grounds, with walks and benches, it is home (if such a word can be used) to six wealthy women, placed under the care of Dr John Foster, a specialist in the treatment of ladies whose husbands have decided, for various reasons, that Cedar House is best suited to lodge and look after them.

There are no locked doors within Cedar House Asylum, no padlock on the gates and no spiked railings, for none of the inhabitants have ever attempted to escape, (a reflection, maybe, on the sort of terrible home lives they endured previously). There is, moreover, a piano, and a tennis court, and carriage rides are occasionally permitted, the patient always accompanied by one of the attendants. For at £420 a year, it is important to their husbands to maintain before the world the fiction that these women are enjoying the same standard of living as heretofore. Only somewhere else.

Lucy Landseer has strolled past Cedar House Asylum on several occasions, each time accompanied by a small toffee-coloured spaniel called Flush. Flush is a playful little dog, and has run onto the lawn to retrieve a red rubber ball, thrown by his mistress, much to the delight of the patients and their attendants, who have clapped their hands and laughed at the little dog's antics.

Now here they are again, Lucy in a fashionably trimmed bonnet and brown coat with brass buttons, and Flush wearing a blue collar, his coat shining like copper flame. They make a handsome pair. Lucy throws the ball; Flush scampers after it, picks it up in his soft mouth and deposits it at her feet. While praising the dog for his agility, Lucy is covertly scanning the ground-floor windows, the conservatory and outdoor benches, almost as if she were seeking out someone.

A final throw. The dog hurtles joyously after the ball. Lucy steps forward. She falls! The ladies gasp in horror! The two attendants rise and run over. They hoist her to her feet, asking whether she is alright. But Lucy is not alright ~ she cannot put her weight upon her left ankle. Oh dear! What should she do?

The attendants support her by an elbow and conduct her gently to a bench. Lucy dimples her thanks, agrees that a cup of tea would be most welcome, and indicates to Flush to sit at her feet. She closes her eyes, letting the warm Autumn sunshine caress her face.

The only other occupant of the bench is a pretty woman in her early thirties. She has a cloud of fair hair, a small retroussé nose and large liquid blue eyes. But her complexion is very pale, and she has an air of melancholy about her. She wears a kind of shapeless russet gown ~ the sort of attire that Lucy has seen on some of the arty women who frequent the British Museum and gawp at the Egyptian mummies.

Lucy opens her eyes, turns and gives her a brave smile. The woman returns it sympathetically.

"That was a nasty fall," she says in a low, but pleasant voice.

"I was clumsy; I should have looked where I was going."

Flush, deciding that he is being unjustifiably excluded, gets to his paws and strolls over to the woman, who reaches down to stroke his velvety head.

"I used to have just such a pretty dog," she says wistfully, fondling his ears.

"You have been here long?" Lucy asks, casually.

"Ah. That is an odd question, coming from a complete stranger."

Lucy introduces herself and the dog, extending her gloved fingers as she does so. Lady Georgiana Lackington (for of course, it is she) reciprocates, then regards her with keen interest.

"A writer? I have never encountered a writer before."

"I have never encountered a member of the aristocracy before," Lucy dimples her reply.

Lady Lackington draws in a quick breath. "Thank you for saying that, my dear."

"But it is true. Why thank me?"

"Because you know what this place is for, and why we are here. You must do, it is common knowledge. And your question suggests it. Yet you have chosen not to remind me. For that, I thank you, Miss Landseer. Indeed, I do."

Lucy gives a dainty little lift of her shoulders, indicating that it is of no account. Flush places his head on Lady Lackington's lap and utters a sigh of contentment. A cup of weak tea is brought, and Lucy receives it gratefully.

The next twenty minutes pass in polite chit-chat, punctuated by dog-worship. At the end, Lucy promises that she will return soon, with Flush. And indeed, she does. The very next day she and her canine companion turn up at exactly the same hour, to be met with much joy by Lady Lackington. It seems to Lucy that there is now more colour in her cheeks, and a slight but perceptible sparkle to her blue eyes.

On her third visit, Georgiana, (things move fast socially when there is nothing to impede their progress) in response to Lucy's artful probing, confides some details about her removal to her current place of sanctuary.

Lucy learns with horror of the cold, brutal aristocrat who whipped his dogs, his horses and his wife in equal amounts. Of her father's determination to marry her off to him, despite her own wishes. Of cruel and demeaning words that slowly seeped into her mind and sapped her life of any enjoyment; of the gradual cutting off of former friends and family, until, one fateful day, when a certain good-looking young artist was hired to paint a portrait of Lord Lackington, the inevitable happened.

"I was so lonely, my dear Lucy," Lady Georgiana says, her eyes brimming with tears. "And he ~ oh, he was everything I desired: kind, affectionate, a gentleman ~ though, of course, he came from a completely different class to my brute of a husband."

"Why, then, has he not come to rescue you?" Lucy inquires, her romantic soul thrilling to the tragic tale, even as her writer's brain is mentally filing it away for future consideration.

"He has left England for good. My husband threatened to destroy him if he ever sets foot in this country again. He is living abroad in Paris, and I, if I only could, desire more than anything else to join him. But I have nothing ~ Lackington has taken every penny I own, ruined my standing in the public eye, got me wrongly declared insane and placed me here. He is an extremely powerful man, with many influential contacts in all the higher echelons of London, so no former friends will help me. They are all too fearful for their own reputations."

"But you have me," Lucy says quietly.

Lady Georgiana turns a disbelieving gaze upon her companion. "You? How can you help me?"

Lucy beams back at her. "I can come up with a plan, Georgiana. That is what we writers do. Leave it to me. Trust me. By our next meeting, I will have devised a way

134

of getting you out of this place, and then out of the country."

****

A London fog is like no other fog on earth. Its ingredients are made up of a million chimneys breathing forth smoke, soot, water vapour, carbonic acid and sulphur, the effect being similar to a vast crater, below which the unhappy inhabitants must creep and live as best they can.

On some days, the smoke hangs about in a grey pall just above the rooftops, resisting the rays of the sun. It is on such a day as this that Mrs Hemmyng-Stratton makes her way to the small tea-room off Bond Street where she has arranged to meet fellow writer and hopefully, saver of her literary reputation, Miss Lucy Landseer.

The Author arrives first and selects a table as far from the door as possible. She has heard nothing from her publisher, despite handing over to him the results of Lucy's research, and the sense that this foul dishonour of her literary integrity is creeping ever nearer is affecting her greatly.

She orders a pot of tea, but no cakes. To indulge in treats at a time like this seems unnecessarily frivolous. No heroine in any of her books would ever partake of nourishment when in the throes of some bitter agony of the soul. So, neither will she. *Così va il mondo.*

By the time Lucy breezes in through the door, minus dog, but plus notebook and radiant smile, the Author has sat for a full ten minutes staring at a cup of weak cooling tea and, metaphorically, at her own doomed future.

"My dear fellow scribe," Lucy says, unpinning her hat and removing her gloves. "What a foul day! A man on the omnibus was smoking some awful tobacco ~ I could barely breathe! I am ready for a cup of tea. Let me drink it, and then I will tell you what I have discovered. It is truly astonishing!"

Mrs Hemmyng-Stratton studies the buttons on her gloves while Lucy pours, sugars and sips her tea. Then she lifts her pallid face and burning eyes to the young writer's face.

"I await your revelation with great hope, Miss Landseer," she murmurs. "I admit that I am currently suffering such agony of soul. I have shed bitter tears over my predicament. Rest and sleep have become strangers to me. As for taking nourishment ..." She lets the sentence fade away, bringing her hand to her forehead in a tragic gesture.

"Ah. I am so sorry. But I shall not disappoint! Oh, where to start? Here, I think. Volume one: The Casual Introduction. Since we last met, I have become acquainted with Lady Georgiana Lackington ~ and no, in answer to the question I see in your face, she is quite definitely NOT mad. Not in the slightest. No more than you or I. She has been wrongfully detained by her cruel husband, though the place she currently inhabits is a blessed relief from his persecution.

"And now, here comes the best of my news: she has confided in me and told me how she used the ideas in your novel to arrange meetings with her lover! Is that not proof positive that you are completely innocent of the accusation made by her husband?"

"It may well be so," Mrs Hemmyng-Stratton says slowly. "But I do not see how it will advance my cause, as she is 'mad' and incarcerated in an asylum. Therefore, her testimony would not be regarded as valid in a court of law, would it?"

"Indeed, you are quite right. But you do not have to rely on it, for she has the actual copy of your novel with her! Yes ~ she keeps it upon her bedside table! She told me she packed it, along with a change of clothing, when the doctor in charge and his attendants came to take her away in a carriage. She could not possibly leave it behind, as every page reminds her of her beloved and the happy times they spent together.

"Now ~ and here is the thing that will clinch the matter: she told me she was given the copy of your book by one of her former friends as a birthday gift: they were all wild about it apparently, and, listen: *the giver has signed the front of the book with birthday wishes, adding the date and year!* So, you could not possibly have based your story upon Lady Georgiana's affair, because, do you see, your book preceded it! There, fellow scribe, have I not done extremely well? Did not I tell you I would help you?"

The Author is speechless!

"But," she says, when at last, the ability to speak returns, "unless I can produce the book itself, I have only your word, and hers, that it is so."

Lucy Landseer wafts the problem away as if it were a pesky fly.

"And so we reach Volume two of the story: The Clever Plan. And here, I will need your assistance. Lady Georgiana wishes to leave the Asylum and join her beloved abroad. But she has no money. I propose offering her enough funds to procure a ticket from London to Dover and thence to Calais, and payment for lodgings and food in France when she reaches the continent, in return for her copy of *Cecil Danvers*. If I enlighten her about what her husband is trying to do to your reputation, I believe her desire for revenge, coupled with her desire to escape, will be motivation enough for her to agree to my suggestion."

"You have thought it all out, Miss Landseer," the Author says, opening her eyes wide. "You are to be congratulated, indeed."

"But the thought must be translated into the deed. And I have no money," Lucy says simply. "My meagre earnings barely cover my rent, my food and the odd bonnet."

"Ah, I understand. Luckily, my earnings, as a result of the unwelcome glare of publicity, have recently grown incrementally. Name the sum and it shall be yours."

Lucy beams at her. "I so hoped you would be able to foot the bill. Shall we say fifty guineas? It sounds a nice round sum and I like guineas. So much more pleasant than mere pounds."

Mrs Hemmyng-Stratton swallows. Truth to tell, she has been stashing away bits of money ever since her first published book, with the aim of buying herself a little cottage in the Lake District (home to the late Mr. William Wordsworth and his friends), to use as a bolthole to escape the noise and unpleasantness of the city.

She has always been sure she would be able to write even better books in the vicinity of the great poets of the not-so-distant past. But, she reminds herself, if she loses the upcoming court case, her home may well be the walls of a prison, and her writing days, good or bad, will be a fleeting memory.

"Let it be so, then," she sighs. "If you care to accompany me to my bank, I will arrange to withdraw the necessary funds."

Lucy claps her hands. "Excellent. I shall finish my tea at once."

"But how on earth do you plan to spirit her away from the Asylum?"

Lucy raises her delicate eyebrows and smiles in a mysterious manner. "Ah. That is for me to work out. Volume three: The Great Escape."

****

Alas, there is no escape for Gerald Daubney, mentally or otherwise. Here he is, his black suit unbrushed, his cravat badly tied, his shoes in need of a good shine, entering the portals of the Antiquaries and Collectors Club. It is an unlikely sighting, given that Daubney has no particular craving for the society and conversation of others, but he has been lured here by the promise of a talk on Travels in Oriental China and Japan by Colonel Liversedge Pittkethly.

The Colonel is not one of the members of the Club, but has recently returned from a long sea-voyage to distant parts, so has become a person of interest to the members. As these distant parts are also where much of Daubney's collection originated, he has been drawn out of seclusion. Perhaps he will learn something that might bring consolation to him in his misery? It is a long shot, but anything is worth a try.

Daubney enters the hallway, hands his outer coat, his umbrella and his top hat to the doorman, and mounts the staircase to the assembly room. The brightness of the chandeliers dazzles his eyes, used as they are to the dim gaslight of his quiet rooms. The noise of boots, the chatter of his fellow antiquarians falls like breaking rocks upon his ear.

For a moment, he contemplates flight. Then his presence is noticed by Charles Warren and Augustus Roach-Smith, who bear down upon him like galleons in full sail. It is clear from their red faces, straining waistcoats and the cigars and balloons of brandy in their hands that they have attended the 'pre-talk dinner' downstairs.

"Daubney, old man!" Roach-Smith exclaims, clapping him on the shoulder. Daubney winces. "Good to see you out and about again. Come, let's find you a seat near the front. Can't have an expert like yourself skulking at the back."

Gerald Daubney, a born skulker, allows himself to be reluctantly propelled through the assembled crowd, acknowledging various greetings and protestations of sympathy by keeping his head down and his eyes fixed firmly on the parquet flooring.

"Here we are," Charles Warren says jovially, indicating, with a curt nod, to the current occupants of three seats in the front row that they had better shift. Before Daubney can protest that he does not wish to cause any trouble, he is plonked down on a seat. His two minders sit either side of him. There is no escape now.

His last chance vanishes completely as the entertainment for the evening enters the rear of the room. Pittkethly is the sort of bluff specimen of muscular Christian Englishman who refers to the inhabitants of other countries as 'Natives'. Daubney has encountered him socially a couple of times, but has never been tempted to read any of his books, which all have titles like: '*Up the Yangtze on a Junk and a Prayer*' or '*Bringing God's Everlasting Light to Darkies*'. He finds both the man and his attitude repellent.

Nevertheless. He is here. And here is the guest speaker for the evening: Colonel Pittkethly, clad in jodhpurs, puttees and a Harris tweed jacket, striding onto the platform. He is preceded by the current chairman of the Antiquarian and Collectors' Club, who rambles through the minutes of the last meeting, then gives a short, glowing eulogy upon the many and varied achievements of their honoured guest, throughout which Pittkethly smirks complacently under his large brown moustache.

Eventually, the chairman talks himself to a standstill, and the colonel gets to his feet, seeming to expand as he does so, until his presence fills the room. His voice is loud and intrusive and Daubney feels himself shrinking back into his chair in response. Nevertheless, some of what Pittkethly says is interesting. His descriptions of Shanghai, with its maze of narrow streets leading to still narrower alleys, reminds him of some of his own night-walks around London.

Peking, with its Forbidden City and beautiful temples, also has resonances. The division into the Tartar City to the North and the Chinese City to the south, divided by a fourteen-mile long wall, makes Daubney think of the river Thames, the liquid 'wall' cutting off south from north. He has never ventured south of the river, regarding it as a place of filth, stinking factories and human horror.

Despite his reservations, he listens entranced to the colonel's depictions of the dealers and native merchants in curios, who'd call daily at the legation and his mouth waters as he pictures the porcelain, jasper, jade, sculptures, lacquer work, silks and textiles they'd spread on the floor for Westerners to buy.

He tunes out Pittkethly's various asides on the superiority and sophistication of the white men compared with the strange and exotic Eastern people with their weird objects, backwards cultures, vile food and even viler customs. He tunes back in when Pittkethly mentions the netsuke and tsuba he acquired on his trip to Nagasaki.

"I shall be offering many of the artefacts to the British Museum, for what I hope will eventually become the Liversedge Pittkethly Collection, an exhibition showing the development from savagery towards civilisation," he announces proudly. "The rest will be offered for sale at Mortlake & Devine's emporium in Sloane Street."

Now he has Daubney's full attention, and as the colonel sits down to hearty applause, Daubney rises and makes his way hastily out of the room, down the stairs and, after collecting his hat, coat and stick, out into the cold and foggy London street.

Tomorrow, he thinks to himself, he will get a cab to Mortlake and Devine and view the netsuke. Perhaps there might be a small ivory cat amongst the treasures there? His heart lurches in his thin chest at the thought, and the thought itself gives wings to his feet.

Gerald Daubney hurries through streets thronged with evening revellers gathering like damp moths outside the brightly lit bars and places of cheap entertainment. Returning to the silent sanctuary of his house, he betakes himself straight to bed, eschewing the cold supper that has been left for him.

But once again, sleep will elude him. Lying awake, Daubney circles the shrinking perimeter of his mind like a caged animal. Night. Darkness. Stars. Shadows. He listens as the minutes slowly creep by. A horse and cart clatter past on a late delivery. Two cats reach a stalemate in their game of feline chess. Occasionally, something clicks open in his mind, a bright tumble of thoughts spilling out.

****

Detective Inspector Stride does most of his thinking while walking to and from his place of work. This habit is a throwback to his days as a beat constable, patrolling the streets of the city. In those days, he got through a lot of boots and a lot of thinking at the same time.

Now, he rarely has the opportunity to lay out an investigation in his head and walk round it, metaphorically studying it from every angle. This is the best way to break the habit of seeing only a single solution. Crime is complex ~ as complex as those who commit it, and it is all too easy to assume the most obvious pathway is the correct one. Which it frequently isn't.

Currently, Stride is trying to track a path through the impenetrable jungle that separates the discovery of the manservant Flashley's body from the arrest of his murderer. The journey is further complicated in that there is a map leading to the murderer, but important chunks of it seem to be missing. He has a strong sense that he is on the edge of understanding the case, but that there are a couple of vital details still hidden. What he desperately needs is more evidence. And some witnesses. But how to find them?

Stride slows. One of the advantages he has, not shared by his younger colleagues, is that he was born and grew up in this city. More specifically, his first posting was to an area of it that he rarely re-visits nowadays. But that does not mean he can't drop by? For old time's sake.

He wheels and changes direction, walking briskly away from Scotland Yard. The mountain of paperwork that waits his attention will have to do just that. Every step Stride takes gladdens his heart. His feet are taking him back to the past, when he was a simple beat constable and knew every rut in the road and crack in a cobble.

That was real policing. Standing in the shadows, while rain sluiced down from some gutter overhead, waiting for the sound of running footsteps that heralded the arrival of some miscreant. Or snatching a quick smoke in a doorway, with only a bright crescent moon and a patchwork of jewelled stars for company.

Stride lets his feet do the walking once more, and eventually they take him down to the river, and deposit him at the entrance to Crutched Friars Court. All human life is here, just as it was then: coalmen, dressmakers, bakers, butchers, housepainters, labourers, builders, street-sellers, coffee vendors, Jews, Hindoo tract-sellers, and quite a bit that is inhuman too. Small undernourished children loiter in the arched alleyways and stray dogs fight over bones, and territory.

Here, in the little labyrinths of tenements, crowded, claustrophobic and huddled up together to the exclusion of light, newly appointed Police Constable Stride first patrolled. Here, in the narrow, dark, irregular alleyways, and streets of small shops and taverns his career began. Everything he knows now was learned in this small area of the city.

And here he is, somewhat older, walking along the same narrow pavements once again, seeing the same dirty streets and old-fashioned shop-fronts with their small panes of glass and wooden lean-tos that he remembers from those far distant days. Eventually, Stride reaches a small street of two-storey brick tenements, joined together by strings of washing.

On the ground floor of Number 6, lives the individual he has come to consult: Mr. Percy Wozenheim, known to all as Pozzy Wozzy. In the past, when he was younger, Pozzy Wozzy was the one who had his fingers in most pies. Or if he didn't, he knew who owned the fingers that were. Stride first met him when he was investigating the disappearance of a local man, and Pozzy's help proved invaluable.

The price of a good informer is above rubies. Now, Stride bangs on the door and waits. After several minutes, he hears slow shuffling footsteps accompanied by a rasping cough, and then a wheezy voice demands:

"Oo's there?"

"Detective Inspector Leo Stride."

The footsteps stop. There is another pause. Then the door is laboriously opened a crack, and Stride finds himself being regarded thoughtfully by two watery pale eyes under a pair of ferocious white eyebrows that swoop across the occupant's face like predatory eagles. The man breaks into a broad grin. Stride shudders. Looking at his teeth is like looking at old gravestones.

"It is you. Give the door a kick would yer; it's got the damp."

Stride takes a step back, then kicks open the door. He steps over the threshold, his nostrils instantly invaded by the pungent mix of overcooked cabbage, drains, strong tobacco and unwashed body. The perfume of poverty. He had forgotten that smell.

"Long time, no see, as the one-legged sailor said to his pet parrot," the old man says, then bends double under a spasm of coughing that sounds hardly human. When it has passed, he leads the way into a back room, where he collapses into a saggy armchair, still wheezing.

"You should look after yourself better. Get out and breathe some fresh air, Pozzy," Stride says, taking the armchair opposite.

A small fire splutters helplessly in the grate. He picks up the poker and stirs it. The room serves as bedroom, sitting room and kitchen. The only light comes from a candle on the mantelpiece. Outside, the sounds of two women arguing filter through the grubby window.

"Can't be doing with fresh air," the old man says, fishing a pipe out of his cardigan pocket and bending towards the flame to light a paper spill. His white hair is long and strays over his bent shoulders. His hands are swollen, the knuckles purple and twisted. But his eyes are still bright, and regard Stride with shrewd amusement as he sucks at the pipe to get it going. "Anyway, why do I need fresh air at my age? What use is a long life to me? Sooner I'm gone, the better."

The universal complaint of the elderly. Stride rolls his eyes.

"So, what do you want?" the old man says. "Don't tell me you came all this way just to ask after my health?

Coz if you did, I can tell you: it ain't any better than what it was last time you came, however long ago that was."

Stride reaches inside his coat and slowly draws out a long-necked brown bottle. The old man regards it with interest.

"Got any cups, Pozzy?"

"In the cupboard by the winder."

Stride helps himself to a couple of chipped cups, their stained brown interiors evidence of much strong tea drinking and precious little washing up afterwards. He runs a handkerchief round the insides, then pours two generous measures from the bottle. He hands one of the cups to the old man, who drinks it off noisily.

"Ah, that's the real stuff. Things are never as bad as they seem so long as there's a drink somewhere about the place," he declares wheezily.

Stride glances round the room. "What happened to all the books, Pozzy?"

"Sold 'em. Burned 'em to keep warm. Can't read 'em anymore, coz me eyes are too weak."

"That's a shame. You were a great reader, as I recall."

"I was a great many things, Stride. And now I'm awaiting the Great Reaper hisself. And something tells me he ain't going to be as long in coming around to see me as you. You caught me just in time, eh?" His rusty laughter descends into another cough.

Stride waits until the fit of coughing has passed. Then he refills the old man's mug. "I am sorry, Pozzy. It's the job. Paperwork, filing, reading reports. That's modern policing for you. I rarely get out of my office nowadays."

"But yet here you are."

Stride acknowledges the implied criticism.

"But here I am, as you rightly remark. Because I want your expert advice. I need to find out everything I can about two local men called Munro and Herbert Black.

They are brothers. Used to live down this way. Names ring any bells?"

"Ding-dong. Why?"

"The older brother owns some gambling clubs. The younger buys and sells stuff. Some of it young and female. And they collect on other people's debts. The older brother is a possible suspect in a robbery and a murder. He's put the frighteners on everyone so nobody will talk to us, and we've not got enough evidence to pin anything on him. Yet."

"So you wants me to find you some pins?"

"Can you use your influence: ask around, turn over a few stones and see what crawls out?"

The old man chuckles. Then nearly falls off his chair as another fit of coughing seizes him.

"Just like the old days eh?" he says, wiping his streaming eyes on his sleeve. "Maybe I will. Maybe I won't. We'll see. Same rate of pay?"

"Of course, Pozzy. And you can keep the bottle," Stride gets to his feet.

"I was going to anyway. Be in touch, then Stride. See yerself out, would yer. I got some drinking to take care of."

Stride heads for the door. As he leaves, he hears the sound of glass chinking on china, and a throaty sigh of contentment.

****

While Detective Inspector Stride is threading his way back to civilization, another traveller is embarking upon a journey. Not upon so perilous a journey, perhaps, though for the traveller, it presents itself with various obstacles that must be overcome before the final destination is reached.

Gerald Daubney has set off bravely from his house, armed with courage, hope and a tightly rolled umbrella. His destination ~ Mortlake and Devine. His mode of travel ~ a boneshaking hackney cab pulled by an underfed grey horse and owned by one of those cabmen who like to talk.

Daubney huddles into his topcoat, feeling his shoulders tense. He has no interest whatsoever in guessing who the cabman had in his cab last week. Really. Yet it is just his luck to be forced to listen to a long list of individuals he has never heard of, but who are supposed to be 'famus'.

This desire to be noticed by people, to be hailed for some accomplishment, has always eluded him. He does not understand it. Yet almost every day he reads in the newspaper of some minor member of society, or a music hall artiste (whatever that is) who has done, or not done something. A 'Pre-Raphaelite' has caused a scandal by painting his friend's mistress semi-naked in a bath. Or was he painting a bath semi-naked? An aristocrat is suing a minor woman writer of novels. The world is going quite mad.

The horse plods slowly through the traffic. The cabman's voice is the wallpaper to Daubney's thoughts, which are building incrementally as the cab wheels trundle him closer to Sloane Street, finally dropping him outside the Emporium of Antique Furniture, Oriental China and Curiosities.

Daubney is not a betting man, nor a praying man, but he is a hoping man, and it is in this frame of mind that he enters through the heavy gilt and glass doors. He glances round the shop. Thomas Mortlake is busy dealing with a customer, while Jacob Devine, a thin saturnine man with high forehead and a nose made to look down upon the world, is carefully arranging a row of Chinese porcelain ginger jars on a glass shelf.

Daubney approaches Jacob Devine and stands at his elbow. He clears his throat. Devine turns, adopting a suitably sombre expression as he recognises who is standing in front of him.

"Ah, good day Mr. Daubney, sir," he says, giving a little bow, because however knowledgeable you are, dealers are men of trade but collectors are gentlemen, and if you are the former, it is profitable to recognise the latter. "May I, on behalf of Mortlake & Devine, commiserate with you in your recent tragedy. We were most upset to read the news. We await your instructions and will try to replace, as best we can, your fine collection of netsuke."

Daubney nods. "Yes. It is about the collection that I am here. I gather you have received some items recently from Colonel Pittkethly. I was hoping that amongst the items might be some netsuke. Is that the case? If so, I would like to see them."

Jacob Devine hesitates. "I have some of the pieces. But I do not think ..."

Daubney cuts him off abruptly, "Let me see them, please. At once, if you would be so kind. I will wait here."

The dealer shrugs, goes into the back room. Daubney suddenly feels light-headed with anticipation. Or lack of nourishment. There was a pot of coffee and some rolls set out in the parlour for him earlier, but he was too eager to get here to break his fast. He feels giddy, and holds on to the edge of the shelf, while the shop and its contents spin around him.

The dealer returns, carrying a familiar small wooden box, which he takes over to the counter. Daubney follows. Devine puts the box on the counter. Daubney picks it up, opens it, and unwraps the netsuke. It is an ugly, squat, fat frog. His face falls. His heart dives.

"But this is an inferior piece. The carving is crude. The wood is poor quality and there is no maker's mark on the bottom."

"I'm afraid this is the type of stuff we get brought in by amateurs," Devine says. "I think the local population just sell them anything, as they know people in the West will buy it. Japanese and Chinese objects are all the rage at the moment. The true collector, like yourself, would spurn such pieces. I did try to alert you, sir."

Daubney's spirits sink. He had such high hopes. Now they have been dashed. He passes a weary hand across his brow. Then, gathering all his inner strength, he turns and heads for the street. Reaching the shop door, he becomes aware that his name is being called. It is Mortlake, now customer-free.

"Mr. Daubney, sir! How good to see you! How are you faring?"

Daubney gives him a stare that goes on a little longer than socially acceptable.

"I am as you see me."

Mortlake raises an eyebrow fractionally. "I am sorry to hear it, Mr. Daubney, sir. Indeed so. And to read of your great tragedy. Your collection of netsuke was one of the finest in London. But maybe, all is not lost. Only the other week I was talking to a detective from Scotland Yard who was here in the emporium making inquiries on your behalf."

Daubney eyes him fixedly. "What did he want to know?"

Mortlake sticks his thumbs into his waistcoat pocket. "He inquired whether Mortlake & Devine supplied anybody else with netsuke. He mentioned a particular individual he was interested in. And he made reference to the Edo cat."

In Daubney's over-taxed brain, this information arrives like a bolt of lightning. He staggers; feels as if he is about to fall. The two shop owners rush to find a chair, a glass of water. Some customers standing nearby regard him with pitying glances.

When equilibrium, or nearest equivalent state, is restored, he asks, his voice still tremulous with supressed emotion, "An individual was mentioned, you say? Do you remember the name of the individual? And what was his connection to the Edo cat?"

Mortlake shakes his head. "I don't recall the name now. I apologise. I wrote it down, but then I threw the paper away. Maybe if you write to Scotland Yard yourself, and ask the detective, he might be able to tell you."

"Yes. Yes. You are right. I should do that. I should do it today. I WILL do it today." Daubney pushes himself out of the chair. His legs still feel unreliable.

"Let me call you a cab, Mr. Daubney, sir. You don't look too clever," Mortlake suggests.

Gerald Daubney makes his way to the front of the shop and leans wearily against the doorframe. As he waits for his cab to arrive, he watches a fashionable young couple exclaiming loudly over the poor-quality netsuke that he has rejected a short while earlier.

"Oh, dearest, look at the little fat frog!" the young woman cries, "Is he not delightful! Just think how good he will look on our drawing-room mantelpiece next to the porcelain vase. I am *wild* for these little Oriental statues. So strange and exotic! Do let us buy him! I shall call him Froggy, and pretend he is a Prince in disguise."

Daubney closes his eyes. Everything jars. Everything is out of kilter. The noise in his head fills the whole room. He allows himself to be handed into a hackney, gives the driver instructions in a faint voice, then sinks back, groaning, against the hard leather seat as the cab bears him steadily away in the direction of his house.

But Daubney's letter to Scotland Yard will not be written for some time. Misfortune, the lodestar of his life, has one more cruel trick to play upon him. On his return, he will go into the parlour, where the pot of cold coffee and the rolls still await, (no butter, as the white cat has helped herself to it earlier).

Overcome with exhaustion and despair, Gerald Daubney will accidentally trip on the edge of the Turkey carpet and fall, hitting the side of his head on a small Japanese lacquer table. He will be found, unconscious, some hours later, by the small parlour maid. The doctor who eventually arrives, will diagnose extreme nervous exhaustion, and prescribe bedrest and a light diet. It will be several days before he is well enough to access his writing desk.

****

Meanwhile, Lucy Landseer, writer, friend and would-be female detective, is making her way across London to spend time with her new acquaintance. She arrives at the asylum and sails in through the front door, to be greeted with welcoming smiles by the female attendants, such is her familiarity with the place.

Flush has a new ribbon bow around his glossy neck, so Lucy has to wait while the little animal is fussed over, fed biscuits, and played with. Finally, she is directed to the conservatory, where Lady Georgiana is eagerly awaiting her arrival. Lucy is greeted with a warm hug, and the promise that there is seed cake for tea, and she and dear Flush will certainly get a slice of it.

Lucy dimples her gratitude, as Lady Georgiana scoops Flush onto her lap and begins to stroke the spaniel's soft ears, remarking forlornly, "Oh how I miss my little pet dog."

Lucy commiserates with her, saying that her own life would be bereft without her furry companion. The two discuss the importance of pets, and horses, about which Lucy knows little, but her companion is happy to enlighten her, having owned a series of ponies in her country childhood, and riding horses as an adult.

"I often think about Overture, my Arab mare," Lady Georgiana sighs. "She was such a gentle mount. I rode her in the Park every afternoon at 4 o'clock. That was where my husband the Brute first saw me. I was so innocent in those days ~ I thought any man in a red coat was a hero. Oh, how little I knew of the world, Lucy and how I have suffered from my ignorance ever since."

"Indeed, I believe it is frequently so," Lucy says solemnly, mining her stock of usefully bland phrases. She pauses, to give her next words greater emphasis. "That is why so many of us turn to fiction, I think ~ to enlighten us, as well as to escape from the cares of the world that surrounds us."

Lady Georgiana clasps her hands together. "I cannot agree more! Where would we be without the great writers of our age: Mrs Ward, Miss Austen, Mr. Richardson ~ I am such an admirer of his novels. *Pamela* ~ is that not a wonderful book? I could not put it down!"

Lucy nods her agreement. "I should be quite lost without a pile of books by my bed. Is there a library here, where you can borrow books to read?"

"Oh yes. Dr Foster believes that we patients must keep busy and cheerful, so that we do not dwell upon our situation too much. But many of the books are so boringly worthy in tone. And some have missing pages."

"But of course, you always have your own copy of *Cecil Danvers*," Lucy smiles. "That must be a great comfort to you."

"It is indeed so, and I often turn the pages and remember a time when I felt happy and free and loved."

"Perhaps that time might come again?" Lucy suggests slyly.

Lady Georgiana shakes her head. "No, it cannot be. My only regret is that I did not pluck up enough courage and follow my beloved abroad. I was too scared of what my husband the Brute might do. I was such a coward and a fool. And this is what he did. Perhaps it is my punishment for not following my heart? What do you think, dearest Lucy?"

"I do not believe that at all," Lucy replies stoutly. "I think you have been badly treated ~ very badly treated indeed. But the power to remedy this lies in your own hands."

Lady Georgiana stares at her in amazement. "My hands? What are you saying?"

Seizing the moment, Lucy now reveals to her the accusations made against the author of *Cecil Danvers* by Lord Lackington, and the court case that his lawyers wish to bring against her. Lady Georgiana listens, the colour dying out of her face. When Lucy has finished speaking, she sits very still for a long time, her hands resting gently on Flush's soft back. Eventually, she speaks.

"What you have told me, dear Lucy, does not come as a surprise, though I am shocked ~ I will admit it. My husband must know that what he is saying is a lie ~ for he has seen me with the book in my hand often enough. He clearly thinks because of his position in society, and the fact that I am here, and my female friends would not be brave enough to stand up in a courtroom and defy him, that he will win this case against Mrs Hemmyng-Stratton.

"And if so, he will then demand a great deal of money in recompense for his 'reputation'. That is what it is all about, dear Lucy. It costs a lot of money to keep me here, and I expect he is running out of funds to pay Dr Foster for my care. He is also a gambler as well as a Brute, so he will have debts he cannot pay on top of the fees. But how can I, imprisoned as I am in this place, help the author of that wonderful book? Tell me at once, if you will. Be assured, I will do anything I can, however small."

Lucy pauses, while an attendant brings in a tea tray loaded with cups, saucers, and a plate of cake. What she has to say is for Lady Georgiana's ears alone. After Lady Georgiana and the other patients in the conservatory have helped themselves, and Flush has been given some water and the biggest slice of cake, she resumes the conversation.

"I have a plan, dear Georgiana. It is a bold plan, but I am confident it can work. And it is this: as I am now a familiar visitor, I shall ask whether I might take you out tomorrow in a hired carriage for a short ride. I am sure that this will be acceptable to the attendants. Only, you won't come back. I will drop you in town, so that you can purchase such items as you will require for travelling, for when we leave this place, we must not look as if you are going any further than around the local area for a little jaunt. No bags or cases. Not even an extra-warm coat.

"Once you are equipped, all you will need to do is arrive at the railway station in time to catch the train to Dover. I shall buy a ticket beforehand, which I will give you in the carriage. The only thing I ask, on behalf of my friend, is that you entrust to me your copy of her book, so that she can prove, once and for all, that she did not base the story upon your relationship and marriage. I have spoken to her, and she has given me sufficient funds to help you leave the country and begin a new life abroad."

Lucy has barely finished speaking when she finds her hands tumultuously clasped between Lady Georgiana's hands, and, raising her eyes to her friend's face, she sees tears streaking her cheeks.

"Oh, dear friend, dearest Lucy! It sounds like the plot of a wonderful novel! Too good to be true!"

"But it is not a novel ~ and I assure you, if you follow my instructions to the letter, and do not mention what we have talked about to a single soul, and remain calm, I believe in a very short time, you could be free of this place and this country, once and forever."

Lady Georgiana stares at her. "Do you really believe it?"

"I do indeed."

There is a pink spot of colour in each of Lady Georgiana's pale cheeks. "Dear Lucy! How lucky for me was that day when you tripped over and had to rest here on a bench. What a fortuitous accident! For you have provided me with an escape route from this place and my Brute of a husband. Of course you shall have my copy of *Cecil Danvers*, if it will help that wonderful writer.

"But tell me, Lucy, you have met the lady ~ what is she like? I picture her as tall and fashionably slender, with a mass of dark curls, large grey eyes and a cunning way of observing the world behind her sweet, open smile."

Lucy agrees that this is *exactly* what the novelist is like, on the basis that Lady Georgiana has had enough of her dreams crushed, and it would be churlish on her part to reveal that the writer of *Cecil Danvers* (and other novels of aristocratic life and loves) is, in reality, a small, dumpy woman who could easily pass for a housekeeper in a domestic staff line-up.

"Now, let us finish our tea and cake, and then I will go and ask the attendants whether I can take you out for a short carriage drive on Thursday," she says. "On their agreement hinges the entire success or failure of the plan. Mrs Hemmyng-Stratton writes that the first day of the trial begins on that day, so we have not a moment to lose."

Lady Georgiana obediently buries her face in her teacup. Meanwhile Lucy retrieves Flush, who is gorging himself on cake at the expense of some of the other residents. She picks him up and takes him out to the lobby, where the attendants are also enjoying the afternoon's refreshment.

Lucy walks up to them, assuming a sad, anxious expression and is immediately questioned as to the origin of it. With a lot of sighing, she reluctantly confides how worried she is by the marked deterioration in Lady Lackington's demeanour. How lacklustre and weary she seems.

It is her opinion, Lucy tells them, that her friend is suffering from a lowering of the spirits, brought on by the prospect of the cold winter approaching. She is sorely in need of some diversion, and what could be more diverting, Lucy suggests slyly, than a carriage ride? Only for a short distance, of course, one would not want to over-excite the poor patient, would one? And naturally, she and dear Flush would accompany Lady Lackington, and return her to the asylum, hopefully a more cheerful individual for her little outing.

The attendants listen, confer amongst themselves, then say they will call Dr Foster and ask him. But Lucy has met the asylum owner, a cadaverous Scotsman who wears a black tail-coat, a high collar and an unctuous expression, on a previous visit, and knows he is no match for her persuasive charm.

Sure enough, after pulling at his moustache, and peering over his glasses, Dr Foster is 'minded to agree, uh-huh, uh-huh' with the charming young visitor that a brief outing would be to the benefit of Lady Georgiana, and no indeed, he does not need to consult her husband on the matter as he is the Medical Superintendent, and the lady has been transferred entirely to his care and therefore her progress is under his direction.

Lucy is almost dancing with glee as she makes her way back to her lodgings. Later, while lingering over her evening meal, and making notes of the meeting for future literary reference, she recalls the words of the Scottish bard, Robert Burns, about the best laid schemes of mice and men. But as she is neither a mouse nor a man, she reminds herself, *her* scheme will definitely not *gang agley*!

****

Detective Inspector Stride is having one of those 'take your problems to work' days. There are new tenants in the house next door, and their loud, persistent, nocturnal quarrelling is keeping him awake, even more so than the snoring of Mrs Stride usually does. For the past week, he has had to bed down in the back room, to be awakened at first light by some wretched bird chirping away at full volume just outside his window.

Stride is not a lover of nature. Or quarrelsome people. And a combination of the two means that his coffee uptake has increased, which is rendering him somewhat peppery of disposition. Thus, he is not in a particularly reasonable frame of mind as he enters Scotland Yard, carrying a mug of hot coffee, to find a small group of elderly citizens clustered in front of the main desk. Their general demeanour is sombre. One old woman is openly sobbing and being comforted by a fellow group member. The desk sergeant catches Stride's eye over the top of their heads.

"Been a bit of an incident, sir. Sorry to say."

"Well, is there nobody here to deal with it then?" Stride snaps. "We employ enough detectives. Where are they all?"

The desk constable consults his list. "It appears everybody is out, sir. Or not in, sir, if you know what I mean. Except for you."

The group, sensing that someone in authority has finally arrived, promptly deserts the desk and regroups in front of him. Stride takes a step back. The group takes a step forward. Stride waits for enlightenment to arrive. The group exchanges nods and glances, then forms up behind an elderly woman ~ the one who is still crying.

"Yes, my good woman," Stride says briskly, trying to keep the impatient tone out of his voice. "How may I assist you?"

The woman sniffs, mops her eyes, fumbles with her handkerchief, clears her throat, fiddles with her bonnet strings, then finally blurts out, "Perce has gone missing."

Oh really! Stride thinks, irritably, instantly presuming that the name refers to a pet dog. He assumes his sternest expression.

"Madam, this is a police station, not a search facility for lost animals."

The woman fixes him with a watery red-rimmed stare. "I know what this place is, right enough. That's why I'm here. Perce told me couple of nights ago he had some *detectoring* job on the go. And now he ain't answering his door, and I ain't seen hide nor hair of him. So what am I supposed to do? Coz he's an old man and his cough is bad at the moment."

Stride feels the day sliding sideways a little further. He gets out his notebook and pencil. "What is the name of the individual who has gone missing, Mrs ...?" he says, mentally crossing his fingers that it isn't who he suspects it might be.

"It's Mr. Percy Wozenheim ~ Pozzy, he's called locally. He rents a room off of Crutched Friars Court. I'm Miss Dorothy Wozenheim, his sister, only everyone calls me Dot. My brother's 68 and he didn't ought to be out in the evenings, with his chest."

Detective Inspector Stride continues to take details from Pozzy's sister, but behind the methodical questioning, his mind is racing ahead of itself. He coaxed the old man out of retirement, so if anything untoward has happened, it will be his fault. And he will have to live with the guilt of that, even though nobody else would know. Which makes it worse, somehow.

After getting as much information as he can, Stride finally makes it to his office. He now has a mug of cold coffee and a bad conscience, neither conducive to a productive morning. Thus, after staring out of his office window for some time, and moving a few files around his desk in a desultory fashion, he pushes back his chair, throws on his topcoat and informs the desk constable that he is going out for some fresh air.

Things have always become clearer in Stride's mind when he is on his feet as opposed to behind his desk. He stands on the front steps of Scotland Yard for a second or two, then sets off at a brisk pace. Once again, he has a lot of thinking, and a lot of walking to do.

****

Stride does not know it, but at some point in his walk, his path will cross with that of Mrs Riva Hemmyng-Stratton, who is making her way, also on foot, to the High Court, where the trial of Lackington v Hemmyng-Stratton is about to begin.

A brief hope that the newspaper evidence garnered by her friend Miss Landseer would stave off the awful day, has failed to produce the desired result. So now, here she is, arriving at the place of judgement. Luckily for her, a mysterious donor has come forward and supplied her with a barrister to fight her case. Mrs Hemmyng-Stratton met with him, briefly, at his book-lined chambers in Bedford Row. He had very large sandy whiskers and frightened the life out of her. She only hopes he will do the same to Strutt & Preening.

But behold! What is this? Why are crowds of people gathered up ahead? The Author falters, her footsteps slowing. Is a riot taking place outside the courtroom? She halts. Suddenly, a voice from the crowd calls, "There she is! That's her! The lady with the veil ~ just like the newspapers described her!" And next minute, to her astonishment, she is surrounded on all sides by cheering men and women, each holding up a copy of *Cecil Danvers*. In various editions.

Pens and pencils are put into her hand. Copies of the book are thrust under her nose, with the instructions to: '*sign it: To Barbara ... To Betsy, with love ... To Sackville, Caroline and little Dubbly*'.

Mrs Hemmyng-Stratton is overwhelmed! Such an effusive welcome from complete strangers is too much. She signs, and signs and expresses her gratitude, and gradually works her way to the steps of the court, where an usher in a dark suit welcomes her and conducts her to the courtroom.

The Author has never set foot inside a court of law before. She takes her place on the wooden bench behind her lawyer, who greets her arrival with a slight nod of acknowledgement. The floor beneath her feet is made up of polished oak tiles, and the witness box looks far too small to accommodate anybody over the age of eleven. Looking around, she sees no sign of Charles Colbourne, nor anyone who could be Lord Lackington, though at a separate table, she spies two bewigged and black-gowned men with piles of papers and expressions hard enough to ice-skate on.

She glances up at the gallery, which is full of eager spectators, mainly, she notes, women in fashionable bonnets, holding copies of her novel. There is a separate area to one side, where a bunch of men in loud waistcoats and even louder suits are writing busily ~ journalists, she guesses. To her horror, she sees that someone is actually sketching her. The Author reaches up, pulls down her veil, and tries to look inconspicuous.

Scarcely has she adjusted her bonnet, when the command to 'All rise' is given, and the judge enters the court. There is a pause while he settles himself, and his various pens and papers are set in front of him by the court clerk. Then Mrs Hemmyng-Stratton takes a deep breath and clasps her hands tightly together in her lap, as one of the black-gowned men, Preening (or is it Strutt?) gets to his feet and begins to lay out Lord Lackington's complaint.

As she listens to his thin monotonous voice droning on and on, using words like 'shameless' and 'polluter of the sacred marriage bond', she finds herself getting more and more irate. This bears no resemblance to the truth whatsoever. It is a tissue of make-believe, and she, more than anyone, can recognise make-believe when she hears it. She utters an exclamation ~ her barrister lifts his right hand in silent admonition.

Mrs Hemmyng-Stratton bows her head and issues a tacit prayer to the irrepressible Miss Landseer. In her youthful hands, she holds the Author's Fate. May those hands be steady and true, because on the basis of what she is now hearing, her chances of returning to rescue and reunite her Heroine and Hero are receding as fast as snow in high summer.

****

162

Meanwhile, far from the official realms of law and order, Maria Barklem sits at her scrubbed kitchen table, her elbows resting upon its surface. How often has she sat here as a girl, watching her mother preparing an evening bowl of bread and milk, with a sprinkle of sugar on top as a treat?

How often has she skipped back from running an errand, or playing outside, her heart going ahead of her to the warm welcoming kitchen and the comforting arms of her dear Mama, who was always on her side, always ready to hear her day's adventures, soothe a wounded feeling with just the right words?

Maria has spent much of her life in this kitchen. She rarely went into the rest of the house, her father's study being particularly out of bounds, for it was there he toiled over his sermons, or met with the various committees and church Elders.

Maria knows that the church authorities are only allowing her and her mother to stay here on the peppercorn rent they pay, out of a sense of guilt. If they hadn't worked her father so hard, if they had allowed him time off, if they had not demanded he took *all* the services, and visited the sick of the parish, when he himself was clearly unwell, then maybe he'd still be alive now.

Of course, that wasn't what the Elders said, when they came to offer their condolences and arrange for the burial to take place. What they *actually* said was that her mother was welcome to avail herself of the property, until such time as it was 'appropriate for her to seek alternative accommodation elsewhere'.

But before long, her mother, too, was failing in health, and until she either recovered, or followed her husband, it was clear that this small cottage would remain their home for the foreseeable future. And now, her mother is dying. Soon, she will pass from this world to that country from whose bourn no traveller ever returns. She is indeed about to seek alternative accommodation elsewhere.

Maria is not sure she'd call it Heaven, but she cannot lose the sense that there must be something more than the miserable eking out of existence that she witnesses every day. She stirs her tea and dips a crust of dry bread in to soften it. She has sat all night by the invalid's bedside, watching as life and death played cards for her mother's soul. It is now abundantly clear who the winner is.

Out in the small garden, a thrush is singing an aubade. She listens to his joyous, carefree notes. Then, with a heavy heart, she finishes her tea and climbs the stairs. Her mother is propped up on two pillows, her face candle-white, the cheekbones so prominent they seem as if they might push through the skin. Her eyes are sunken and heavy-lidded.

Maria sits beside her and takes the paper-skinned hands with their traceries of blue veins, in her own. In a movement that seems to take forever, her mother turns her head and fixes her eyes upon her face.

"Do you hear our thrush?" she whispers, each word an effort.

Maria nods.

"Ah, it is good to die while listening to such heavenly music," her mother says, a ghost of a smile shadowing her pale lips. She closes her eyes. As Maria watches, she takes a long breath in. Lets it out. And is gone.

For a moment, the world seems to pause, as if awaiting its next instructions. Maria sits, motionless with shock. Then the thrush sings once more, his notes spiralling upwards into the grey sky, as if serenading her mother's soul on its final journey.

Once more, Stride walks, letting his feet take him where they will. They decide to take him to Russell Square, where he pauses for a while at the north end, silently contemplating the long line of terraced townhouses, with their chess-board front tiles and green wrought-iron railings and balconies.

His attention lingers upon Number 55, currently shuttered, with its Venetian blinds drawn down at every window, where lives the man who is currently at the forefront of his mind. Stride stares at the house, wishing he had the means to see what is going on behind the white-painted walls.

Nothing moves. Rather like the investigation. Stride knows that all investigations stall at some point. Detective work is always a long game, unless members of the press get involved. Then it is still a long game, only you have to pretend that it isn't.

A maid comes out of Number 55 carrying a shopping basket. Stride watches her walk down the street. She is of no particular interest to him. Learning what to ignore, and whom, is part of the job. He puts his trust in his experience, which tells him that something nearly always turns up in the end.

Eventually, when he has stood watching the house for some time, his feet tell him it is time for lunch. He has a quick word with one of the constables in a Watch Box, who confirms that he has not seen anyone matching the descriptions of Munro and Herbert Black arriving or departing from Number 55, so far.

Stride turns and heads for Sally's, reminding himself that he has not been wasting his time. A lot of police work consists of standing around, having lunch, drinking coffee and staring out of the window. All of which is infinitely preferable to dealing with paperwork, which is, sadly, what awaits him after his lunch.

****

Lucy Landseer, on the other hand, has no time for luncheon. From the moment her eyes opened upon the day, she has been in a whirl of busyness. You seek her here, you seek her there ~ one minute she is at Charing Cross Station, purchasing a ticket for the Dover train, and the boat to Calais. Next minute, she is visiting a cab rank, and inspecting the animals and vehicles in order to find the fastest.

And now, wearing a merry bonnet, with a basket of provisions, and accompanied by Flush, who is taking rather too much interest in the contents of the basket, she is being carried to Cedar House Asylum.

The day is cloudy, with rain hovering in the background. Lucy has taken the precaution of bringing an umbrella and a travelling rug, which she has wrapped around herself, as the horse clip-clops through the traffic.

The cab finally pulls up at the gate of Cedar House Asylum. Lucy and Flush alight and make their way up the gravel path to the foyer, where they are greeted by one of the attendants, who invites her to sit and wait while they fetch Lady Georgiana from her room.

Lucy sits. Flush guards. She tries not to think about the implications of what she's undertaking. Instead, she runs a mental checklist of everything that is about to happen and the order in which it needs to happen for it to succeed. Meanwhile, her partner in crime yawns and scratches himself behind his left ear.

At last, the double doors open, and Lady Georgiana walks through. She is draped in a warm shawl and carries a small reticule. Her expression is so terribly innocent that, for a split second, Lucy fears they will be rumbled by the staff. Luckily, Flush chooses this moment to be sick on the carpet.

As the attendants rush to find mops, buckets and a cake of soap, Lucy steers Lady Georgiana quietly out of the front door, down the front steps, along the gravel drive, and installs her in the waiting hansom.

"*Good* dog," she murmurs, hauling the spaniel on board.

The driver cracks his whip and the hansom sets off at a trot. Lucy passes Lady Georgiana the travelling rug and lifts the lid of the basket of provisions. They are on their way! Lady Georgiana turns her shining eyes to her rescuer's face.

"I cannot begin to thank you for this, dear, dear Lucy," she says, and opening her reticule, she draws out her copy of *Cecil Danvers,* and hands it across the carriage.

Lucy glances inside the book. There, exactly as described, is the inscription.

"Venetia was one of my closest friends. Oh, how I miss her and all the happy times we spent together."

"There will be plenty of other happy times," Lucy reassures her. Then she taps on the hansom's roof and gives the driver new instructions.

"I must deliver this book to the courtroom at once," she says. "That is where I shall leave you. The driver has instructions to take you to Regent's Street. Now let us eat something to fortify us for the next part of the adventure. I see Flush is eyeing the ham sandwiches already!"

Meanwhile, back at the High Court, Preening (or is it Strutt?) has finished laying out the case against Mrs Hemmyng-Stratton. The lunch recess is over; not that the Author has partaken of any food; she is much too distressed by the adjectives used to describe her. The court has risen for the judge's re-entry, and now it is the turn of her own barrister to fight her corner. He shuffles his papers, gets to his feet, sways a couple of times, shoots a venomous glance at Strutt & Preening, and launches into a spirited defence of his client, who sits behind him, twitching.

Halfway through his speech, a hansom draws up outside the court building and a slender young woman alights. She lifts down a spaniel, who immediately heads for the nearest lamp-post. The young woman leans in to say something to the remaining occupant of the cab. Then she waves farewell, hauls on the dog's lead, and hurries into the building. The cab drives away.

Lucy Landseer goes up to the first usher she sees and asks where the Lackington case is being heard. She is directed to court three. On arrival at the door, the usher takes one look at Flush, and tells her sternly she cannot enter.

Lucy frowns. Then, giving the man her most persuasive smile, she says,

"In that case, sir, will you please inform me how I can give this book to Mrs Hemmyng-Stratton, the lady who is the subject of the case. I cannot stress how important it is that she receives it *at once*. I believe her barrister would be *very angry* if he knew this vital piece of evidence was being withheld."

The usher bites his lower lip. Lucy regards him steadily. In the end, he gives in.

"Well, if it is as important as you say, I could always slip it into the courtroom and pass it to the lady."

"Oh, would you? Thank you. Thank you so much," Lucy says, handing him the book, which is now wrapped in a note. The usher takes it, opens the wooden double doors, and returns in a couple of minutes.

"She has it," he says.

Lucy nods her thanks. Then, tugging on Flush's lead, she heads back to the main entrance. Time to take the dog for a brief walk before the court rises for the day.

Inside the packed courtroom, the barrister is winding up the case for the defence. He sits down. Mrs Hemmyng-Stratton rises to her feet, leans forward and gently edges the book onto the desk in front of him. The barrister picks it up, reads the letter, opens the book and reads the inscription. The judge continues to make notes.

Barely breathing, the Author sits and waits.

Next minute, the barrister is on his feet.

"M'lud, I have just been in receipt of an important piece of evidence. With your permission, may I share it with the court?"

The judge sets down his pen.

"If you believe it is relevant, you may."

"Not only is it relevant, it casts a whole new light upon the allegations of libel and infamy made against my client by Lord Lackington. On the balance of probability, I now declare the allegations to be utterly false from first to last!"

He pauses for dramatic effect. There are gasps from the gallery.

"M'lud, members of the court, I have in my hand a copy of *Cecil Danvers* ~ this is the actual copy of the book owned by Lady Georgiana Lackington. I open it at the flyleaf, as you see, and I read:

To dearest Georgie, on the occasion of her 30th birthday. A copy of our favourite novel. Your loving friend, Venetia."

He unfolds the accompanying letter.

"I gather that the signature is that of the Honourable Mrs Venetia Ackwynd of Knightsbridge Mansions, London. May I remind the court that it was in the months *after* Lady Lackington's 30th birthday that the affair with the portrait artist, known as Mr. X, began, *according to the written testimony of her husband, Lord Lackington.*

"Yet, according to the plaintiff, the writer, my client, used events from the affair and the marriage in her work. This inscription clearly indicates that Lady Georgiana Lackington had read the novel BEFORE the unfortunate events that broke up the marriage. I quote: *'A copy of our favourite novel'.*"

"M'lud, I intend to send an urgent telegram to the husband of the Honourable Mrs Ackwynd, requesting that he allow her to appear in this court to answer my questions. I ask, therefore, for an adjournment until tomorrow morning."

There is a pause. Then uproar breaks out in the spectators' gallery. Copies of the book are waved aloft in gloved hands to cries of 'Shame!' 'She is innocent!' and 'Case dismissed!' The judge bangs on the table as he struggles to make himself heard. Strutt & Preening throw their court papers around as they try to make their objections over the hullabaloo.

And in the midst of it all, Mrs Riva Hemmyng-Stratton quietly rises to her feet, lowers her veil and walks out of the court. Crossing the vestibule, she hears her name being called. At first, she does not acknowledge the appellant, too overcome by the events of the previous few hours. And the past five minutes. Then she realises that the person calling her name is Lucy Landseer. Accompanied by a dog. She hurries over. Lucy's face is wreathed in smiles.

"Have I not done well, fellow scribe? A book delivered, an unhappy and wronged woman released from captivity, and best of all, a fellow author vindicated. I think I might definitely take this up as a profession; I seem to have a knack for it."

Mrs Hemmyng-Stratton allows a faint smile to embroider itself along her lips.

"I am extremely grateful to you, Miss Landseer. I believe that you have indeed, as they say, saved the day."

Lucy beams at her. "It was my pleasure and delight. Anything for another writer. I shall now leave you to your adoring readers," she says, indicating the clatter of footsteps descending the gallery stairs. "I await the final outcome ~ although I believe it is a foregone conclusion. Come Flush, we must return you to your owner, with our deep gratitude. You have played your part to perfection."

And with another enchanting smile, she is gone.

Later, alone in her small sitting room, Lucy Landseer will pick up a piece of paper from the pile by her desk, and, after chewing the top of her pen for a while, will write *The Case of the Lunatic Lady* at the top. It will be the first story in her exciting and popular series of books depicting the adventures of dashing female detective Miss Belle Batchelor and her faithful canine sidekick, Harris.

****

It is a dark and stormy night ~ which could well be the opening of one of the Author's novels, but in this case, is an accurate meteorological observation. The rain gushes in gutters, pours from downpipes and rushes from rooftiles. It is a filthy night to be out, and most decent citizens are venturing no further than their firesides.

Here, in St John's Wood, in the peace of a loose box at Bob Miller's Livery Stables, the storm is mere scenery. For Brixston, a day spent mucking out horses, wheeling barrows piled with muck, and cleaning tack, means that sleep comes in an instant. The sky might throw hailstones or diamonds upon the earth, but curled up in the straw, one arm flung over the back of Molly, he sleeps peacefully on.

Only Molly, the black and white sheepdog is still awake, her ears pricked for any sound other than the gentle breathing of the boy, and the snuffling of her pups as they root around for food. So it is Molly who hears the gate opening; Molly who hears the heavy footsteps crossing the yard; Molly who gets to her feet, her hackles rising at the unfamiliar tread of someone she does not know, but recognises with every fibre of her being as an enemy.

The footsteps pause outside each loose box. Molly sees a dark lantern being swung into the interiors, hears the snorting and pawing of the horses as they react to the sudden intrusion into their rest. The sheep dog instinctively returns to her pups and the boy, who has now taken on the role of friend and master, and begins to paw at the straw in an attempt to cover those she loves and knows she must protect, even at the risk of her own life, from whatever evil is coming their way.

The footsteps reach the end box. The bolt is pulled back. Molly waits, growling softly at the back of her throat, her eyes fixed on the triangle of light. The intruder steps into the loose box. He has a knife in one hand. Molly opens her jaws in a roar of rage and launches herself straight at him, like a small black and white thunderbolt from hell.

The rain continues to fall, silently, persistently, turning the stable yard into a sea of noxious mud. When William Smith arrives early in the morning, the first thing he notices is the half-open gate. He hurries into the yard, sure that he definitely locked the gate, and that blame for anything he discovers, especially any stolen or injured horse, will be his fault.

The second thing he sees is a body, lying in a pool of liquid. The colour and viscosity of the liquid suggests that it is not horse-generated. William feels a thickening in his throat and a singing in his ears. He can hear his heart hammering furiously under his coat. Bending down, he grasps the body by a soaking wet shoulder and flips it over.

****

Detective Sergeant Jack Cully has received a strange and slightly disturbing communication from Gerald Daubney, in which the collector accuses Scotland Yard of withholding important information pertaining to the theft of his collection of priceless Japanese netsuke and Cully himself of being an accessory to the decision. There are also vague threats of an undefined but unpleasant nature involving members of the legal profession.

The letter is written in a scrawling hand, various words crossed out, and, from the blots and deep indentation marks on the paper, it is clear that the writer was enduring some strong emotions while penning it.

Cully frowns. He cannot see where Mr. Daubney has got the idea from. He knows he was extremely discreet last time they met. And now this? Cully skim-reads the letter once more. The most worrying part comes at the end, when the collector suggests he might be forced to take matters into his own hands, and offer a reward for information leading to the return of his precious items, as the detective police seem both unable and unwilling to track down the thief.

This threat is never taken idly. Too many investigations have foundered on some victim's decision to bypass the legitimate channels and go rogue instead. The thought of weeks of wasting precious time interviewing the sort of people who always came in to 'confess' to every crime committed, or claim part of the reward for information that turns out to be useless, resulting in public criticism from the press, and wild goose chases across the city, is not to be contemplated.

After thinking about his next move for a while, Cully decides to go and consult Lachlan Greig. He finds his colleague in the day room, also perusing a letter, which Greig stuffs hastily into his jacket pocket as soon as he sees him.

"Don't tell me Mr. Daubney has been writing to you as well!" Cully says, rolling his eyes. "The man is obsessed. He cares more about those little wooden carvings than about the death of his manservant."

Greig shakes his head. "No, he has not written to me," he says.

Cully regards him curiously. There is something reticent behind his colleague's tone of voice, and his usually frank gaze is clouded. This, coupled with the speedy way he put up the letter raises immediate warning signals. He wonders whether there might be something amiss. A medical problem, perhaps? Cully is on the cusp of framing some innocuous remark that might lead to a shared confidence, when the door is flung open. One of the day constables stands upon the threshold, panting and breathless.

"Detective inspector, sir, please ~ you have to come with me at once," he says. "There's a dead body at a livery stable in St John's Wood, and you've been sent for."

Greig leaps to his feet, "Come with me, Jack," he cries, reaching for his coat and hat, "And let's pray this isn't the young lad I left in Will's charge ~ because if any harm has come to him through my actions, it is my fault entirely, and I will never forgive myself."

The two detectives hail a cab and arrive shortly at the gate of Bob Miller's Livery Stables, where they find a crowd of eager local bystanders, each with their own lugubrious contribution to make to the situation.

"I allus knew there'd be trouble eventually," a grizzled old man says, shaking his grey locks, as they push through. "Stands to reason ~ where you got h'airystocratic horses, it's bound to 'appen sooner or later."

"Oi, Mr. P'licemen ~ you ask about the screams," a woman at the back calls out, as they pass through the gate, now being guarded by a Marylebone constable with folded arms and a warning expression. "Horrible screams there was. And *rending* sounds. Like someone was being torn in pieces. Kept me awake all night."

Greig and Cully ignore the various strange and unhelpful suggestions being made, and enter the yard. Will Smith, his face the colour of a corpse candle, steps forward to greet them.

"Thanks for coming so prompt, gents. I didn't know who else to send for. I found him lying in the yard," he says, leading the way. "I remembered not to touch anything ~ only I did turn him over, just to make sure."

By the end of Will's speech, they have reached the centre of the yard, where the ring of grooms and stable lads, standing in a solemn circle, part to allow them access to the body, covered by a stable rug. Taking a deep breath, Greig lifts one end of the rug and stares down.

Into the face of a complete stranger. He meets Cully's eye and sees the same relief echoed in his expression.

"It's not the lad," Will says. "I was afraid it was too. In a dim light, it could've been anyone. I was dreading telling you he'd gone ~ especially after his escaping the fire."

"Where is Brixston?" Greig asks, looking round.

"Over here, Mr. Detective," says a voice from the back of the stable lads, and the boy advances, closely followed by the black and white sheepdog, who is limping and looking decidedly the worse for wear. Brixston squats down and curls his arm gently around her neck.

"My friend Molly saved me, Mr. Detective. When the man came to kill me, she tried to cover me and the pups up in the straw so he wouldn't find us. Then she fought off the man ~ went straight for his throat and wouldn't let go. She's a hero, this dog. A bloomin' hero."

Cully gestures towards the body. "I see the puncture wounds in the throat, but I don't think that was the only thing that caused his demise. Look here: he also suffered a blow to the back of his neck, which is one of the most vulnerable areas of the body. I don't know how that happened, though."

Greig sees a quick significant glance pass between Will and Brixston.

"As far as I could make it out," Will says, "The dog went for his throat, then the hand holding the knife, and as he tried to push her off, he must've stepped back and tripped over one of the stone mounting blocks, it being dark, like, and hit his head upon it. 'Course, I'm not a detective, but that's how I see it."

Greig decides not to pursue matters. He turns to the boy. "You said the man came to find you. How do you know that?"

"Coz I recognised him," Brixston said. "Remember I told you there was two men in the pub that night? Black and another one. This was t'other one. I saw him in the street a coupla days ago. Besides, he had a knife. So someone must've sent him to get rid of me. Coz of what I saw."

Will interjects, "We found a knife outside the stable door. It's still there. I told the lads not to touch it."

Greig turns his gaze to Will. "I thought I told you not to let the boy out of your sight," he says reproachfully.

Will Smith shuffles his feet guiltily, like a ten-year old caught with his fingers in the jam. "I can't watch him every minute of the day," he says. "Sometimes I'm away from the yard visiting a client. Besides, he ain't a prisoner; he's done nothing wrong. If he wants to go out for a walk and sitch, that's his decision."

"A decision that meant he was spotted, and nearly killed?" Greig says sternly. "No, it won't do, Will. It really won't."

"So where do we go from here?" Will asks.

"We need to find somewhere else to keep the boy. It is clear his hiding place has been revealed, so he is no longer safe."

"I could take him to my place," Will says. "Josephine will be back from her business trip next week, and I'm sure that's what she'd want to happen."

"It might be for the best," Greig says.

All the while Brixston has been looking from one man to the other, following the conversation keenly. Now he speaks. "I ain't going anywhere, gents. Sorry an' all that. This is my home now, and Molly and the pups are my fambly. She put her life on the line for me, and I ain't going to leave her. Not now, not ever. You'll haveter carry me out of here feet first, and that's my last word."

He turns, and stomps across the yard to the open stable door at the far end. The sheepdog limps after him, her ears pricked. The men watch their progress, then exchange wry smiles.

"I'll fit a new lock on the gate," Will says. "And we'll all try to keep a better eye on the boy from now on."

While the two men are talking, and Brixston is voicing his objections, Cully is kneeling beside the body. He lays his fingers carefully across the throat. Then behind an ear. He senses nothing. Then he places his palm flat on the man's chest. Very faintly, but quite definitely, he feels a flutter of movement. He looks up at the others.

"I think this man is still alive, though only just."

Will exclaims, "But he can't be! I'm sure he was dead when I checked him over."

Cully stands up. "You'd be amazed how many dead men turn out to be fit and well after someone has pronounced them dead. I've read of cases where a man was almost buried alive, but for a mourner at the funeral hearing knocking on the coffin roof.

"I think we'd better get this man off the damp floor and into a warm police cell as soon as possible. Robertson can take a look at him ~ it cannot be beyond his expertise to suggest what should be done to bring him back to enough consciousness for us to question him."

"Finally, the breakthrough we've been waiting for!" Greig exclaims. "I'll get the constable at the gate to send for a stretcher party at once."

He hurries away. Meanwhile Cully covers the man back over with the blanket, being careful to leave his face free this time. He decides to use the intervening time to examine the knife. He walks over to the stable door and studies it. Carefully. It is an unusual knife ~ in the sense that most fatal stabbings are committed with kitchen or domestic or pocket-knives of various sorts and sizes.

This knife looks neither culinary, nor domestic. He decides it is more like a dagger than a knife. It has a curved blade with a slightly serrated edge, and a shiny carved handle that glints goldenly up at him. It is covered in muck, but even so, he is pretty certain he has seen something similar in the recent past. Cully racks his brains, but the location stubbornly refuses to reveal itself. He returns to find Greig issuing final instructions to Will and the stable boys. The two detectives wait until the man has been carefully placed on a stretcher and carried out of the yard.

"What Will told us back there, about the mounting block and the fall wasn't the whole truth," Greig says, as they both set off in the direction of Scotland Yard. "Apparently the boy picked up a shovel and lamped the man on the back of his head when he saw him punching and kicking the sheepdog."

Cully nods silently. "Ah. Self-defence?"

"I'd be prepared to say so, if it ever came to court, which it won't. After all, the original intention was to kill him. Therefore, he was quite justified in taking whatever means he could to preserve his life."

"I agree. And we have a shrewd suspicion who sent this individual to silence him."

"We do. But once again, we have no direct proof," Greig says gloomily. "Our best hope is that this man regains consciousness. Let us alert Robertson and hope he can bring him back from whatever state he currently occupies. It will make a nice change for him! Usually he deals with the recently dead, not the barely alive."

****

Mrs Riva Hemmyng-Stratton has been kept awake by the storm raging outside her window. And the anger and indignation raging in her writer's breast. That some man should use her novel to try to make her pay for his own marital failings! That she should be made to forfeit her hard-earned income to fund his impecunious habits! That she should endure shame and suffering while he, because of his position in society, could impugn her reputation!

It is too much!

At three am, with sleep eluding her, and a branch of the tree outside her window beating a tattoo upon the glass, she had risen, lit a candle and placed it on her desk. Taking up her pen, she had poured out her soul onto a virgin sheet of paper, blotting the words with hot tears, then, in an ecstasy of rage, she had torn and crushed the paper again and again between her hands.

Now here she is, tempest-toss't, making her way once more into the court room, where her barrister greets her arrival with a slight shake of his head, which she is unable to interpret. She presumes it refers to the tardiness of her arrival.

Mrs Hemmyng-Stratton slides onto the hard, wooden bench seat. After the fracas and near riots of the day before, the judge has declared that members of the public may only attend the hearing in limited numbers, so the spectators' gallery is sparsely filled. The press has been told their presence is not welcome.

She glances across to where Strutt & Preening are sitting. They are in earnest discussion with each other, seeming oblivious to anything else happening in the court. Even when the usher announces: "All rise", they merely elevate themselves a couple of inches before resuming their seats. She assumes they are mentally sharpening the knife, ready to expunge her from the literary world for evermore.

The judge shuffles his papers, peers over his spectacles, and addresses her barrister.

"Mr. Fladgate, the floor is yours."

The barrister rises, bows.

"Thank you, M'lud. As you know, I have been awaiting an acknowledgement of my telegram from the husband of the Honourable Mrs Venetia Ackwynd. I have to inform you, and the court that no such acknowledgement has been received, and therefore I am, as of the present time, unable to call the lady to act as a witness in the defence of my client."

Mrs Hemmyng-Stratton hears someone utter a groan. To her horror, she realises it emanates from her own throat. The judge turns to Lord Lackington's lawyers.

"Before I rule on this case, do you have anything you wish to add on behalf of your client?"

The pause after his question seems, to the hapless Author, to go on for an eternity. Finally, Strutt (or is it Preening?) gets to his feet. He clears his throat.

"M'lud, my client wishes to withdraw his accusation."

Consternation in the court!

Slowly, the judge sets down his pen.

"Have I heard you correctly? Lord Lackington does not wish to pursue his claim for libel and defamation against the author Mrs Hemmyng-Stratton?"

"Correct, M'lud."

"I see. Then the matter is no longer the concern of this court. Case dismissed."

Cheers erupt from the small crowd in the gallery. Her barrister turns around and congratulates the Author, who gapes at him, unable to grasp what has just happened. Certain members of the press, who have managed to gain access to the courtroom by some mysterious process only known to the journalistic profession, now advance, notebooks in hand.

A short while later, the Author and her barrister reconvene in one of the small rooms off the main hallway.

"I congratulate you, Mrs Hemmyng-Stratton," he says, his voice booming round the walls. "An unexpected capitulation, but a capitulation *nevertheless.* You live to write another day. The introduction of the novel, albeit at the last minute, has frightened them off. You must be delighted with the outcome."

Mrs Hemmyng-Stratton purses her lips. "Oh, I am," she says. "And I thank you, and my unknown benefactor for your invaluable assistance."

"It was an honour, dear lady," the barrister purrs loudly. "Now, I suggest you celebrate your success ~ for you have won a great victory for the female writing profession. Nay, the writing profession in general. All that remains is the public restoration of your reputation, which I shall take great pleasure in arranging."

And indeed, she has won a great victory. Or rather, Lucy Landseer has. But was it just the production of the novel, Mrs Hemmyng-Stratton wonders, as she makes her way home? She will never know.

(*The truth is slightly more prosaic. Stephen Ackwynd, a fellow pupil at Harrow with Lord Lackington, and a man with an acute sense of his social position, was horrified by the thought that his wife might have to debase herself by speaking in a public courtroom.*

As soon as he received the barrister's telegram, Ackwynd went straight round to see his former schoolmate Edwin Lackington. In the ensuing violent row, overheard with great relish by all the Lackington servants, he made it quite clear that unless Lackington withdrew his accusation forthwith, he'd make sure his old Harrovian chum would be blackballed from every club in town, the local Hunt, the Gentlemen's Private Gambling Society, the Casino de Royaume etc.

Ackwynd also made mention of Lackington's patronage of certain bookshops in Holywell Street, which might be of interest to members of the press and the police. And finally, for good measure, he threw in a pretty little horse-breaker, who lived in some style in a nice house in Maida Vale, which she could not possibly afford. It was more than enough to persuade the ignoble lord to withdraw.)

The discovery of the truth is currently the focus of Greig and Cully's attention. Here they are standing next to a makeshift bed in one of the whitewashed interview rooms. On the bed lies the man who isn't dead. A fire has been lit, and Robertson, the police surgeon, is gently probing various of the man's orifices with a steel instrument.

"Interesting," he says, straightening up from his brief examination. "Your man was lucky the temperature dropped last night to near freezing, causing his blood to clot, and thus preventing him from bleeding to death. And it lowered his heart rate, making him go into a state of suspended animation. Of course, you are both familiar with the three forms of suspended animation: syncope, asphyxia and trance? No? I am happy to enlighten you, if you so wish."

"Could you, perhaps, just tell us when we might expect this man to wake up," Cully says hastily.

Robertson purses his lips. "Of course, there is always the fourth form ~ wherein the subject deliberately brings on a state of apparent death. I refer to the case of the Honourable Colonel Townsend, who claimed he could, by an act of will, expire and then come to life again, though in this case before me, I think the judicious application of a scalpel … here … might be aidant and remediate in the recovery process."

Sure enough, as he pokes a scalpel into the man's side, the detectives see the man's fingers twitch convulsively. Then his breathing becomes louder and his eyelids begin to flicker.

"Ah. And there you go, gentlemen," Robertson nods complacently. "From death unto life." He packs his instruments away into their velvet-lined case. "Mind you, I have always thought that the case of Townsend should be taken *cum grano selis*. And the state of trance is usually only seen in females. On that note, having fulfilled my duties, I leave you to your interrogation. *Ego sum dominus mortis*, as it were. Shame the good detective inspector was not able to grace us with his presence. I think this is one he would rather have enjoyed. Oh well."

He gives them a small formal bow, then walks out of the room. Cully and Greig sigh in unison, before turning their focus upon the man, who is slowly regaining consciousness. As they watch, his eyes open, his tongue moistens his lips. He moves his head very slowly, groans, and stares round the room, his gaze finally coming to rest on the two detectives, at the sight of whom he swears copiously.

"Ow ~ my 'ead hurts. And where the hell am I?" he says, levering himself painfully up on his elbows.

"Good morning, sir," Greig says affably. "You are currently a guest of Scotland Yard's detective division. This is one of the holding cells. I am Detective Inspector Greig; this is Detective Sergeant Cully. And your name is?"

The man sits up. He is a hefty-built type, who probably couldn't run fast, but could hand out a beating without breaking into a sweat. His eyes are cold and hard, his mouth a vicious tear. He stares at them.

"I ain't saying nothing."

"Really, *sir*? You cannot remember your own name? Shall I send for the doctor again?" Greig suggests, lifting his eyebrows fractionally.

"You can send for the Queen of England for all I care."

"If you are unable to remember your name, maybe you won't 'remember' where you were last night? Let me jog your memory," Cully says, folding his arms. "A certain livery stable in St Johns Wood? You broke in, armed with a knife and with intent to commit a murder."

The man notices his bandaged hand. He lifts it to his face and examines it. "What the ...?"

"You were attacked by a dog. It was defending its master from you."

Something dark and unpleasant flits across the man's face. He mutters under his breath.

"I'm sorry, *sir*, I did not quite catch that," Greig says, smiling pleasantly.

"I said vicious dogs like that oughter be put down."

"Ah ~ so you DO remember the dog. Excellent. Now we are making progress. Mr. ...?"

The man clamps his lips together.

"Still no memory? Perhaps the name Munro Black might bring it back?

A flicker of fear appears momentarily behind the hard eyes. And disappears leaving only blankness.

"This Mr. Black, whose name you do not recognise, is wanted for various crimes and misdemeanours. You are quite sure you have never heard of him? You don't know him? You never met up with him at the Ship Inn? No? Strange, because we can produce several witnesses who say they saw you both there," Greig presses on. "Including the lad you attempted to murder last night."

The man stares fixedly at the opposite wall, as if his gaze could bore an escape-hole in it.

"Shall we do that, *sir*? Shall we ask our witnesses to come in and identify you? Better still, maybe we could ask Mr. Munro Black to come down to Scotland Yard and take a look at you for himself. We might suggest to him that, having failed to carry out his request to attack one of our witnesses, and to save your own skin, you told us who was behind the attack. Then, we could release you, and wait to see what he chooses to do. Might that 'help' you to remember your name, and other things?"

"You wouldn't dare!"

"Ah, detective sergeant: he speaks!"

"He does indeed, detective inspector. Now, I'm sure he'd appreciate a cup of tea. Let us send for one. I suggest we also ask one of the day constables to trot round to Russell Square." Cully says. "You'd like a cup of tea, wouldn't you, Mr. ...?"

"Albert Norris."

"Mr. Norris. Your memory has returned! I shall make a note of that," Greig goes through an elaborate pantomime with a notebook and pencil. "And your address, Mr. Norris?"

"I'm temp'rily between lodgings."

"We are getting on famously, Mr. Norris. So, before we send for that cup of tea, and my officer pays that morning call upon Mr. Black ... let us return to the night of September the 2nd. The place: The Ship Inn. Cast your mind back to that night, Mr. Norris, and let us see what you now recall."

****

Detective Inspector Stride is attacking a plate of food in a back booth at Sally's Chop House, when a shadow falls across his plate. Looking up, he sees the tall figure of Detective Inspector Lachlan Greig, who eases himself onto the opposite bench. "Here you are," he says.

Stride mutters words to the effect that it is lunchtime, so where else would he be? He moves a small chop around with his knife. He is not in a good place (metaphorically). It has now been several days since Pozzy Wozzy was reported missing, and there still hasn't been any sighting of him. Stride doesn't feel good about it. There is an awful lot of London for an old man to get lost in, and a lot of people who might want to help him do it. One in particular springs to mind.

Stride has sent a description of Pozzy round all the local police offices, asking the beat constables to check alleyways and doorways for an old man. They have. No old man answering Pozzy's description has been found. Other old men, yes. Many of them dead or dying. The nights are turning cold. Stride is trying to console himself with the thought that if no actual body has turned up, then his former informer must still be alive, somewhere.

Greig ignores his colleague's downcast manner. "I am the bearer of good news," he says.

"They've found him?" Stride leans eagerly forward in his seat.

Greig frowns, "Found who?"

Stride sighs. So Pozzy has not turned up. He signals to Sally to clear his plate. He has suddenly lost his appetite.

"Let me tell you who we have got in custody," Greig says. "Finally, we have the breakthrough we've all been waiting for." He describes the interview with Mr. Albert Norris, Munro Black's enforcer. "We now know both men were in the Ship Inn on the night James Flashley died. We also know they met him later that evening. Norris told us that when they met up, Flashley was carrying a sack ~ he does not know what was in it, he says. According to Norris, Black and Flashley got into an argument about debts and money, at which point, he says, he decided he'd had enough and left."

"And you believe his story?"

"Up until the leaving part. We know Flashley didn't hang himself from that scaffolding, and it would take more than one man to string him up. We have no proof Albert Norris was involved, but his presence at the livery stable, and his attempt to finish off young Brixston gives us enough to keep him locked up, and eventually charged for attempted murder."

187

"Good work," Stride says. "Yes. And where do we go from here?"

"I suggest we drop a hint to the newspapers that we have received new evidence and are on the point of making an arrest in the Bridge Murder case. That might flush Black out of his lair. It will certainly get him worried, and worried men are inclined to make mistakes."

Stride nods. "It is worth a try. But we still have no witnesses who place him at the murder scene itself. Nobody who saw him tie that rope round Flashley's neck and string him up. What he did before, or even after, is of no account. It is all circumstantial. We need hard evidence; that is the only thing a judge and jury are interested in. No hard evidence, and we might as well throw in the towel."

They sit in silence for a while. Then,

"Was there anything else?" Stride asks.

Greig shakes his head. Pauses. Seems to hesitate, works his mouth for a while, then stands up. "No. I shall see you back at Scotland Yard? You might care to interview Mr. Norris for yourself. Perhaps you can elicit something from him that he was reluctant to tell us."

Privately, Stride doubts this. "I can try, certainly. But it will not change where we are. We have the monkey, Lachlan, but the organ-grinder is still free to pursue his trade. The game is not over yet."

"Indeed, it is not. I gather that chess-players have a particular name for this stage," Greig says thoughtfully. "I cannot now quite recall what it is."

"A waste of time?" Stride grunts. He does not play chess.

"The endgame. That is what it is called. We are in the endgame."

Later, after questioning Albert Norris and eliciting nothing further from him than his food preferences,

Stride decides to call it a day. It is clear that the threat of reprisals from his employer are so real that Norris is not prepared to admit to playing any part in the murder of Flashley.

He has confessed to the attempted silencing of Brixton, but on all other counts, his lips are sealed. Stride also has the distinct impression that Albert Norris would far rather be tucked up in a police cell, than walking the streets as a free man.

It demonstrates, clearly, the power and control that Munro Black exerts on all those whom he employs, Stride thinks. Which means the sooner they rid the city of his malign presence, the better for all concerned. He sends up a silent prayer that a certain cantankerous old man and his cough have not fallen into his evil clutches.

****

Izzy Harding walks the streets of the greatest city on earth. The day has worn itself away. Twilight advances; the lights begin to start up in shops. The lamplighter, with his ladder, runs along the margin of the pavement. Izzy walks and walks, until the moon and stars are bright in the cold black sky above her.

It has been a strange day. A difficult day. A day that started out in the usual way ~ she woke in the cold crepuscular dawn to the familiar smell of rot, filth and bacon being fried for her landlady's numerous progeny.

She turned over to find an empty space beside her, where her mother had been. Izzy had felt under her mattress, relieved when her fingers touched the shiny brass button, the length of bright scarlet ribbon, the sheet of gold leaf, the six farthings, the miniature dolls' tea-set, the green velvet pincushion and the silver sixpence.

She'd got up, rubbed sleep out of her eyes, combed her hair and tied it with the scarlet ribbon because today was going to be a special day. She left the lodging house and set off for the dolls' furniture workshop. Once again, the city had been her library: **Author Accused in Copyright Caper ~ Case Dismissed!** she'd read on a newspaper seller's board. Passing a dining room, she'd read a sign for *Leg of Beef Soup, 2d per bowl*.

A poster for Madam Tussauds was slightly less reassuring, as it invited passers-by to visit the Chamber of Horrors to see a portrait model of '*William Fish, The Blackburn Murderer*'. She had hurried past that one, head averted.

Izzy had paused by the small shoeblack, who'd recently appeared on her walk to work, pitching his box and brushes by a convenient wall. His sign: *Brushup and Polish for 1/3d* and his cheerful whistling blended almost seamlessly into her daily morning route. The boy had lifted his cap and they'd exchanged a few words of greeting before Izzy plodded on.

Izzy reached the Colonnade just as the church clock was striking the half-hour. All along the street, shutters were being taken down, doorsteps were being sluiced or swept, and small trestle tables were being brought out and erected, ready to be piled with goods for sale.

She spotted a wooden box of oranges on a table outside the small greengrocer's shop. The shop owner was not around. Izzy had hesitated, then she'd dipped a hand in and grabbed one. The fruit was soft and oozy. She'd bitten a hole in the peel and sucked on it, letting the sweet juice fill her mouth. It was a long way to suppertime.

Reaching the small alleyway that ran alongside the confectioner's shop, ending at the back in the rickety iron staircase to the first floor, she'd been surprised to see a couple of her fellow painters sitting on the steps.

"Can't get in," one of the painters had informed her laconically.

"Door's locked," another added.

"Been kicking it," Izzy's nemesis said, glaring at Izzy as if it were her fault.

Izzy'd placed herself on the bottom step, fished the orange out of her pocket and continued making inroads into it. Time passed. The girl overseer arrived, tried the door, leaned her weight against it, then shrugged and walked away. The hour struck, then the quarter-hour. Eventually the half-hour struck. Then the next hour. They waited for her to come back. She didn't come back.

Izzy's legs were getting cold. She rose and went down to the confectioner's shop on the ground floor, where she inquired politely whether the woman behind the counter knew what had happened to the people renting the upstairs space. The woman looked at her pityingly.

"They cleared off, my duck. Did a moonlight flit. Owed the landlord rent. Was you one of the painters?"

Izzy nodded dumbly.

"Well, I'm sorry for you. But there's no point hanging around here. They've gone, and they ain't coming back and that's all there is to it. What I heard was they were going up north ~ Manchester, coz it's cheaper to rent a property and they can pay lower wages." She eyed Izzy's downcast face. "Here, have a sweet. Cheer you up. Don't fret. There's plenty of other jobs for a bright girl like you."

Izzy returned and conveyed the dispiriting news to her co-workers. There were a few tears from some of the smaller ones, for whom life's disappointments were still novel. The rest shuffled resignedly down the stairs and dispersed to various parts of the city. Izzy would never see them again.

The orange and the sweet kept her going for the rest of the day. A long day, in which Izzy Harding was turned away from job after job. It appeared that nobody wanted a small work-slave to clean, sweep, run errands, mind babies, hold horses, or carry parcels.

It seemed she had entered an over-crowded market. Flower-sellers told her there wasn't room for another girl. Street-sweepers shook their heads and said all the pitches were taken. Costers told her they only employed their own, and she wasn't. Other possible employers took one look at her frayed and worn work clothes and her forlorn bonnet, and pinch-poor face, and shook their heads.

After hours of knock-backs, Izzy finally arrived at the kitchen entrance to Mrs Sarah McAdam's Select City Dining Room. She was exhausted from walking the streets of the city, asking at every shop and business whether they needed a good reliable worker.

She found her apron, pulled the stool up to the deep butler sink, and began to tackle the mountain of greasy plates. Occasionally, she slid a piece of discarded chop rind into her mouth. The act of chewing gave the impression that she was eating, even though what was in her mouth provided little nourishment and was soon spat out.

Izzy tried to find some positives in her situation. She reminded herself that she had a roof over her head for now, which was a blessing, given the state of some of the homeless children she saw every day, gathered around some workmen's brazier, warming their blue hands, their clothes ragged and unwashed.

And she had family ~ when it chose to turn up. A job would materialize sooner or later, because she would keep on looking until it did. Meanwhile, the steam from the kitchen was warm and comforting, and there was the prospect of something to eat when she finished the washing up.

At the end of her shift, Izzy had received her usual wages of leftover bread. She wrapped it in her apron, together with some leftover pie from a dinner plate, which she hid while nobody was looking, then slipped out of the back door, darting up the dark alleyway like a scrawny stray cat.

And now here she is, her meagre supper consumed, making her way to her teacher's house. It is not a class night, but Izzy feels the need for some sympathetic company. Preferably with a cup of hot sugared tea, cake, and a warm-up by the kitchen range. Her teacher always manages to make her feel optimistic about her future. Right now, she needs all the optimism she can get.

Izzy passes the church, with its rows of gravestones pointing to the sky, then stops outside Maria Barklem's cottage. The blinds are all drawn down. There is a black ribbon bow on the door knocker, all unmistakable signals that someone in the house has died. For a second, her heart stands still, then she recalls mention of her teacher's elderly infirm mother, remembers a tea tray being born aloft.

Izzy stands outside the house for a while, trying to imagine what it must be like to lose your mother. For all her faults, her mother has been a constant, if erratic, presence. She could not imagine life without the sense of her mother's body, smelling of tobacco and beer and cheap scent, lying next to her on their shared mattress.

Thinking about her own mother brings back memories of Izzy's last birthday. It was a special day. Her mother had met her from work, and they'd walked to a food stall down New Cut, where her mother had spent some of her money on hot potato and fried fish, which they'd eaten by the light of a swinging oil lamp. The stall holder had put his arm round her mother's shoulders, whispering in her ear. The rest of the memory was blurred, but the taste of that lovely hot fish lingered on.

She takes a final look at the house of mourning, sending kind thoughts towards her grieving teacher, then sets off back to the small section of shared floor that she calls home. As she walks, Izzy looks up, up at the shining stars. She takes a breath of cold tingly air. Today is her eleventh birthday. That was why she'd put on her scarlet ribbon this morning when she got up. Today will be remembered as a special day too, but not for the same reasons as last year.

****

The city is emptying as Stride walks home. There has been paperwork; there will be more paperwork. Now all he craves is the comfort of his own hearth. He pauses at the newsboy's stand on the corner of the Piazza, but the headlines this evening are all about the disappearance of Lady Someone who has escaped from a privately-run asylum.

Stride does not blame her. In his opinion, there are more people walking the streets who should be incarcerated in lunatic asylums, than ever have been. Good luck to the lady, he thinks, even though wishing anything positive upon the upper classes goes against his moral grain. His thoughts linger briefly on Mr. Gerald Daubney. There is a man so close to the edge of madness that it would only take a slight push to tip him over.

He reaches his street, where the gas-lamps have been lit, and spies his house in the distance. Smoke is rising from the chimney, a sign that supper is being cooked. He quickens his pace and is just about to unlatch the front gate, when he has the distinct sensation that somebody has stepped out from the shadows and is standing right behind him.

Stride whirls round, fists raised, ready to strike the first blow. Then, recognising whom he is about to strike, he lowers his hands and grips the putative assailant by his shoulders instead. "Pozzy! For the love of God! Where have you been?"

The old man wheezes himself into voice. "Bin here an' there, Mr. Stride. Duckin' and divin', wheelin' and dealin'. Like you do."

"Did you know your sister has been down to Scotland Yard and reported you missing? She is very upset about you."

The old man laughs. It sounds like a rusty knife scraping along a brick wall. "Has she now? Silly cow. She oughter know me better. I allus turns up, eventually. Like the proverbial bad penny, I am. Serves her right. Coming round the house, telling me what to eat an' when to change my socks. As I keeps saying to her: I eat what I likes, and I don't need clean socks at my time of life."

The old man sniffs the air. "Smells like good stew cooking somewhere," he says. He regards Stride with watery, but hopeful eyes. "Bit of supper wouldn't go amiss. Then I might be up to tellin' you wot I found out."

Stride shudders at the thought of Mrs Stride's reaction if he turns up with Pozzy in tow, but he marches him to the front door and, bidding him wait on the step, enters the house, carefully taking off his boots first. After a short interval, he returns, carrying a brimming plate.

"You sit down here on the step and enjoy your meal, Pozzy," he says. "Then we'll go for a pint or two, shall we?"

The old man's mouth waters as he takes the plate in his hands. "Fair enough, Mr. Stride. Fair enough," he says, sitting down carefully so as not to spill any of the rich gravy. Stride hands him a spoon, then goes back to the kitchen where, even with the door closed, he can hear the noises of the old man enjoying his food.

A short while later, Stride and Pozzy set out for the Black Horse, the nearest public house. Stride doesn't drink there normally. Partly because it is the nearest public house and partly because Mrs Stride, who was brought up strict Presbyterian, does not approve of strong drink.

Nevertheless, an exception has been made, and now Stride places the old man in a quiet back booth while he orders drinks at the bar. When his pint arrives, Pozzy takes a long pull of his ale, wipes his moustache, then sits back contentedly.

"That's better, Mr. Stride. Nothing like a plate of good stew and a pint to set a man up for the evening. Now then, I expects you're wanting to know what I has to tell yer?"

"In your own time, Pozzy," Stride says. He is rather relishing the excuse to have an evening out: Mrs Stride has been leaving paint charts on the kitchen table again, an ominous sign that more decorating is being planned. Stride hates decorating. He has barely recovered from the last bout.

"So, where have you been staying, Pozzy?" he asks.

The old man looks vague. "Got a mate down Deptford way. Owed me a favour. Been kipping at his place while I made some inquiries for you. And the word on the cobbles is that it's not just you who wants Mr. Munro Black caught. There are a lot of people in that queue.

"See, it's not just the gambling, currency rackets and loan sharking what he does, but right now he is bad for business generally, coz whenever you get policemen investigating somebody, they always end up seeing more than they should. The sooner he clears off or someone puts him behind bars, the better for local businesses round here, and for certain people who'll sleep safer, and stop looking over their shoulders."

Stride sees the logic of this. "But if that is so, why won't anybody talk to us?" he asks.

"Nobody wants to be known as a snitch, is why. And they're scared, Mr. Stride. They don't like Munro Black, but he's got a lot of muscle and the muscle is paid to put the frighteners on anybody who might get in his way. That's why he did what he did. Show who's top dog. Ain't no one going to take him on if they know they might end up swingin' from a rope somewhere, are they? Stands to reason. And that's the long and short of it."

"Did you find anyone who'd be prepared to stand up in court and swear it was Munro Black who murdered James Flashley?"

Pozzy shakes his head. "Nobody was there, nobody saw nothin'."

Stride pulls a face. "Well, you did your best, Pozzy," he said. "At least you kept yourself safe."

"Oi, Mr. Stride! Hold up a bit. I ain't finished. I might not be able to help you out with Munro Black, but I got some interesting stuff about his younger brother."

"I thought he had gone abroad."

"He comes and goes. He trades in *hooman flesh*, as them newspapers puts it. Picks up girls in London and takes them over to France or to Belgium."

"We know this," Stride says. "We can't stop him. These girls are old enough to choose where they want to work. If we arrested every 'actress' on the street, there wouldn't be room for the real criminals."

Pozzy waves a dismissive hand, "Ah, but wait a bit ~ we ain't talking about your usual judies, Mr. Stride. These are very young ones, but they are being sold on the Continent as older girls."

Stride leans forward, his gaze fixed intently upon the old man's face. "Go on …"

"What they do, see, is they gets hold of a birth certificate of another girl, maybe she has a similar name, and then they pass off their girl as that one. Mr. Black senior turns up at the Register General's office, all suited and booted, and pays the fee for a copy of the birth certificate. Then Mr. Black junior ships the girl over to the Continent, with the copy, and shows it to the Continental police, who think it is an official document.

"They have to do it like that because taking a young girl abroad is a crime. And I got the address of the woman who looks after the girls until they are collected," Pozzy grins crazily at Stride, "Coz why? Coz I am still the best-informed informer in town, Mr. Stride. And that's God's own truth."

They finish their drinks. Stride gives the old man the agreed reward for his services, which Pozzy pockets with a grunt of satisfaction. Then, having made a note of the address of the woman, he walks the old man to the nearest cab stand and puts him in a hansom. It is far too late for an old man, unsteady on his feet, to walk home on his own.

Stride waits until the cab has disappeared into the night, after which he sets off in the direction of home once more. The walk will enable him to clear his head. And to plot the next stage of the investigation. Finally, the net is closing on Munro Black, but they must move carefully and with stealth. It is absolutely vital that there are no holes for him to slip through.

****

The night wears on. Mrs Hemmyng-Stratton sits at her writing-desk, chin resting on one cupped hand, staring out of her window at the starlit sky. Venus is rising, an auspicious portent.

On her desk, as yet unopened, sits a letter, written in the familiar hand of her barrister's clerk. It was delivered earlier this evening, while the Author was at table. Now, she rests her other hand upon the superscript, thinking that this moment is like that point in a novel when the turning of a page will finally reveal the true destiny of a fair, but misjudged heroine.

Her current Heroine is still languishing in the sloughs of unrequited affection, even though it is a bright and brilliant June (her favourite month); a triumphant summer has banished the pitiful spring and the meadows are all perfume and colour. She (the Heroine) awaits her fate, even as her creator, the Author, awaits sufficient courage to open the letter she has received.

At last she turns her gaze away from the celestial realm. It is time. She picks up an ivory letter-opener and inserts it under the red waxed seal. Inside the envelope is a letter, written on rich cream paper in the same sloping, clerkish hand.

Dear Mrs Hemmyng-Stratton, (she reads)

I have now received official written confirmation from Strutt & Preening (lawyers) that the allegation made against you by Lord Edwin Lackington has been formally withdrawn. In the circumstances and given the adverse effect upon your esteemed literary reputation, I will be making an application to the court for compensation.

It is my intention to request that the sum of two hundred guineas, which I think is an appropriate amount given the social position of the litigant and the seriousness of the accusation made against you, should be paid into your bank account at the earliest opportunity, on the understanding that we will not pursue Lord Lackington through the courts for his wrongful and malicious accusation.

I trust this meets with your approval.

The letter is signed by the barrister himself (she presumes it is his signature, like the signature of most professional men, it is totally illegible to the layman's eye).

Mrs Hemmyng-Stratton stares at the letter for some considerable time, trying to take in the contents. She remembers reading, in her youth, some saying in the bible on the lines that if one cast one's bread upon the waters, it would return one hundredfold or thereabout. Here is tangible proof. She spent fifty guineas; she will receive two hundred guineas in return. All being well.

She decides that, should it come to pass, some of the money must be given to Miss Landseer, in recompense for her successful efforts in clearing her name. The rest will be saved towards her eventual purchase of a little writer's nook in the Lake District.

The Author sets the letter aside. All this is for another time. Meanwhile, outside her window is the clear sky, upholding the never-ending pomp of night, and the ever-new prospect of dawn. With a grateful sigh, Mrs Hemmyng-Stratton takes up her pen, dips it into her ink-pot, and begins to write.

****

It is the following morning, and Maria Barklem is meeting with the church Elders to discuss her future occupation of the cottage. The meeting is taking place in the church parlour, a plain room, barely warmed by a sputtering coal fire. The room has a large polished table. The Elders sit behind the polished table. Behind the Elders are the words GOD IS LOVE, painted on the white wall.

It is just over two weeks since her mother was buried in the churchyard, next to her father. The mound of earth is still fresh on her grave. The headstone has not been set in place yet. But the living (and the houses they currently occupy) are more important than the dead, so here she is, clothed in full mourning, waiting the judgement of these three wise men.

And here they are, elderly and upright, elected to carry out God's Will to the letter, if not the Spirit. They regard her cautiously across the wide brown shininess of the table, as if she were some strange alien on a far-off shore. An Egyptian facing the Chosen People. Which is what she certainly feels like.

"Let us now open the meeting with prayer," one of the Elders intones solemnly.

Heads are bowed. The Almighty is called upon to bless and guide. The departed are mentioned, briefly, but not dwelt upon for too long, as the absence of their presence plays no part in what is to be discussed.

Maria lets the words float above her. Her lips instinctively frame an 'amen' at the close of the prayer, but she does not inhabit it. It is not just the black clothes that separate her from the world, but her whole existence. She does not know who she is any more. Can you be a daughter when you have no mother?

One of the Elders, (his name is Samuel Cutclyffe-Hyne) clears his throat. Meaningfully. Maria raises her eyes and fixes them upon him. He is the man who grudgingly agreed to allow her mother to stay on in the cottage. In his face there is little expression, but behind the pale eyes, some ruthless calculation is in progress. He is the business end of the meeting. The other two Elders are here in a scenic capacity.

"We meet, albeit in sad circumstances, to consider the future of the church cottage," he begins. "More particularly, the future use of the church's dwelling place, which has been the topic of much prayer and debate, and which I, as senior Elder, have now been instructed to share with you."

Maria stares at him. She says nothing in response. She is damned if she is going to help him out. His dislike of her has always been hidden in plain sight. She works. She earns money. She has opinions. Which she expresses. She does not conform to his idea of what a young unmarried Christian female should be. Plus, he strongly suspects (correctly) that she seems to be poking every utterance of his with a stick.

"It has always been the intention of the church that the cottage should be offered to somebody who is in the employ of the diocese," Cutclyffe-Hyne says. "In the past, that was your father, who served the parish in the role of assistant minister. Then, as a concession to her situation and her declining health, your mother and you were permitted to reside there. Now, we face a new prospect, and so a new solution must be sought. Do you not agree?"

Maria folds her black-gloved hands in her black silk lap and lets the black thoughts circle inside her head like predatory birds. "So, in which particular gutter would you like me to take up residence, then?" she says, sharply, in a voice that she does not recognise as hers.

There is a swift indrawing of Elderly breath.

"Now, now, young woman, I do not see the necessity for such a remark," Cutclyffe-Hyne says, his face reddening. "I am sure an amicable outcome is the one we all wish to see enacted."

Maria holds his words up for scrutiny. "You want to throw me out of the home I have lived in since I was a child. How is that 'amicable'?"

"Nobody is speaking of throwing you out. Far from it. We have a proposal that, once you hear it, we are all sure will suit your current circumstances admirably."

Maria sidles up to this and sniffs it cautiously. "I am listening."

Cutclyffe-Hyne shoots a quick glance at his fellow Elders.

"Now then. Miss Barklem. As you know, the church has recently appointed a new curate. He and his family of four will be joining us from Northumberland in a few weeks. What we propose is that you stay on in the house as cook and general housekeeper to the family."

"I see. Where would I sleep?"

"I believe, from my recollection, that the scullery adjoining the kitchen is capacious enough to hold a small truckle bed, is it not? The church itself is in need of a cleaner, so you could easily combine the two roles. Of course, you would live rent-free. A small emolument might be provided in recompense for your Christian services. What do you say?"

Maria grips her hands tightly together. "I say I would rather die in a ditch than skivvy day and night."

"Hoity-toity young miss! You are not in a position to turn down such an offer of Christian charity, I think?"

"Well, I have to inform you, gentlemen, that you are wrong. I have made my plans, and they do not include working my fingers to the bone for a pittance." She stands. "I bid you good day. Be assured, by the time your new curate arrives, I shall be gone. You will see me no more, other than when I visit the graves of my father and mother, whose lives you made thoroughly miserable. You call this Christian charity? A dog in the street has more charity than you."

Maria thrusts her arms into the sleeves of her coat and stalks out of the room, slamming the door behind her for good measure. Anger gets her most of the way home. Then, the cold reality of her situation punches her in the face.

She sits down on the red plush chair that was her mother's favourite, covering her face with her hands. She has lied to the Elders. Lied. She has nowhere to go once she quits this home. And her job at the bakery will not pay her enough for both rent and food. Bravado without back-up. Her jibe about living on the street may well become a reality unless something turns up. And it doesn't have long to do so.

****

A short while later, a cab pulls up outside a certain respectable-looking house in Portland Place. The blinds are lowered at some of the upper story windows, suggesting that there might be illness in the house. Out of the cab steps Detective Inspector Stride. He is accompanied by an inspector and a couple of constables from C-Division.

Stride and the inspector walk up the spotless path, stand on the spotless step and rap on the door, which is opened by a small boy dressed in the uniform of a page. His eyes open like saucers when he sees who is demanding access. Stride hastily places a foot on the doorstep and leans his elbow against the door.

"Is the lady of the house receiving visitors?" he says, managing to put air-quotes around the appellation 'lady'.

The small boy mentally counts the number of men standing on the front path, realises that he is outnumbered, mutters something about going to see if she is.

While they wait for him to return, the two men enter. The interior of the house is lavishly furnished, maroon button-backed sofas compete for space with small rosewood tables displaying Chinese vases and flower glasses. The walls are adorned with Japanese fans. Chandeliers hang from the ceilings and the curtains and pelmets are a handsome green colour.

Eventually, the lady of the house makes her appearance. She is a tall, tightly corseted woman in her forties, preceded by a strong smell of pipe tobacco and some spicy scent that makes Stride want to sneeze. He recognises her instantly as the woman he saw going into Number 55, Russell Square, accompanied by two girls.

"Good day, gents. Bit early for a morning call, isn't it?" she says. She has an upmarket voice with downmarket vowels and a smile that does not quite reach her eyes.

Stride steps forward. "It is Mrs Gresham, I presume? Mrs Bella Gresham? I am Detective Inspector Stride from Scotland Yard. This is Inspector Fitch from the local branch of the Metropolitan Police. We wish to talk to you about your connection with two men: Mr. Munro and Mr. Herbert Black. May we sit?"

Mrs Gresham's perfectly pencilled eyebrows shoot up her forehead until they almost disappear under her false fringe of yellow curls. "I am sorry, gents, I do not reckernise either of those names."

"Let me place them in context for you, Mrs Gresham," Stride says amiably. "The gentlemen in question reside at Number 55, Russell Square. Have you ever been to that address?"

The false front of curls bobs and dances as Mrs Gresham shakes her head. Unperturbed, Stride presses on. "The matter we are investigating is that of procuring young girls and shipping them over the Channel to work in brothels in France and Belgium. To do this, the gentlemen have been obtaining birth certificates under false pretences so that the girls would not fall foul of the Continental police, who do not take kindly to underage girls working as prostitutes in their countries.

"We showed pictures of one of the men to the clerks in the Registrar General's Office, and they were able confirm that it was Mr. Munro Black, and that he had obtained many certificates over time. Now ~ and here, I think, you might like to tread warily, Mrs Gresham, my men have been watching Number 55, Russell Square, and both they and I have seen you get out of a carriage with some young girls, and enter the house. So, let me ask you again: do you, or do you not know Mr. Munro Black and his brother? Take your time, Mrs Gresham. Please. We are not going anywhere."

Stride's smile is so stiff and wooden you could use it as an ironing-board. The inspector folds his arms and stares at the chandelier in a fascinated manner as if he has never seen one like it before. Mrs Gresham clamps her lips together. The silence extends and settles round them.

"Construction can be put upon silence," Stride observes quietly.

"I ain't done anything wrong," she says at last. "I was only doing what I was asked."

And getting paid handsomely for doing it, Stride thinks. He has seen the inside of many houses of assignation. Few boast the fixtures and fittings of this one.

"What you are doing is aiding and abetting a criminal," Fitch says. "Have you got any girls on the premises at the moment? We should like to interview them."

The woman adopts a mulish expression. "I may have some paying guests, but I don't have to let you talk to them. It ain't against the law, is it ~ to have paying guests?"

Fitch gestures towards the window. "If you would care to take a look outside, Madam, you will see a cab. Inside the cab are several of my best men. If I give them the signal, they will enter your premises, making as much of a row as they can, and disturbing the whole street in the process. Do you want that to happen? Also, given the unfortunate nature of the times we live in, somebody is bound to contact the press. They always do, don't they? I expect this is a 'respectable house'? Do you want to see your name splashed across the front of the newspapers for all your neighbours to see?"

The woman sends him a hate-filled glare. She heaves herself out of her seat. "Follow me, then."

She leads them up the carpeted stairs and knocks on a door. It is opened a crack by a very pretty but very youthful girl, her hair in curling rags. Behind her, the men can just see two other girls sitting on a bed, dressed in morning wrappers.

"Now then, my love," Mrs Gresham says in a cooing voice, "These gents mean you no harm so do not be afraid. They just want to ask you a few questions."

Stride steps up to the crack in the door.

"What is your name, my dear?" Stride asks.

The girl flashes a quick crafty look at Mrs Gresham, then back at Stride. "Bluebell Herring," she says.

"And how old are you, Bluebell?"

Another knowing glance. "Twenty-one."

Take off five years and you'd be nearer the truth, Stride thinks grimly.

"And why are you staying here, Miss Herring?"

"I'm going to be an actress in Paree."

"I see. When are you setting off for Paris?"

"Tonight, ain't we, girls? Can't wait. Gay Paree!"

There is a faint chorus of agreement from the other occupants.

Stride thanks her, indicating that he has nothing more to ask. The door is closed once more. The men return to the parlour. Mrs Gresham regards them sullenly.

"I hope you are satisfied, officers. Nobody is forcing them girls to go abroad. They are free to change their minds any time."

"Who has the girls' birth certificates?"

Mrs Gresham shrugs. "I just delivers the girls to the train station. I don't know about anything else."

"Which station, and at what time?" Fitch asks.

With grudging reluctance, the woman tells him.

"Thank you, Mrs Gresham, you have been most helpful," Stride says. "Bear in mind that a man will be watching the house until you leave with the girls, so I suggest you do not try to contact anybody in the interim, or it will be the worse for you."

He sends a tacit signal to the inspector. The two men return to the street.

"You'd be hard put to find a charge that would stick," Fitch says. "It isn't a crime to take young girls abroad."

"But once they are abroad, it is a crime to possess a false birth certificate," Stride says. "The police control the trade in prostitutes over there, and they take a dim view of those who run foul of the law."

Leaving one of Fitch's men outside the house, the two men part company and return to their various police offices. Later, Stride will telegraph the Calais police force and alert them to the young women and the false birth certificates. He is also going to place a man on the train, to follow the younger Black brother, and his three 'actresses' to the French coast, where he will make sure he is detained by the French authorities.

Stride has little doubt that Miss Bluebell Herring and her friends will find alternative employment somewhere else. The younger brother can eke out his time in a French gaol. For now. *And so, Mr. Munro Black,* he reflects, *the net closes a little tighter.*

****

Unlike her youthful contemporaries, Maria Barklem is not looking for alternative employment, far from it. She currently has employment. Rather, she is seeking a new roof over her head. So far alas, with little success. After her day's work is done, she returns to the home that will soon belong to another family and prepares herself for her evening class.

Yes, Maria knows that in the eyes of the church, and social convention, she is not supposed to engage in public activities during the set period of mourning for a parent, but if she does not break the convention, she risks losing her chance to gain her valuable certificate. She is pretty sure that evicting her from her home also does not feature in any 'How to Treat Those Recently Bereaved' booklets, but that isn't stopping the church Elders from throwing her out, is it?

In between sessions on geography and arithmetic, Maria joins some of her fellow students in the canteen. Over coffee and buns, she finds herself confiding about her prospective homelessness. She is comforted by the sympathy, and the shared stories of her fellows. It seems that every girl has some similar misfortune in their background.

Later, just after the close of the final session, as she is gathering up her folders and buttoning her coat, she is unexpectedly approached by one of the female lecturers, Miss Letitia Simpkins.

"Miss Barklem, may I trouble you for a private word in my teaching room?" she asks.

Maria follows her into the classroom and is invited to take a seat. Miss Simpkins draws up another chair, and to her surprise, takes one of Maria's gloved hands in her own.

"I overheard your conversation in the canteen," she says. "Allow me to offer my deepest sympathy upon the death of your mother. I also lost my Mama at a young age, and the loss of the one person who believed in me made all the difference to the course of my life."

There is a pause. Maria withdraws the hand, fumbles for her handkerchief and mops her eyes. Miss Simpkins waits patiently for her attention to return. Eventually it does.

"I was lucky enough to be given the chance of an education, Miss Barklem, although I had to fight for it. It may seem strange to you, but five years ago, it was almost unthinkable for a girl from a 'nice' family to want to have a profession. We were supposed to stay at home until some man came and asked for our hand in marriage."

Maria studies her lecturer. Letitia Simpkins is tall, flat-chested and gawky, her clothes unfashionable, her mousy hair scraped back in a bun, her face plain and without the slightest vestige of prettiness. Her eyes are hidden behind a pair of spectacles. She does not seem like the sort to ever attract a suitor.

And yet there is a glow about her that has nothing to do with her physical appearance; she walks with a sense of purpose, and the eyes behind the thick lenses are bright with enthusiasm. Miss Simpkins has a way of disseminating information in a lively and interesting way. All the students enjoy her classes.

"I had to face the disagreeable revelation that my father was not my real parent, and upon the death of my mother, I, too, faced the prospect of being made homeless," Miss Simpkins continues. "Even now, I am sometimes haunted by the memory of packing my small trunk and carrying it out into the street. Were it not for the help of an old schoolfriend, who took me in, which in turn allowed me the opportunity to complete my studies, my life might have turned out very differently indeed."

Maria sits and processes this for a while. Then she nods slowly.

"I sense in you, Miss Barklem, a kindred spirit," her lecturer says. "I have also marked you out as having an exceptional talent for pedagogy. Your essays and your contributions in class discussion demonstrate that you would be a great asset to the profession. It would be a dereliction of my duty not to offer you what assistance I could to complete your studies and gain your certificate."

"I am grateful," Maria replies. "Indeed I am. But unless I can find somewhere to live ~ with a rent I can afford on my meagre salary, I do not see how that is to happen."

"May I offer a suggestion? I have good friends who run a kind of ladies' club, based in Langham Place, off Regent Street. They have a few rooms they rent out to young women in similar situations to yourself, who are in need of temporary accommodation while they finish their education. I could write a letter of introduction, recommending you for one of their places, if you wish? The rent is nominal and some meals are provided."

Maria is overcome. Tears fill her eyes. After a lifetime struggling against opposition in the form of some malign authority or another, such kindness is like balm to her battered soul.

"I cannot express how grateful I am, Miss Simpkins," she says, brokenly.

"Then it shall be done at once. If you care to wait in the canteen, I will write the letter of introduction for you. I sense some urgency in your situation, am I correct?"

Maria nods mutely.

"If all goes well, you will have a place to stay before the week is out. And I urge you also to consider going in for the Cambridge Junior Locals ~ they have been open to girls for the last two years and are a stepping-stone to the next stage of education. Now, I shall write that letter. I wish you well, Miss Barklem. You have the chance of a good career. Seize it with both hands."

Miss Simpkins goes to her desk to write her letter, leaving Maria to return to the canteen and bury her grateful nose in another cup of coffee. Although she doesn't yet know it, this evening will be the turning point in her life. She will indeed go on to take the Locals, and after them, the Higher Locals, which in turn will lead her to a place at Benslow House in the small market town of Hitchin. Under the tuition of Emily Davies, and with support from visiting professors from Cambridge, Maria Barklem will be amongst the first women to study a degree course at any English university.

****

But all these events will take place several years in the future. Now, it is night-time, and a wolf's howl of wind whips against the window and rattles the chimneypots. Midnight finds Gerald Daubney still lying awake in his bed, letting his thoughts wander down the dark labyrinthine streets of his mind. The house is silent, but even an empty house can still be loud with ghosts.

Outside, the moonlit city is a haunted tangle of shadows and threats, a world of creatures that scream and howl. Far from being a sanctuary, somewhere to hide from predators, he now sees it for what it is: a place of noise, foul smells, a dark landscape of chaos.

Since his accident, he has not ventured further than his front door. It is as if an invisible hand holds him back from crossing his own threshold. He wanders from room to room, as he once wandered the restless nocturnal streets. Occasionally, the doorbell rings and he hears the girl whose name he cannot remember opening the front door and speaking to someone. At which point he cowers silently. It is the kind of silence that wraps itself round someone who doesn't want to be discovered.

Church bells chime. The watchman calls the hour. Sleep is a fugitive who has escaped and will not return. Daubney rises, wraps himself in a dressing gown, lights his candle and pens another letter to Detective Sergeant Cully.

This letter informs Cully that, having once again had no news of his missing collection, nor any visits from Scotland Yard to keep him abreast of the latest developments, nor a response to his last letter, he will be attending the detective in his office tomorrow morning. It is reasonably polite but with sharp critical undertones. He rereads it a couple of times and is satisfied that it strikes the right note. He does not want to leave the officer in any doubt of his dissatisfaction.

He places the letter in an envelope, addresses it, and leaves it on the hall table with written instructions to the servant girl to post it as soon as she comes in. Daubney then returns to bed. He must be at his intellectual zenith tomorrow, to extract from the elusive detective why he was asking Mortlake, the dealer, about other collectors of netsuke, and why he brought up the Edo cat. There is some mystery here about which he is being kept in the dark.

Eventually, Daubney sleeps, blissfully unaware that Zanthe, the real white cat, is busy chasing moths downstairs. In hot pursuit of a particularly big juicy one, she will jump onto the hall table, skid across it, and knock his letter down the back next to the wall, where it will lie, unnoticed, for many weeks.

****

It is not often that Detective Inspector Stride views the front pages of the London papers with any sense of equanimity, but today, even *The Inquirer* has managed to surpass itself in his estimation. Over a rather dramatic picture of a couple of women clad in what the artist clearly wishes the reader to understand is the sort of attire worn by ladies of negotiable affections, is the headline: ***Metropolitan Police Foil Filthy Foreign Trade in Female Flesh.*** The two women are depicted walking down a gangplank accompanied by a figure in police uniform, while a villainously bearded man looks on from the deck rails.

Stride checks the other newspapers on his desk, noting with satisfaction that each presents a variant on the same headline. *The Times* even goes into some technical details about the purchase and use of forged birth certificates, having conducted its own investigation on the back of the tip-off.

He tries to imagine the effect of this upon Munro Black. He hopes that the arrest of his brother, combined with the disappearance of his 'heavy', will be enough to throw him off his guard. So far, he has heard nothing from the constables patrolling the area, but it cannot be long before Mr. Black reacts. And when he does, Scotland Yard's finest, in the form of Greig and Cully, will be there to apprehend him.

Stride is just about to send out for his second mug of coffee, when there is a knock at his door. The on-duty constable appears.

"There's a gentleman in the outer office to see Detective Sergeant Cully, sir," he says.

"So, go and tell him," Stride growls.

"He isn't here, sir."

Stride rolls his eyes. "Does the gentleman have a name?"

The constable tells him.

Stride groans.

"Are you quite sure Jack Cully isn't on the premises?" he asks.

"I've checked the rota, sir. He isn't due in until after lunch," the constable says. "Shall I tell the gentleman to call back later? Only he seemed to think he had an appointment arranged."

Stride waves a dismissive hand, "No, no, don't do that; I'll see him. If I must. Give me five minutes, then show him into Detective Sergeant Cully's office. And bring me a mug of coffee, would you? Strong and black. I have a feeling I'm going to need it."

It is with a deep sense of foreboding that Stride levers himself out of his seat and goes to sit behind the small desk in the room Cully shares with several other detectives. After a suitable interval, Gerald Daubney is shown in. The constable places a mug of coffee on the desk.

Stride finds a chair for the collector to sit on, then opens the folder of Cully's interviews and reports on his investigation into the missing netsuke. He leans on the desk and smiles in what he hopes is a professional, and not a fed-up-with-being-pestered manner.

"Good morning, Mr. Daubney. As my constable has told you the detective sergeant is out at the moment. How may I assist you?"

Two bright spots of anger burn in Daubney's corpse-candle face.

"But this is not good enough! Not good enough at all! I wrote to Detective Sergeant Cully informing him that I would be coming to Scotland Yard to see him today. This is the second time I have written! And now you inform me he is 'out'? Out?"

Stride riffles through the folder. "No sign of a letter here, sir. Perhaps it went astray? It happens. This is a big police office and we deal with a lot of cases."

"But not, apparently, mine," Daubney says bitterly. "I have been waiting for a letter telling me what progress has been made. I have received nothing. I have waited for a call. Again, nothing. The only news I have had, came from Mr. Mortlake, of Mortlake & Devine, who told me your detective was round at his showroom asking all sorts of questions about who else collects netsuke.

"When pressed by myself, he also informed me that the detective was particularly interested in a man called Mr. Munro Black. Who is this man, inspector? And what is his connection to my burglary and my netsuke?"

Damn, Stride thinks.

"I am afraid I am not at liberty to tell you anything at the moment, sir, as the person concerned is currently the focus of an investigation."

Daubney twitches violently in his seat.

"Mr. Mortlake, from whom I learned more in five minutes than I have from you in five weeks, said your detective was asking about the Edo Cat."

"Possibly he was, sir. But like I said, I am not at liberty to share with you details of an ongoing investigation."

If you had run Daubney through with an ancient collectable Japanese sword, he couldn't have looked more astonished.

"But it is my netsuke. My Edo cat. If this man has taken it, then of course I must know."

"And you will know, sir. As soon as we have collected the evidence we need. That is the way we deal with cases. In the meantime, I'd appreciate it if we could be allowed to pursue our inquiries, on your behalf as well as on behalf of Mr. Flashley's friends and family. As I said, we will be in touch. Now, if you would excuse me, sir, I have other urgent matters to deal with."

Daubney hesitates. A stubborn expression crosses his face.

"And what if I refuse to go? What if I don't believe you?"

"We are on the cusp of making an arrest, sir," Stride says, wondering why interviewing the non-criminal was even harder than extracting a confession from the malefactor. "Soon, we hope to be able to return your stolen property to you. It would assist us greatly if you'd allow us to proceed at our own pace."

He is mentally crossing his fingers that the collector will see the logic of this, and that the deity he doesn't really believe in won't hold the lie against him long term.

Daubney sinks his face into his hands. A tremor passes through his etiolated frame.

"Would you like some water, sir?" Stride asks, rising. "I will ask one of the men to bring you a glass."

He stands up and hurries out of the room, closing the door behind him. Daubney raises his face from the sieve of his hands. He listens. Then he darts over to the desk, turns the folder round, and looks at the top report.

As luck would have it, the report is the one detailing Cully's first interview with Munro Black and contains the reference to the ivory cat that he noticed on the hall mantelpiece. Daubney skim reads it, making a mental note of the address. Then, hearing footsteps returning, he turns the folder back round to its original position and resumes his seat.

Some time later, Gerald Daubney leaves Scotland Yard, a determined expression on his face. He knows where he is now, and where he is going, and what he will do when he gets there.

****

While all this is happening, Constable Dean, newly appointed to the Metropolitan Police, and as keen as mustard, is on duty in one of the cramped Watch Boxes that fringe the perimeter of Russell Square.

He has a whistle, a rattle and a copy of the *Police Gazette* for company. Every now and then, he peers out of the narrow wooden aperture and checks for suspicious characters. The very wealthy inhabitants in their big houses do not want the hoi-polloi to loiter on their exclusive pavements, nor lean against their pristine iron railings.

Constable Dean is aware that one house in particular has to be carefully observed, but he has been watching it for so long that, as is often the way of it, he has forgotten why, and so he has stopped. At midday, he unwraps the packed lunch his landlady has put up for him and enjoys the two juicy ham sandwiches and slice of cake. His landlady believes that young men, especially good-looking ones, need plenty of wholesome sustenance.

While Constable Dean is lunching, some men start to rake the leaves into piles, a very fashionably dressed woman takes her small dog into the gardens to relieve itself, and a horse-drawn furniture van pulls into the square. It stops in front of Number 55. Two men in the brown-overalled livery of Beales & Co., Storage & Shipping, dismount. They knock at the door and are admitted by a parlour maid. After a while they return and begin to unload packing crates from the back of the van.

Constable Dean shakes the crumbs from his lunch out of the aperture, and notices that there is a certain amount of activity taking place at Number 55, at which point he remembers a vague instruction from his superior to keep an eye on the place and report anything unusual.

As he watches, he sees packing crates being manhandled down the steps and loaded into the van, which then drives off. It is now afternoon. He decides to take a turn about the square ~ what, in universal police parlance, is known as 'proceeding'. He is proceeding past Number 55 when the door opens, and a couple of female servants emerge. They are wearing outdoor clothes and carrying bags. They do not look happy.

Seizing the initiative, he approaches and engages them in polite conversation, from which he learns that the house is being packed up, as the master is leaving. The servants have all been let go, without the usual notice and, more importantly, without receiving their proper wages.

Constable Dean returns thoughtfully to his Watch Box. He is sure this information needs to be relayed to somebody higher up the food chain. He makes copious notes, waits an hour until his replacement turns up, then inquires of him what he should do.

Luckily, the replacement is the man who received the original briefing from Detective Inspector Stride and so, after a brief discussion, Constable Dean is sent hot-foot over to Scotland Yard to deliver his carefully written observations straight into the hands of the appropriate authority.

****

It is early evening when Greig and Cully arrive at Russell Square. The gas-lamps have recently been lit, their muted golden glow casting patches of light interspersed with pools of shadow. The two detectives make their way to Number 55. The house is in total darkness, except for the hallway and first floor, where more light slants out between the slats of the Venetian blind. Cully tries the door. To his surprise, it opens.

They enter quietly but find nobody to challenge them or bar their way. There appears to be no servants in the house, confirming what they have been told. Greig places a finger to his lips and nods in the direction of the rear sitting room, from whence comes sounds of hammering.

"I think we will find our man in there," he whispers. "Proceed with caution."

The two detectives approach. Through the half-open door, they spy Munro Black. He is wearing outdoor clothing and is busily hammering down the lid of a wooden packing crate. Other crates are stacked against the walls.

"Just in time, eh," Greig murmurs. "A while longer, and it is clear our bird would have flown. Let us confront him, and end this once and for all."

He steps boldly into the room. "Good evening, Mr. Black," he says breezily. "I see you are planning a house move?"

Munro Black straightens up and stares at the two detectives. He appears totally unfazed by their unexpected appearance.

"Evening, gents," he says coolly. "Bit late for a social call? I'd offer you a sherry, but as you can see, I am rather busy. So, why don't you just state your business and be on your way, eh?"

He turns his attention back to the crate and continues hammering down the lid.

"Why don't you put down that hammer first," Cully suggests. "You may find it better to concentrate upon what we have come to say."

Black turns to him with a sneer. "I doubt you have anything to say to me that'd be of the slightest importance."

"Is that so? Does the name Albert Norris mean anything to you?"

Black's expression is impenetrable. "Never heard of him. Why?"

"That's odd," Greig says, picking up the conversational reins. "He has told us that he was employed by you specifically to deal with people who owed you money, or were threatening to make your life difficult by reporting you to the authorities. Men like James Flashley, for instance."

"Yeah, well, you don't want to go believing everything you get told."

"He is lying? Really? Strange. Because he was able to give us chapter and verse on several 'punishments' he swears you ordered him to carry out. And when we investigated his statements, they all checked out. So, I ask you once more: do you know this man?"

Black shrugs his massive shoulders, then gently taps his open palm with the head of the hammer in a 'not threatening, just suggesting' sort of way.

"Stop wasting my time, gents. If you have anything important to say, spit it out. I am a busy man."

"Where are you going?" Greig asks evenly.

"None of your business officer. Now, if you'll excuse me ..."

"Not so fast. Not so fast. There are still matters to discuss. Like what happened after you and Mr. Norris left the Ship Inn public house. At the end of that evening, a man was left swinging from a rope. Mr. Norris denies any knowledge of his death. Which only leaves your actions unaccounted for. Would you care to account for them now, to us?"

Black's face darkens, and the hand gripping the wooden handle of the hammer tightens, until his knuckles go white.

"You haven't got a shred of evidence," he snarls. "You come here accusing me in my own house of this and that, but you can't prove a single thing. Once and for all: I did not steal whatever it was you think I stole. I did not murder whoever you think I murdered. I have nothing more to say. Now get lost, both of you! I want you to leave. Before I get really cross. There are laws about intimidating people."

"And I expect you know them all, don't you, Mr. Black? Doesn't seem to stop you though, does it?" Greig replies smoothly.

Meanwhile, Cully is glancing round the empty room, searching for clues and inspiration. His gaze finally comes to rest on the space above the marble fireplace. Whatever was hanging there has been packed, but the evidence of its presence remains in the ghostly outlines left on the sun-lightened wallpaper. And suddenly, Cully makes the link.

Last time he was in this room, there were two oriental daggers with fancy gold handles displayed over the mantelpiece. Cully is absolutely sure that one of them is currently the property of the Metropolitan Police, having been picked up at Bob Miller's Livery Stable by himself.

He tugs at Greig's elbow and, speaking in a low urgent voice, quickly appraises him of what he has realised. Greig makes no outward sign that he understands, but something in his demeanour shifts, subtly.

"You are quite correct, Mr. Black. We do not have the proof to accuse you of theft. You must be relieved, eh? And we have no actual proof that you participated in the killing of James Flashley. Oh, we suspect that you did, very much so," he pauses, "but obtaining false birth certificates for young women, Mr. Black ~ that is something we'd very much like to look into with you. As would the Registrar General's Office.

"And then there is the attempted murder of the young potboy from the Ship Inn, still under investigation. My colleague reminds me that we have the dagger from that incident in our possession. It is an unusual oriental dagger, Mr. Black. We picked it up at the scene, along with your man Norris."

Cully takes a step towards Munro Black.

"We believe the fire that destroyed the Ship Inn was set at your command to intimidate the local community," he says. "But the boy survived the flames and is in our safekeeping. As is the murder weapon. I would be extremely interested to see whether the dagger is one of the pair that used to hang over your fireplace. I remember seeing it there on a previous visit. Therefore, I request that you accompany us to Scotland Yard, as we need to ask further questions."

Munro Black does not answer, but his hand snakes into his coat pocket. It emerges, clutching a small pistol. He raises his right arm and points the pistol straight at Cully's head. His hand is perfectly steady; his eyes are like black ice.

"Don't make me regret anything, gents," he says quietly. "Accidents can happen so easily. One shot, and it's lights out, eh? Now, this is how it's going to go: I'm leaving London, and there's nothing you or any Scotland Yarders can do to stop me. You have no proof of anything. No court in the land would convict me. If they could find me in the first place, which they won't. So, if you're sensible, you'll just stay here for a while. And then you'll forget you ever saw me or heard of me. Right?"

Greig and Cully do not move. Black makes some mock shooting gestures at them, laughs scornfully, then quits the room, slamming the door after him. They hear his heavy footsteps going down the hallway towards the front door.

Suddenly the sound of a gunshot cracks the silence. Greig wrenches open the door and they both rush out. Amy Feacham is standing in the hallway, her back to the open front door, a gun gripped in both hands.

As they watch, Black spins, staggers, brings his hand to his chest. A crimson stain begins to spread. He jerks forward and falls, blood bubbling from his mouth. His body writhes on the floor. He gasps for breath, a hoarse choking sound. Then a great shudder passes through him and he lies still.

Cully and Greig edge slowly towards the youthful assassin. At the sight of them, Amy sets down the gun and walks over to the body. She stares down at it for a long, silent time. Then she glances up at the two detectives. She seems completely unsurprised to see them in the house.

"Good riddance!" she says.

Cully breathes in sharply, "How on earth did you get hold of a gun?"

"Jonas gave it me when he returned. For my protection. He said I wasn't safe anymore. Not after talking to you and then coming here to find Rosa." Amy gestures towards the street door. "He's waiting for me down at the docks, with Ma, my little sister and our luggage. We're off to a new life in America. Got our passage all booked. We sail tonight on the tide. Nothing left here for us, is there? Just one last thing I had to take care of before we set sail. And now I have."

"But why did …" Greig begins.

She closes him down with a fierce look.

"You know why I did it ~ for Rosa, and all the other innocent young girls what they took and soiled, and then sold on to be used by men for their pleasure. And what I think, being decent gents both, is that you ain't going to arrest me, coz we know it's exactly what he deserved, right?"

Amy Feacham waits for a second, staring at them, daring them to lay hands on her. Neither man takes a step towards her. Eventually, she nods at them.

"Well then, I'll bid you both good-night. Got a ship to catch. It's been a bad time for us, but it's over at last. We may not have got poor Rosa back, but we're still a family; we got each other, and that's all what counts in the end."

She turns and walks away, closing the front door quietly behind her. Greig and Cully wait for the silence to die down a bit. Then Greig goes over to the gun and starts edging it carefully towards the body with his boot, until the handle is almost touching the dead man's hand.

"Suicide?" he murmurs thoughtfully.

"Indeed," Cully replies. "As Mr. Robertson never tires of telling us: *In suicidal cases, the instrument of death is generally found near the body.*"

"It is." Greig nods. "*And the wound is frequently inflicted in the region of the head or the heart.* I think our work here is done, detective sergeant."

"I agree, detective inspector."

The two men make a quick final check of the house. Just in case they have missed anything, or anybody. They find nothing, only empty rooms, packing crates, and furniture covered by dustsheets. Just before they leave, Greig switches out the lights.

****

But unbeknown to them, Greig and Cully won't be the only visitors to the house this evening. In the small hours, the dead time, when the bright places in the West End of the city have emptied out of people, leaving only those who have no home, and so are forced to inhabit the streets at night, another noctambulant enters the square.

Clad in a black overcoat, his hat pulled low over his brow, Gerald Daubney opens the gate to Number 55. He is here to reclaim his treasures. He has been thinking and planning for this moment ever since he left Scotland Yard earlier in the day, the address burning bright in his fevered brain. He is about to enact upon the sleeping occupants what was done to him ~ he even has a house-brick, wrapped in a cloth, under his coat.

Daubney slips down the basement steps. There is a strange ringing in his ears; his head seems bursting. Something dark and monstrous is rising up inside him, its wings beating in his chest. He smashes the brick against one of the side-windows, then uses his cane to clear enough of the glass to clamber through.

Once inside, he palms his way around the walls until he comes to the door leading up to the ground floor. He feels constricted by the weight of his clothing, but he climbs the stairs, one hand always supporting himself on the wall. Reaching the hallway, he makes his way in pitch darkness, towards the front of the house. There is a mantelpiece there and the Edo cat is waiting for him. He read it in the report.

One step. Another step. Suddenly his foot slips on a wet, sticky patch and he goes down, vainly flailing to get a grip on thin air. His hands reach out and touch a cold something that feels like … but … no … it cannot be! Gerald Daubney throws back his head and screams in horror as he realises what he has stumbled upon.

When the night-duty constable eventually gains entrance through the front door and switches on the electric light, he finds a black clad man with wild staring eyes, crouching beside a dead body. The man's face has the pallor of a three-day corpse, and his hands are covered in blood.

****

Resolutions and conclusions take some time to outwork, and so it is a good few days before Stride and Cully meet to discuss and finally close the Flashley murder investigation.

"It was just as well that you and Lachlan were able to verify Munro Black's suicide," Stride says. "The outcome for Mr. Daubney, had you not, would have meant a trial for murder, leading assuredly to a guilty verdict and to the rope. Ironic, isn't it?"

Cully keeps his facial expression neutral. To his surprise, Robertson has agreed with the presumption of *felo de se* as he calls it. Cully vies between amusement that their carefully structured set-up worked and guilt. Mostly he is amused.

Stride stares intently at the far wall. "That house again. It is almost as if it sucks in evil. If I were a superstitious man, I could well believe that it is cursed in some malign way."

"Better not tell the new tenants, whoever they are," Cully says drily.

"Indeed." Stride makes a mouth. "Well, Munro Black is dead, which means our investigation does not have a satisfactory conclusion. We were unable to extract a confession of murder from him before he died. And we may have found an oriental knife amongst his possessions that matches the one dropped at the livery stables, but we did not find any of Mr. Daubney's stolen property," he pauses, "Do we know what has happened to the poor man?"

"I gather that some of his fellow collectors have taken him to a safe place, where he can be properly looked after," Cully says.

"I did not warm to him, I own it. But to discover the body of a suicide, as he did, no wonder he was upset. We forget that members of the public are not so accustomed to the gruesome things that we encounter on a daily basis. So Munro Black has eluded justice, just as he has eluded us. I am not happy about it, I tell you plainly. It should have ended with that man facing the full force of the law."

"We have the younger brother in custody in Calais," Cully reminds him. "Perhaps he might be able to shed light upon the case. He will be allowed to return for Black's funeral. May I suggest we pull him in for questioning when he does."

Stride nods curtly. "We shall be at that funeral. I am interested to see who else turns up. The man seems to have made so many enemies. I expect some of them will be there just to check he is really dead."

And some won't, Cully thinks. Amy Feacham, for one. She and her family will still be on the high seas. He hopes they land safely and go on to make a good life for themselves in America.

There is a light knock at the door. Detective Inspector Greig enters. "Ah, gentlemen, good: I was hoping I'd find you both together," he says. "I have some important news that I wish to share with you."

Cully feels a frisson of apprehension. He has noted his colleague's air of preoccupation over the past weeks, the staring off into space. And then there was the letter, put up quickly before he could inquire about it.

Greig moves a couple of folders aside and perches on the edge of the desk. Stride and Cully wait to hear what he has to divulge. "I am delighted to be able to tell you that Miss Josephine King and I are engaged to be married," he says.

There is a nanosecond's pause. Then both men jump to their feet, uttering congratulations. Stride shakes his hand. Cully claps him on the shoulder.

"Aye. It is amazing, even to me," Greig says, smiling broadly. "I would have told you sooner, but I was waiting for a reply to my letter from Jeannie, my sister in Scotland. She is all the family I have, so without her approval, I couldn't have asked Josephine. But she is as delighted as you both."

"When is the wedding day to be?" Stride asks.

"We are hoping for a Christmas wedding," Greig says. "And on that matter, I have a favour to ask: as I have no menfolk to stand up with me at the altar, would you both be my groomsmen?"

Stride's smile is as wide as Africa. "My dear chap, it would be an honour ~ for us both, eh Jack?"

"Indeed, it would," Cully nods.

"Good. That is settled then. In the meantime, we are hosting a small party this Sunday afternoon to celebrate the engagement. It will be at the Lily Lounge, of course. I hope you and your families will be free to join us?"

"Wild horses, Lachlan," Cully laughs. "You wait until I tell Emily. She will be planning her and the girls' frocks as soon as she hears the news. I am so happy for you. This is the best news I have heard in an age."

"I agree," Stride agrees. He picks up his pen and signs off the Flashley case file with a flourish. "Gentlemen, I think this news calls for a celebratory lunch. Let us betake ourselves to Sally's, where I will stand you both a plate of the finest chops and a glass of something to toast the health and happiness of the future Mr. and Mrs. Greig."

****

Sadly, alas, there is little to celebrate in this place. Sometimes it is light. Then it is dark. There seems no logic to it. Time has gone runny at the edges. He does not know why it has happened. But now it is light once more, and he is here, and this is his spoon. His. Spoon. They tried to take it away when he first came here. He resisted them. It is his spoon.

He picks up his spoon, turning it so that the bowl catches the early morning sun shining through the window of his room. Nobody will take his spoon away from him, as they took his cat. He still recalls her crying as she was picked up by the scruff of her neck, thrust into a basket and removed from his house.

That was just before he was put into a carriage and removed as well. He didn't even have time to finish his pudding. But he kept hold of his spoon. And his dreams. Some nights, he dreams about her. Some nights, his dreams are of another cat. A small carved ivory cat. So small that he can hold it in the palm of his hand. A smooth cat, with green jewel eyes that shine. Whenever he dreams about that cat, he wakes up in the morning to find tears shivering down his cheeks and his pillow is wet.

Sometimes, he hears noises in the night. People elsewhere screaming and shouting. He hears running footsteps in the corridor beyond his door. After a while, the noises cease. Out there, on the other side of the door, are people who want to take his spoon away. That is why he stays in this room, with its white walls and bars on the window. And his spoon. They cannot hurt him while he has his spoon. As long as he has his spoon, he is safe.

****

Izzy Harding wakes up to find herself unexpectedly sleeping on the floor. Her mattress has been turned over in the night, tipping her off. She slides her hand underneath it to discover that all the treasures she secretly kept there have gone: the shiny brass button, the length of bright scarlet ribbon, the sheet of gold leaf, the six farthings, the miniature dolls' tea-set, the green velvet pincushion and the silver sixpence.

There is no sign of her mother either. She suspects that the two events are not unlinked. Izzy goes downstairs, where Mrs O'Shaughnessy informs her that her mother came in very late with a man, both the worst for drink. There was a blazing row, after which her mother packed her belongings and left. This information is followed by the polite but firm request that Izzy follows her mother, as Mrs O'Shaughnessy keeps 'a clane house' and the Hardings are no longer considered suitable lodgers.

Now Izzy walks along the Thames foreshore, the hand of Fate snipping the threads behind her. Early morning light is slanting through the mist and her boots make squelching sounds as they sink into the black mud. Since waking up, she has lost all her treasured possessions, her mother and her home. It seems a lot for a person of so few years. She hopes the rest of the day will be more uneventful.

Izzy walks towards one of the great iron bridges that crosses the river like so many heavy rainbows. The light shivers, then settles. A ripple of sunshine. Diamonds dance on the grey water. At the foot of the bridge she pauses as something catches her eye. It gleams in the mud, ivory-white. She sees a small triangular face. Two pricked ears. Two green eyes. Izzy squats, scraping away the filth with a piece of stick. She reaches down. The Edo cat is gently lifted from its muddy bed.

Izzy rolls the thing she has found between her cupped hands, studying it curiously. She hasn't a clue what it is. She has never seen anything like it before. She turns it over a couple of times, running a finger lightly along the smooth ivory back, marvelling at its small perfection, the tiny tongue poking out, the segmented paws, the cat-stare eyes.

She has found a new treasure. It must be a sign: the door to her better life is opening. Izzy Harding scrambles to her feet, tucking the Edo cat into her pocket. Then she walks on, gradually disappearing into the morning mist, like a figment of the city's turbulent imagination.

Finis

Thank you for reading this book. If you have enjoyed it, why not leave a review on Amazon and recommend it to other readers. All reviews, however long or short, help me to continue doing what I do.

Printed in Great Britain
by Amazon